JESSI ELLIOTT

Twisted Fate
Published by Jessi Elliott
Copyright © 2018 by Jessi Elliott
All rights reserved.

ISBN: 978-1775004202

Visit my website at www.jessielliott.com
Proofreader: Kim Chance
Editor: Maggie Morris, The Indie Editor
Cover Design: Sarah Hansen, Okay Creations
Formatting: Stacey Blake, Champagne Book Design

Dedication

In memory of Wayne Elliott. I miss you, Dad.

Playlist

Poison by Felicity

War of Hearts by Ruelle

Haunted by Maty Noyes

Emerald by Lyra

Skinny Love by Birdy

The Other Side by Ruelle

Helium by Sia

Murder Song (Acoustic) by Aurora

Holy Ground by BANNERS

Blue by Troye Sivan

Kingdom Fall by Claire Wyndham

Heal by Tom Odell

The Scientist by Corinne Bailey Rae

Chapter One

A GENTLE HAND RESTS ON MY ARM, AND I MOMENTARILY consider breaking it. I'm tired, overworked, and in desperate need of caffeine. I sat at the back of the lecture hall for a reason. Still, someone has the nerve to bother me.

"You might want to at least pretend to be awake," says a male voice, his tone laced with amusement.

I lift my head from the fold-out desk and blow the hair away from my face before turning toward the unfamiliar voice. The first thing I notice is the grass-green color of his eyes. I recognize his face now. It's an embarrassing reminder of the many times he's caught me noticing him around campus. I saw him for the first time during freshman year at Taylor's Brew—a popular student hangout a few blocks from campus. My best friend and roommate Allison was convinced he was checking me out, but she didn't miss a beat in warning me he was too old.

He sticks his hand out. "I'm Grant, the teaching assistant. I'm also in this class." He must be pretty smart to land that position while still being a student himself.

"Aurora," I say. His palm is rough against mine, as though he works with his hands often.

He passes me the class outline and syllabus, which I scan while he drops into the seat next to me. The keys in the pocket of his worn denim jeans jingle, drawing my attention back to him.

"What's your major?" he asks, flicking back a bit of brown hair that's sticking out from a beanie hat. Grant rocks the over-done hipster look, I'll give him that.

"Business," I answer. "My last year, thank god."

He nods as if he understands. "A busy year."

I groan in agreement, fighting the urge to let my head fall back onto the desk and go back to sleep before the lecture starts.

Grant leans over and nudges my shoulder. "It's Friday. You should take the weekend off. You'll have all semester to stress over papers and exams. Try to think about it this way: only two semesters until graduation, then you can work for some huge company or open your own. You can do whatever you want."

Opening my own business *is* the goal. Since I was young, I've known I wanted to open a bookstore. Now it's even more important I succeed. My brother was diagnosed with cancer three years ago. My parents would never ask me to pay them back for my tuition, but with the amount of time they've both taken off work, they need the money.

I sigh before casting him a sideways glance and say, "I hope you're right."

He grins. "Stick with me, and you'll see I'm always right."

My only response is a short burst of laughter.

"Listen, there's a party off campus tonight. You should

come." He scribbles the address on a piece of paper and hands it to me. "No better way to ring in the new school year than with cheap beer and free pizza."

I press my lips together. "You make a good point," I say. "I'll think about it."

The lecture ends late as they often do. It's after nine when I say goodbye to Grant and cross the street to walk through the cobblestone courtyard toward the dorms. Located in the middle of downtown, Rockdale University's campus has beautifully landscaped gardens paired with tall, glass buildings. The entire campus is spread out across ten blocks.

My shoulder smacks into someone walking the opposite way, and I immediately turn to apologize, catching a stranger's intense blue eyes.

"My fault," he mutters, continuing on his way.

My feet feel like concrete, stuck in place as my stomach churns, unable to erase the sharp expression on the man's face. I swallow, sucking in a breath when my phone buzzes in my back pocket. "Hey, Mom," I answer, a little breathless as I force my legs to move again.

"How was your week?" she asks. "I wish I could've been there for your first day as a senior." What she means is she still wishes I'd gone to the college in my hometown of Mapleville, where both she and my dad are professors. That was never my plan. I didn't want my education handed to me on a shiny silver platter.

"It's been a fairly uneventful week." I walk into the lobby of my dorm and wait for the elevator.

"Any news on your placement?"

"Interviews are in a couple of weeks." I'm hoping for something that has the potential for a job offer at the end. Knowing I have a job after graduation would make me feel better.

"Sounds good," she says. "Adam misses you already."

"Tell him I miss him, too. Love you guys."

We say goodbye as I step into the elevator with a few other students. I arrive back at my room and find the door wide open. Oliver is lounging on my bed in his normal, casual attire of jeans and a plain T-shirt, and Allison is sitting on her own bed. I shoot him a look. "What did I say about shoes on my bed, Oliver?"

He takes his time kicking them off, staring at me the whole time. That's Oliver, though—always teasing, like an annoying brother. He's also Allison's boyfriend, but he may as well be chopped liver right now with how focused she is on her computer screen. Allison's dedication to school is something I love about her. I think it's part of what made us such good friends when we met in freshman year. We're practically sisters. Hell, we look so alike we *could* be. That paired with our shared love of reading sealed the deal. Our friendship was fate. She's been my rock since Adam got sick the first time, which is only further proof that we'd do anything for each other.

I drop my backpack and fall into the chair with a heavy sigh. Our standard size room couldn't fit more than two beds, two dressers, and two desks, which is a shame because I'd love to have a bookshelf in here.

"Did you get homework dumped on you this week, too?" I ask Allison.

She nods without looking up and pushes her wavy blond hair away from her round face. She must've had an early class this morning because she skipped her makeup routine.

"It's not fair," she mumbles, continuing her typing rampage.

Oliver hollers and shoots his fist into the air, startling both

Allison and me.

"What the hell, Oliver?" Allison huffs as she closes her laptop.

He looks up from his phone. "We're going to a party. Tonight. Get ready. Right now."

My stomach flutters. "The one off campus?" Was he talking about the one Grant invited me to?

"Hell, yeah. C'mon!" He jumps off my bed and shoves his hand through his sandy brown curls. He puts his shoes back on while humming under his breath before standing upright. Oliver towers over my five-foot-three frame, but he doesn't have much muscle on him.

Allison and I exchange looks, trying not to laugh at his adorable, childlike behavior.

"You're awfully excited for this party," I tease.

"The first kegger is always the craziest. It's the best party of the year. Now quit your stalling and put on some clothes that don't make you look like a homeless person." Apparently Allison's shorts and crop top are sufficient for this party, considering he doesn't comment on them.

In the small, three-piece bathroom, I change into jean shorts and a flowy tank top and shrug on a cardigan as I second-guess going to this party. I'm not one to frequent them throughout the semester, but I've tagged along with Allison and Oliver on a few occasions. I always have a good time; I would tonight, but I *should* stay home.

Screw it.

It's my senior year of college. I want to start it off with a bang.

The cab drops the three of us off at the curb of a student property on the less urban side of Rockdale. The music from inside is vibrating through the house, and Allison is already swaying her hips to whatever pop song is playing.

The house is huge, which is not what I expected for a student rental in the city. Where most are run-down bungalows, this place is three stories of gray stone. Several trees cover the yard, all glowing with the soft hues of twinkling lights strung through the branches. An empty beer can crunches under my foot as we're walking across the lawn.

We approach the door, and Oliver, without knocking, lets himself in. Far too many people fill the house to notice more entering, so Allison and I follow him. We make our way through the hallway, and my eyes flick to the vaulted ceiling before we make it into the open concept kitchen, furnished to the nines with stainless steel appliances and granite countertops—most of which are covered in empty beer bottles and pizza boxes.

Oliver shouts at the guy manning the keg near the French doors which lead to the backyard where more people are dancing, and the two of them spark up some conversation about a party they were at last semester.

Allison and I grab a couple of beers, leave Oliver talking to his friend, and migrate into the living room where people are singing and dancing.

"Allison! Aurora!" We both spin around at the high-pitched squeal of Danielle, a girl from my program who lives on our floor. Her cheeks are rosy; the beer in her hand probably isn't her first.

"Danielle." I smile as she clinks her bottle against mine, then Allison's. "How's it going?"

Her eyes shift between Allison and me. "Great! This place

is packed!"

She's right. I wrinkle my nose at the overwhelming smell of pizza, beer, and a mixture of perfume, cologne, and body odor.

Allison nods and takes a drink of her beer. I flick my eyes over to her, wondering why she's glaring at Danielle.

"We'll catch up later, okay?" I say.

"Sure." Danielle giggles. "Have fun, ladies."

When she's out of earshot, I turn to Allison. "What was that about?"

She shrugs. "Nothing. Let's dance." She plasters a smile on her face as if it's been practiced, and I frown before following her through the crowd. Allison and I stick together, dancing side by side, chatting with the people around us, while Oliver hangs with the guys in the kitchen.

Hours pass in a blur of drinking and dancing, talking over the music. The country songs aren't anything I'm a huge fan of, but the beer I'm tossing back makes it easier to enjoy.

I manage to break away from the crowd and leave Allison with a group of girls from our building while I look for the bathroom.

You don't buy beer; you rent it, my mom always says.

"Upstairs." A deep, newly familiar voice catches my attention, and I glance toward the sound to find Grant grinning at me.

I smile in greeting and arch a brow at him. "Excuse me?"

He tips his head back against the wall, the hair in front of his face falling away. "The bathroom. It's upstairs." He points to a set of stairs a few feet away.

"Oh," I mumble. "Thanks."

He nods. "I'll be honest, I didn't think you'd come. I figured you'd crash after class earlier."

"It's not my fault Professor Boring talks so low. It's a miracle anyone could hear him." Grant laughs before I continue. "And don't get me started on his PowerPoints."

He whistles. "Those are some harsh words, but I have to agree. I offered to work on them for him, but the guy wouldn't let me. Being a TA only means so much, I guess." He laughs again. "I won't keep you here talking. I'll see you around, Aurora." He touches my shoulder briefly and offers a smile. The butterflies in my stomach give a healthy flutter. Grant's attention is rather nice.

My head spins as I jog up the stairs, having to grab the railing a couple of times to keep my balance, and almost get lost trying to find the damn bathroom. This house has way too many hallways and doors. That, and I've had a few too many beers—an annoying reminder I'm a lightweight.

Groaning when I round another corner and see the line, I make my way to the back of it and pull my phone out. I scroll through Twitter, my most recent social media addiction, until the line moves and it's my turn. I'm quick and hurry out of the bathroom, knowing how many people are still waiting.

Trying to retrace my steps is more difficult than it should be. Turned around, I end up in an empty hallway. The skin on the back of my neck tingles, making me pause. I debate calling Allison or Oliver to come find me when a door opens, sending me stumbling back, clutching my chest as a guy steps into the hallway.

"My bad," he says, sounding unapologetic. He runs a hand through his short, dark brown hair, and his gaze holds mine as his eyes narrow. He inhales slowly. "Well, it's my lucky night. Looks like I'm going to be able to wrap this up in a jiffy." He tugs on the lapels of his jacket as if to straighten them and then claps his hands together.

My brows inch closer. "Do I know you?"

"I'm Max." He smirks, his teeth straight and white—too perfect. "You don't know me, but I know you."

I shake my head, sobering up a bit, and peek around the empty hallway. *Where the hell is everyone?* I can hear voices shouting over the music downstairs, but there's not a person in sight. "I don't think so." Hold on. Those eyes . . . This is the guy I ran into on my way home from class.

He presses his lips together and exhales through his nose as if he's trying to calm himself.

My gut tells me I need to get out of here. *Now.*

"I should get back to the party," I say in a forced, level tone. "My friends are waiting for me."

He tilts his head to the side, and the curve of his lips turns my stomach as I shift the weight between my feet. His eyes follow me closely, as if each move I make is intriguing.

I take a step back in the same moment he steps forward. "What are you doing?" My voice cracks, as tightness clamps down on my chest.

He chuckles. "You," he pauses, "are in a lot of trouble, blondie." His hand shoots forward, pressing flat against my chest, and my skin tingles under my shirt.

I should scream. I should slap his hand away and bolt. I should do a lot of things, but everything happens so fast. Black dots swim across my vision, and my ears ring over the pounding of my heart. Then my legs give out, and I collapse onto the hardwood floor.

chapter Two

OPENING MY EYES FOR WHAT FEELS LIKE THE FIRST TIME in days, I squint at a chandelier hanging from the ceiling. I blink until I can see clearly, and the sharp, heavy sound of metal chains startles me when I try to move. I take a deep breath to keep myself from panicking. It doesn't do much good. My hands are bound and attached to the chair I'm in. Cursing under my breath, I tug on them, but the cold chains bite into my skin; I wince before letting them go slack. I sniff a few times. I can't have been here too long, considering I don't smell particularly bad.

Am I still at the house where the party was held? The room looks more like a luxury hotel suite. It even has a fireplace surrounded by a seating area. But one thing's missing: a window. If this place *is* a hotel, I doubt they have guests staying in this room.

The door swings open, and my entire body goes rigid. It's the guy from the party—Max. Being stuck in a sitting position isn't ideal when I want to kick his ass. He swaggers into the room, with his hair messily framing his face as if he hasn't brushed it in a while.

"You're awake," he says with a menacing smile, and I fear the worst. Did he spike my drink at the party? Would I know if I were drugged? Oh god . . . Did he touch me?

"Observant. Well done," I shoot back, my hands clenching into fists. *Don't show him weakness*, I chant to myself as my fists shake.

"You've got a mouth on you, blondie." He walks closer, leaving the door open as he pulls on heavy gloves. He yanks the chains off the chair and forces me into a standing position, leaving my arms chained together.

I glance past him, but all there is to see beyond the doorway is a long, dimly lit hallway. "Who are you? Where am I? Why did you bring me here?"

Max rolls his eyes. "You ask a lot of questions."

I swallow the lump in my throat, blinking back hot tears. "What the hell do you expect?" Each word is laced with a combination of fear and anger, making my tone sharp and lower than normal.

He ignores what I said and inhales as he did at the party, grinning in a twisted way that turns my stomach. "Your fear . . . it's delicious."

My lip curls in disgust. "Excuse me?"

"I'm hungry." He sighs. "There's never much to eat around here. Nothing I'm allowed to, anyway."

"I suggest a McDonald's drive thru," I remark, bitterness heavy in my tone.

He laughs. "You're funny, too. Good to know." He reaches out and grasps my chin in his gloved hand.

Panic floods through me, and I react without thinking, kneeing him in the stomach.

He reels back a step, growling, and his eyes darken. "You stupid girl."

"I like my personal space," I say in a defensive tone.

Without a word, his hand shoots forward, and his fingers wrap around my throat. "Forgive me," he mutters with fake sincerity. "I tend to get a bit irritable"—he pauses and tightens his grip on my neck—"when I'm hungry."

Black dots dance across my vision, my heart slamming against my chest as I struggle to breathe. My eyes roll back, but Max scoffs and releases his grip on my throat before I pass out. When I cough and wheeze, he takes a step back, his face contorted with disgust. I suck in a breath, greedily filling my lungs with air as he removes the chains from my wrists.

"Please," I force out as the chains hit the floor. "I want to go home." I fold my arms over my chest, staring at the wall to avoid looking at my captor.

"What? No 'thank you'?" he bites back. Max throws the gloves off and places a hand on my collarbone, backing me against the wall before shoving his leg between my thighs.

I scream at the top of my lungs, aiming my knee a little lower this time to catch him hard in the groin. When he doubles over, clutching himself, I bolt for the door.

The hallway beyond the door is longer than I thought. I make it to the end, my flat shoes slapping against the marble floor as I run, too afraid to look behind me. As I round the corner, I'm grabbed from behind by impossibly strong arms and thrown against the wall. My head throbs, and I reach up and touch my forehead with a shaky hand. I'm unsurprised to find blood when I pull it away. A trail of warmth trickles down my face, dripping blood onto the floor at my feet.

"I've decided that I don't like you," Max hisses in my ear, and I shudder. "I did a nice thing for you, taking the chains off, and this is how you thank me?" He barks out a laugh and grabs my face, forcing me to look at him. "Your fear . . ." He slams me back into the wall again, and I cry out. "It's stronger now. Lucky me." He grins, but all I can focus on is the darkness in his eyes as he leans in.

"Seriously?" A sharp, female voice says. "You can't follow the simplest directions, can you?"

Max scowls, turning his face to look at the tall Asian woman approaching us with brows raised. She stops off to the side, radiating elegance in a dark purple dress. The woman is wearing heels, but I didn't hear her approach. Her black hair falls almost to her waist.

"Back off, Sky, this has nothing to do with you."

She rolls her eyes, sparing me a brief glance. "I'm looking out for *you*, asshat."

Max pulls his hand away from my face, shifting his body away from mine to face the woman. "What would you have me do? Let her go?"

"That's not your call," she says.

I flick my eyes back and forth between them, and then I bolt again. I have no idea where I am or where I'm going, but when an elevator comes into view, I sprint toward it, slamming my fist against the button.

"You're going to let her get away?" Max hollers, making the panic in my chest dig its claws deeper.

"Let her try." The woman seems uninterested whether I escape or not.

The elevator slides open, and I throw myself forward—right

into a solid wall of muscle. The force knocks the air out of my lungs, but I still open my mouth to scream. I reel back as my eyes snap upward to meet a pair of brilliant lapis lazuli irises. They're like the darkest parts of the ocean woven with lighter, softer hues, and surrounded by dark, thick lashes.

Max grabs me again, pulling me away from the new arrival as he steps off the elevator.

"Max," Blue Eyes says in a calm, measured voice. "Remove your hands from the girl. Now."

My kidnapper hesitates, growling low in his throat before he lets go. My face stings like a bitch where blood continues to trickle from the gash on my forehead. I touch it again and wince at the sharp pain that follows.

The stranger in front of me is tall—at least a foot taller than I am—and built. I think he's a bit older than me, considering the expensive-looking dark gray suit he's wearing.

His eyes stare into mine as he waves a hand to dismiss Max. "Leave us."

Max nods once and takes off down another hallway with his head hung low.

The man blocks the elevator, which is the only way out of here—the only one I can see, anyway. He cocks his head to the side.

"Move," I demand, surprising myself by the harsh tone of my voice.

The man raises his brows; I've surprised him, too. "Where are you off to?" He sounds curious.

"I'm not going to die here," I say, my determination clear.

"I'm glad to hear that." His jaw is sharp and shadowed with stubble. He steps forward, bringing his hand toward my face, and huffs in annoyance when I flinch.

"Hands off! Who *are* you?"

"That doesn't matter right now. Allow me? It will help." He lifts his hand to my face again and gently holds me in place while his fingers brush along my jaw. The throbbing from before fades, leaving a warm, tingling sensation.

My eyes widen, and I turn my face away from his hand. "What the hell was *that*?" My heart is beating fast, but I try not to let the shock show on my face.

"You're welcome," he says dryly.

"Who are you?" I repeat.

"You may call me—"

"Tristan, there are more important things to deal with right now." The woman from before is back with an armful of file folders.

He arches a brow at her. "I'll deal with what I decide needs to be dealt with, Skylar."

"Or you could let me out of here," I suggest. "No need to deal with me at all."

"The human makes an excellent suggestion, and that's coming from me."

Human?

Tristan makes a sound of frustration, a deep rumble in his throat, and then, with a subtle flick of his wrist, Skylar vanishes. She was standing no more than four feet from me, and now she's gone.

My hand flies to my mouth, my mind reeling. "You . . ." I can't form words. "What just . . . ?" The ability to finish a sentence escapes me. My eyes fill with tears, and I start shaking.

"Yes?" he murmurs.

I jerk my fingers through my hair, pressing them into my scalp, urging myself to wake up. "I'm going insane," I groan.

When Tristan steps forward, I reel back, my body springing into a defensive stance, my hands clenched into fists, ready to swing. "Did you kill her?" My voice cracks.

He chuckles. "I didn't kill her. I simply shifted her back to her office. Aurora, I need you to listen to me," he says in a calm voice. *How does he know my name?*

I shake my head adamantly. "You stay away from me!"

"I'm afraid that's not going to work."

In an instant, I lose it. I try to push him away, slamming my hands against his solid chest, but he doesn't move an inch. "What the hell are you?" I demand through chattering teeth, fighting to keep tears back.

His eyes flicker across my face, and he sighs. "Calm down," he says. "Take a deep breath." He waits until I exhale before he continues. "I'm the leader of the fae, Aurora. I imagine that means nothing to you." My brows rise, and he says, "I thought not."

"Why am I here?" I ask and force myself to hold his steely gaze.

"That is the eternal question, isn't it?"

"You said you're the leader of the fae?" I'm no expert, but I did take a mythology class last year to boost my average. Tristan doesn't look like what I think he should if my textbook is to hold any merit. No physical traits one might associate with a supposed supernatural being. He doesn't have pointy ears or sharp teeth.

He's lying. He must be. But then, how else could I explain his ability to heal my injuries? His ability to make that woman disappear?

He nods. "Precisely. However, I'm sure your idea of what we are is purely fictional."

16

I shrug, weary of his proximity. As much as I want to deny everything, what I saw with my own eyes *is* making it difficult to discredit. It's possible I'm suffering from some wicked hallucinations, or maybe Max *did* drug me at the party and again after he brought me here.

"I'm curious." He cocks his head to the side, his light brown, almost blond hair, falling into his face. "What is it you believe you know about my kind? Care to offer any theories?"

I press my lips together. If I'm to believe what Tristan says—though I'm not sure what to think right now—maybe I can use this opportunity to get some information. Or at least play along until I figure out an escape plan. "I'll tell you what I believe if you tell me why I'm here."

"You wish to trade information? This could be amusing. Please, go ahead."

"You're immortal," I say, recalling the basics of most inhuman creatures.

He offers a charming grin. "For the most part."

"You can't lie."

The grin remains. "True, though we are masters at evading."

"Iron is poisonous to you."

The grin slips a bit. "Yes."

"Why am I here?" I finally ask.

He looks at me, a thoughtful expression painting his features. "You don't wish to know more about me?"

"I think I know enough. Your name is Tristan. If I'm to take what you've told me as the truth, you're the leader of the fae. You made your girlfriend disappear—which I'm sure all guys would love to be able to do occasionally—and that other guy was trying to eat my emotions. How am I doing?"

His laugh is a deeply sensual, caressing sound, making my

eyes widen. "Skylar is of no romantic significance to me. As for Max, you're right about that. It's one of the ways we feed."

I fold my arms across my chest. "On emotions?"

"On *human* emotions," he corrects. "And energy. The two are closely related. We feed by contact, or, if we're in a large crowd of humans, we can absorb it without touching. So long as we don't take too much energy, the only effect on the human is exhaustion."

"Right . . ." I feel like my head is pretty damn close to exploding.

"It's how the immortal stay immortal, Aurora."

Immortality. This can't be real. "I'm here—to be fed off of? Are you . . . ?" My voice trails off as my stomach churns.

Tristan shakes his head. "I'm not going to feed from you. That's not why you're here. Though I have to agree with your statement about Max. He gets carried away. I will speak with him." He checks his watch and looks annoyed. "Later."

"Lovely." I sigh, tipping my head back against the wall. "If I wasn't brought here to be a human vending machine, why am I here?" I'm still in denial, but the words tumble out of my mouth as if I believe what he's been saying.

"It was an honest mistake."

"Of course it was. You can't lie," I remark dryly.

He smirks. "It was a case of mistaken identity," he explains. "Max was sent out to retrieve someone, and he mistook you for her."

"When he discovered I wasn't who he thought, he kidnapped me anyway?"

Tristan nods. "Yes, well, Max doesn't always pay as much attention to detail as he should."

"If I'm not who you want, then why am I still here? And

how did you know my name?"

"A mistake was made, and you were involved. There is certain protocol to be followed when something like this happens. Keeping you wasn't a decision Max made. I did. However, you weren't meant to be handled the way you were. Max wasn't supposed to go into the room. As for your name, I had one of my guys run your prints."

My eyes widen. This guy is certifiably insane—they all are. "I have a family, you know. And the last time I checked, kidnapping is a crime."

"You'll find that your laws mean nothing to us. We have our own laws—our own moral code." He seems to believe what he's telling me. Or he's a damn good actor. "As for the family you mentioned . . ." He rubs his jaw as if he's deciding what to say. "It seems they are partly to blame for the unfortunate mix-up."

I lick the dryness from my lips and shake my head. "You're insane."

"Max *can* be a little unfocused at times, especially under the circumstances last night." He huffs out an agitated sigh. "He wasn't exactly sober, but I can understand how he mistook you for the intended target."

This keeps getting crazier. "What are you talking about?"

His eyes take on a curious light as they flicker across my face. "You truly have no idea, do you?"

I glare at him. "No, I don't."

"You have fae ancestors. I'd guess hundreds of years back, and considering your surname, they'd be on your father's side. None related closely enough to make *you* fae, but close enough that a small remnant of their magic lies dormant within you. That's why Max thought you were the one he was assigned to collect."

I burst out laughing. "I'm not sure where you're getting this shit from. I don't think you understand how crazy you sound." The throbbing behind my eyes returns, but more from the stress and how fast my head is spinning than from Max's assault.

The corner of his mouth quirks. "You don't believe me." It's not a question.

"I just met you," I say in a quiet voice. "I don't believe anything." He's trying to use my family to make me buy his story.

He steps closer and places a finger under my chin, gently tilting it upward, as if he's concerned he'll hurt me.

I freeze as his eyes dance across my face, as though he's studying every inch meticulously.

He slowly traces the line of my jaw, brushing my hair back and tucking it behind my ear. "Are you hurt anywhere else?" he asks, his voice soft.

I swallow and shake my head. "No."

"Aurora."

"Tristan," I level.

He smiles. "You're not afraid of me."

I consider what he says and decide he's right. As much as I probably should fear him—the alleged leader of the fae—I don't.

"You silly, silly human," he says, shaking his head in exasperation, his fingers lingering against my cheek. "It's a good thing you aren't going to remember any of this."

His fingers warm against my skin, and his eyes capture mine in a gaze that goes on too long. Then, his eyebrows rise, and he adjusts his hand, squinting slightly as he peers into my eyes.

I blink at him. "What are you doing?"

He drops his hand and lets loose a surprised laugh. "This is going to be a problem."

"Hold on. What did you mean by *you aren't going to remember any of this*? Holy shit, were you trying to give me some freaky ass fae amnesia?"

His lips twitch. "It would seem my manipulation doesn't work on you."

Despite the pounding of my heart, I smile. He can't control me.

chapter Three

TRISTAN SEEMS CIVILIZED FOR A FAE, NOT THAT I'VE come across any before today. I'm finding it hard to wrap my head around the possible existence of them. He looks deceptively human, aside from his vivid eyes. It makes my head spin, more so when I consider there's a tiny chance he's being truthful. I could be living among the fae without any knowledge. I could have *family ties* to the fae.

I scan the undecorated hallway outside the elevator, searching for a sign of hidden cameras, but find nothing. I'm cold, disconnected from my body, as if someone is going to jump out and tell me this whole thing is a prank. Or I'll wake up any second, lying in my dorm room in a cold sweat, shivering from this nightmare.

Tristan asks me to follow him, and I concede, figuring I have a better chance at escaping if I'm somewhere with a window or a door. We step into the small elevator, and I put as much distance between us as possible. Tristan's lips twitch in amusement, but I ignore him.

He doesn't look at me as he speaks. "You'll have to forgive me for Max's behavior."

I press my lips into a tight line and keep my eyes forward. "I don't blame you for his behavior," I say in a low voice. "I blame you for the fact that I'm still here."

He nods. "I see."

I lean against the wall and cross my arms. "You can't keep me here." My voice is quieter than I want. It lacks assurance, and I hate that.

"Have I said anything to lead you to believe I'm keeping you here?" he asks.

"Actions speak louder," I retort. "I was chained to a fucking chair."

He shifts his gaze over to me, but I refuse to meet it. "I had no plans to keep you here once I adjusted your memory. I don't particularly enjoy keeping the company of someone who does not wish to keep mine."

"Right, so then where does that leave us?"

He scratches along his jaw. "I can't let you go yet. Not knowing what you do."

I scowl. "How the hell is that my fault? I didn't ask for this!"

"I understand that," he says, his voice strained.

I shake my head, "Listen, I won't tell anyone about what happened. About you, okay? You don't have to be concerned about me."

Tristan's chest rises as he takes a deep breath. "This isn't an ideal situation for either side. I put my people above all else."

"That's cool. Really. But I can't stay here. You've got to find some way to convince your 'people' that I'm not a threat."

His expression remains impassive. "Aren't you?"

23

"Tristan, *you* kidnapped *me*. I don't exactly have the upper hand here."

His brows tug closer. "Let me offer you a deal."

My eyes widen. "A deal?"

"There's a female fae on your campus. I need her located."

"Why?" I ask without thinking, as if I've accepted the existence of fae.

"That's not your concern. You locate the girl and contact me to collect her."

"Why would I do that?"

"To show me I can trust you. It's simple enough." Simple. How can he use a word like that in this situation? Nothing about this is simple. He's acting as if I'll go home, and this will no longer affect me, but no matter what happens when I leave, this—meeting him—will impact my future. I have a million questions I'm too scared to ask. There are so many possibilities I'm not allowing myself to entertain. All because of *him*.

A flash of anger lights up my entire body. "And if I refuse?"

"Don't refuse," he advises.

I swallow. "How would I know who you're looking for?"

He seems pleased—almost relieved—that I'm both considering the offer and asking the right questions. "I can provide you with a charm that will allow you to identify her as one of my kind." He's put some thought into this.

"Magic," I mutter under my breath.

"Just so," he says as the elevator signals we've reached the top floor. The door slides open, revealing the large entryway of a penthouse suite.

Tristan sweeps his arm out and gestures for me to walk ahead. I don't trust him, and it's obvious from my expression. With a quick smirk, he exits first. At least I know I'm not walking into a trap. We stop at a door, which Tristan unlocks and opens before stepping inside.

I follow him, taking in my surroundings as I walk further into the suite. The sunrise beams through expansive windows that overlook the city, and the autumn sky illuminates the living room. Plush, black furnishings frame a glass coffee table, and a flat screen is attached to the wall above a lavish fireplace. The suite smells fresh and a bit like lemons, as if it's just been cleaned. It also smells like *him*. A crisp, alluring scent I haven't quite figured out, and one I'm fighting not to like.

I roll my eyes. "Of course you're rich."

"I'm a successful businessman." He shrugs.

My cheeks burn. "So what? You glamour people into giving you money?"

Tristan bristles. "I have earned my wealth honestly."

I walk past him and stand against the wall, that way I can't be surprised from behind. I prop my foot against it, trying to look casual despite my racing pulse. He eyes my shoe and his lips twist; I've annoyed him. I decide in a matter of seconds that I don't care.

"Where are we?" I glance around. "Earth?"

He presses his lips together against a smile. "I live in the human world, yes. We are able to reside here because we appear the same as you or any other human." I want to roll my eyes again. He looks far too perfect to *appear the same* as anyone.

"Okay. *Is* there another, like, realm or whatever?"

He nods tightly.

My brows draw closer. "And you chose this one?"

He almost smiles. "Chose is a strong word. I think that's a story for another time."

I wrinkle my nose, shooting him a look that lets him

know there won't be another time. "Let's get back to me going home. Because I'd like to. Now."

"You're uncomfortable," he says, watching me with a spark of curiosity in his eyes.

"I'm confused." I don't elaborate. I won't give Tristan any more ammunition to use against me.

None of this makes any sense. Tristan made someone disappear with the wave of his hand. There's a good chance if he's not the leader of the fae as he claims to be, he's part of the mob with a wicked budget for special effects.

"This has been inconvenient for everyone involved." He shrugs out of his suit jacket and drapes it over a chair before rolling up the sleeves of his white dress shirt. My eyes follow the movement, and I swallow thickly. *Those arms . . .*

I shake my head. "Inconvenient?" I remark incredulously, pushing away from the wall. "You think this was just a dent in my weekend plans? You kidnapped me! And now you want me help you kidnap someone else!"

He waits until I've finished shouting, then says, "However this seems, you're not the only one at a disadvantage. You were kidnapped by accident, Aurora, but now you know about us. The fae magic that clings to you isn't letting me remove your memories. My people expect me to protect their existence— that's what being their leader means. Having you out there is a liability. I have no desire to kill a woman over a mistake, let alone one that is part fae. Work with me on this. It will help me sell my decision to . . . spare you."

"Why do you need me for this? If you're some powerful fae leader, don't you have, like, an army of fae or something to go after your enemies? She's one girl. I don't get it."

His jaw is clenched so tight his teeth must be screaming.

"This matter isn't one I'd like to make known on a large scale. Sending you resolves that problem."

I lick my lips. "If it's so serious, why are you trusting me with it?"

"You seem like a competent person, Aurora. Consider me impressed with your ability to escape Max." He chuckles. "As for the girl in question, this is more of a preventative measure."

My brows inch closer. "Meaning?"

"That's not something you need to worry about." He reaches into his pocket. "To ensure you identify the correct fae, here is a photo of Miss—"

"Fine," I cut him off, snatching the wallet-sized photo from him without looking at it. "Let me go home, Tristan." Maybe I should feel grateful that he doesn't want to hurt me. No, screw that. Neither of us would be stuck in this position if *he* hadn't sent Max out to kidnap someone. I push the thought away. I can't allow myself to consider the possibility he's telling the truth—that fae exist.

"Very well." He walks toward another room, but I stay put and wait for him to come back. He returns and holds out his hand. Sitting in his palm is a bracelet with a circular, dark turquoise charm set around a dainty-looking silver band crafted to look like delicate tree branches. It's pulsing with light. It must have batteries inside. "Put this on," he instructs.

I take it from him, slipping it onto my wrist. Only after it's on do I consider its potential negative effects on me. My eagerness to get the hell out of here is making me reckless. I need to keep it together. Nothing happens while I stand there staring at it, so I force myself to relax. "Great. Can I go now?"

"Once you have returned home, you will keep this bracelet on no matter what. Do you understand?"

I bite back my retort. I want to take the bracelet off and throw the damn thing at his head, but instead I nod. My teeth hurt from keeping my jaw locked, and I'm pretty sure I look feral.

"Charming," he says. "The stone will illuminate in the presence of my kind." He reiterates, reaching into his pocket and pulling out a business card. "Here's my cell phone number. Call me directly and try your best not to alert her." If this is a joke, his acting is impeccable. I almost believe him. This back and forth in my head is going to give me whiplash.

I take his card and slip it into my back pocket. "What if she notices?"

"It's not a difficult task, Aurora."

"Is that what you told Max?" I remark, my voice dripping sarcasm. "What's to keep me from bailing on this little adventure once I'm home?"

"You'd like to test me?" he inquires, sizing me up like an animal surveying its prey.

I force a neutral expression. "It doesn't seem like many do."

A dark look passes over his face. "There's a reason for that."

"I've witnessed a lot of crazy today. If you want to scare me, you'll have to do better than that." We're so close that his cologne tickles my nostrils, and I can feel his breath on my cheek.

His eyes narrow. "Who *are* you?"

"Guess you should've done your research before you kidnapped me," I say.

"Had it been my intention to bring you here, I would have." He licks his bottom lip.

Instead of replying, I glance at the bracelet around my wrist. The turquoise stone continues to pulse in his presence. I tug the sleeve of my cardigan to cover it. An uncomfortable weight settles on my shoulders, and a familiar tightness fills my chest. I try to swallow, but my mouth is too dry. I notice a slight shake in my hands and an increase in the pounding of my heart. I think I'm having a panic attack.

Tristan regards me with an odd expression. "Aurora?"

I shake my head and turn away, looking out the window as I try to force myself to breathe. Not a minute later, I feel his presence behind me and refuse to turn around.

"What are you studying?" he asks.

My forehead creases. "I . . . what?"

"Your major," he clarifies. "What is it?"

I take a deep breath. "Business."

"What year?"

"Fourth." I take another breath, relieved to find my heart rate returning to a normal pace. "I'll graduate in the spring."

"Impressive. What are your plans after graduation?"

I laugh, leaving his question unanswered. I'm not about to bond with my kidnapper.

I turn around. "What are you doing?" I know what he's doing, he's talking me through my panic attack.

"Making conversation," he answers.

"Well, don't. We aren't friends. After this situation is dealt with, we will never speak again," I say, all of my anger and confusion backing the fierceness in my voice.

"Feel better?" he asks.

"Excuse me?"

"Does your pseudo sense of control over the situation make you feel better?"

I scowl and look away. "Don't pretend you know anything about me."

"A person learns a lot about someone when they pay attention."

I need to get out of here. "You've given me the bracelet and your phone number. I know what I'm supposed to do. Now take me home."

"All right, all right." Tristan picks up his jacket and pulls it back on, buttoning the front, and nods toward the elevator. I follow him but stay on the opposite side. I may not be afraid of him, but that doesn't mean I want him in my personal space.

The elevator stops on the main level. When we step out into the lobby, it's clear I'm in one of the fanciest hotels in the city. The white marble floor and crystal chandeliers are a dead giveaway. A few men in dark suits pass by, nodding at Tristan, but shooting me hungry looks. *Great.* More arrogant men who stare at me like I'm something to eat.

"This is yours?" I ask, unable to hide my surprise. Under different circumstances, I would use this opportunity to pick his brain about business, but I'm not about to ask him for help.

"Yes," he answers.

The lobby has a subdued atmosphere that comes with wealth. I've never considered a career in hotel management, but I feel an uncomfortable sliver of respect for my kidnapper. I immediately want to slap myself and insist it's strictly professional interest.

Or Stockholm Syndrome.

"Good afternoon, Mr. Westbrook," a chipper voice greets Tristan.

He smiles politely. "Good afternoon, Gloria," he says and dismisses her with a nod. The older-looking woman walks over to the lunch buffet in the attached dining room.

"Friend of yours?" I ask with an arched brow, following him out the door.

"Her husband passed away a little over a year ago. She's been staying here ever since," he explains.

"That's terrible," I say. "And expensive."

He stops at the curb in front of a fancy black town car. "My driver will take you home."

I nod. It suddenly feels awkward, like I should say goodbye or something, which is insane. This wasn't a pleasant visit or a meeting between friends. I'm lucky to be standing outside and not locked in that room.

Tristan opens the backseat door for me and stands behind it, waiting for me to get in. I slip into the car and buckle my belt.

Tristan leans inside. "Remember our deal, Aurora."

I force a brilliant smile. "Has anyone ever told you how much of an ass you are?"

He mirrors my smile. "No one alive."

I roll my eyes. "Good one."

He closes the door and steps back onto the sidewalk. Keeping my eyes on Tristan, I tell the driver where to go. As we pull out into traffic, I watch as Tristan stands at the curb until I'm out of sight.

I stare out the window for a while before I realize I'm crying. I wipe the tears away only for more to fall. I'm no longer running on adrenaline. It's quiet, and I have time to think. I catch a glimpse of myself in the rearview mirror. I look, well, like a girl who was kidnapped and held captive for hours. My hair is in a tangle of messy, matted curls, and both my eyeliner and mascara have smudged almost all the way off since the party last night. The sight of myself sobers me up.

31

I glance at the clock on the dash; it's just after noon. Last night seems like a long time ago.

I was *kidnapped*.

The driver clears his throat, and I startle from my reverie, unaware that the car has stopped moving. I glance at him for a moment and then go through the motions of undoing my seatbelt and opening the door to get out.

I wrap my arms around my waist and hug my cardigan closer as the car pulls away. It's September, and the weather is still warm, but I'm shivering.

Allison isn't home when I get to our room. I consider texting her but realize I don't have my phone. *Dammit.* I must've lost it at some point during my escapades. I make a mental note to go out and get a new one. I don't have the money for it, but I need a cell phone.

My eyes can't stay away from the bracelet snaked around my wrist. The charm stares at me and makes my heart pound unevenly. This entire situation is so insane. I still can't wrap my head around it. I can't tell anyone. I wouldn't risk putting any of the people I love in danger.

After a shower, I change into a pair of high-waisted shorts and a plain black tank top. I'm blow-drying my hair when I hear the door slam shut. I turn the blow-dryer off and peek into the bedroom to find Allison tossing her purse onto her bed.

She turns and looks at me. "There you are. You disappeared last night."

Not by choice. "Yeah, I sort of met someone, and we went somewhere quiet to talk."

She gives me a suggestive look and wiggles her eyebrows.

"Oh, I got you."

I cringe. "No, that's not what I meant."

"I'm sad I missed your walk of shame," she teases.

I frown. "Thanks."

"Are you hungover?" she asks.

I wish that's what this was. "No. I'm fine."

"You look like you need some strong coffee." Her eyes flick across my face. "Dark circles for days."

"I'm fine." Okay, now I *am* lying. To my best friend. To her face.

"Okay then," she mumbles.

I run my fingers through my hair. "I'm—"

"What the heck is that?" she cuts me off, her eyes wide.

I shake my head. "What is what?" I follow her gaze down to my wrist, and my mouth goes dry. The stone in the bracelet Tristan gave me, the charm supposedly designed to detect fae, is pulsing with light.

chapter Four

ALLISON STAGGERS BACK, BUT HER EYES STAY LOCKED ON the bracelet. As if waking from a trance, her wide hazel eyes find mine. "Aurora, where did you get that?"

This can't be happening. Not after all the shit I went through. This is *not* happening. Maybe it's a trick of the light.

"Where did you get that bracelet?" she asks again.

I shake my head. "Um . . ." I shift my arm behind my back as I debate lying. Honestly, I wish I could climb my ass out the window, but I don't think I'll fit. That, and we're not on the ground floor.

Allison's face is a mask. "Where did you get it?"

I swallow the lump in my throat. "He's looking for you."

Allison pushes past me like I'm a piece of furniture, letting loose a string of expletives. As if remembering the source of her fear, she grabs my arm and rips the bracelet off. It hits the floor with little sound. Gritting her teeth, Allison lifts her foot and brings it down. Over and over. Until the charm is no longer illuminated.

"How the hell did you meet him?" she demands in between shallow breaths.

"Some guy at the party thought I was you, so he knocked me out and brought me to *him*," I answer in a quiet voice. "Oh god . . . It's true?" I shove my hand into my pocket and pull out the folded photo Tristan gave me. I open it, and the familiar face staring back at me knocks the breath out of my lungs.

Allison stands in front of me, brows furrowed as if she's trying to come up with an answer. Abruptly, she rushes around, grabbing clothing, books, and anything else she can get her hands on. "I have to get out of here." She throws things into a suitcase, not looking my way once.

I watch her, unable to find words. *This is Allison*, I tell myself. My roommate. My best friend. The person who busts my ass during exams and lifts me up at the same time. I have no idea how to feel. "You—the fae—they're *real*?"

She nods, her lips pressed into a tight line.

My jaw clenches. "Why is Tristan looking for you?"

Allison grabs my hands and holds them, ignoring my question. "Leave with me." Her plea is desperate.

"What? I can't!" I pull my hands away from hers. "I need to finish school and get my degree. I have a life, a normal freaking life despite everything I've seen and learned in the last twelve hours!" I shake my head to clear it and take a step back. Allison stands there with an unsure look on her face. She turns away without a word and wrestles a dress from its hanger. Her knuckles are white; her grip is sure.

Allison's voice is rough with unshed tears. "I never wanted you to find out what I am. You didn't need to know. It isn't safe."

"Safe? Tristan told me my ancestors were fae. Now I find

out you are too, and you're on the run from him. All of a sudden you're worried about *safe*?"

She freezes. "Wait, you're part of a fae bloodline?" Something like recognition passes over her face. "That's why—I've always sensed *something* on you, but I never knew what, and I couldn't bring myself to say anything. It was clear you didn't know or you would've known about me, so I ignored it."

My eyes widen, and my forehead creases. "I have no idea what's going on right now! I just found out about the fae!"

Her gaze softens. "I know. Let's get out of here. We'll figure it out, I promise, but we need to leave."

My eyes burn as the tightness in my chest threatens to suffocate me. "I'm not going anywhere," I force out in a hoarse voice.

Allison throws the dress into her suitcase. The only sound in the room is the loud zip of her luggage. She looks at me for a long moment, but I can't read her expression. "I'm so sorry. I have to leave," Allison whispers. She takes off, leaving the door wide open.

Her quick footsteps retreat down the hall, but I don't follow. Tears spill free and wet my cheeks. I want to go after her. Shake her and demand answers. I have a million questions, but my feet are glued to the floor.

I stand there as the minutes tick by and stare at the almost empty side of our room. Allison's bed is unmade like usual, but all of her dresser drawers are askew, the clothes she left behind falling out of some of them.

The fae are real.

I might not have believed the crazy guy who kidnapped me, but Allison—my best friend—I believe. I've lived with her for years. How did I not know something wasn't human about her?

There must've been clues. I sink down onto my hard mattress and push my palms against my eyes.

I stand and pace my room until I'm dizzy, trying to come up with some brilliant plan to figure this whole thing out, to keep Tristan from finding Allison, to keep the fae off my back. None of my plans are feasible. Leaving would only take the issue elsewhere, not get rid of it. Facing it head-on looks like my only option right now.

Huffing out a heavy sigh, I fall onto my bed and curse. I bash my fists against the mattress, but none of it takes away the ache left behind by Allison's absence or what she hid from me. I thrust my fingers through my hair and groan.

I spend the rest of the afternoon trying to get in contact with her, checking with her friends to see whether they've heard from her—none of them have—and scouting out every place on campus she might go to. I've run out of all options except one. Maybe there's a chance Oliver knows something. I head to his room and bang on the door until he opens it. I was hoping to keep him out of this, but that isn't going to be possible. I don't know what else to do at this point.

He pokes his head out the door and frowns. "Aurora, what's up?"

"Have you heard from Allison today?"

He shakes his head and opens the door to let me in. "She did mention going to visit her parents, so maybe she went home."

"I'm worried, Oliver." I don't tell him she packed her bags and took off. I don't mention that there's a dangerous, potentially psychotic fae looking for her. If I didn't know about Allison, I can't see that Oliver would.

He laughs. "It's Allison. I'm sure she's fine."

I blow out a breath, but it does nothing to alleviate the

weight on my chest. "I have a bad feeling. Please help me find her."

"Okay." He sighs. "Hold on. We both have the Track Your Friend app."

"Like a GPS sort of thing?"

"Yeah," he answers.

"Okay, can you try to find her?" I chew my bottom lip as he taps away on this phone.

His eyes brighten when it chimes. "I got her," he says. "She's still in the city but nowhere near campus." He frowns. "It looks like she's across town somewhere."

"Why would she go there?" I ask.

He shrugs. "Her cousin runs a bar around there. Maybe she went to see him?"

"Do you know which bar?" I ask, and he nods. "Can you take me? I want to make sure she's okay." I have no idea why Allison isn't tearing it out of town while she's got the chance. Could this cousin of hers know something about her situation? Maybe he knows how to keep her safe. I want to believe that.

We walk down to the student parking lot and get in his car. As we're pulling out of the lot, Oliver asks me to call her. Shame licks at my insides.

I bite my lip. "I think I lost my phone at the party."

His eyes flit to me for a second before returning to the road. "That doesn't seem like you."

"I didn't do it on purpose," I snap and regret it when he frowns. "I'm sorry. I didn't mean to sound so snippy. Give me your phone, and I'll try her again."

She's still not answering. Not that I blame her. She's scared out of her mind right now and on the run. I might not under-stand what's going on, but I do know that I'll fight to protect my best friend.

"Anything?" Oliver asks.

"Nope." I hang up as it clicks over to voicemail. "We have to find her, Oliver."

She's got some major explaining to do.

Oliver pulls into a parking space and kills the engine. "The bar is a few blocks away. This is as close as we're going to get on a Saturday."

A quick Google search shows me that the club is only open forty-eight hours a week. Friday and Saturday, all day and all night. I nod. "Let's go."

The place is packed wall to wall with hot, sweaty, dancing bodies, and it's so loud the building is vibrating. Oliver throws his arm around me and shouts in my ear. "I think we should split up. If you find her first, wait for me at the bar, and I'll do the same."

Eager to find Allison, Oliver and I turn in different directions. I comb through the crowd, but it's a mess of unfamiliar faces. I try my best not to push people as I squeeze through, holding my breath at the heavy smell of liquor, cologne, and perfume, but it's difficult with all of the flailing arms and grinding hips everywhere.

I scout out the bar before I fight my way through to the bathrooms. I'm walking down the narrow, poorly lit hallway when someone grabs me around the waist and pulls me into a dark room. I try to scream, but a hand covers my mouth and muffles the sound. My pulse surges, and when the lights flick on, I squint against the sudden brightness of what appears to be a storeroom for stock. Boxes fill most of the shelves, and the rest are lined with bottles of liquor. It looks like there was a window, but it's been boarded up.

I recognize my captor instantly, and my eyes narrow.

"What the hell are you doing here?" I growl when he moves his hand away from my mouth.

"I could ask you the same question, sweetheart." Tristan slips his arm from my waist and steps back. "Did you come to see me?" he purrs. His voice is sensual but dangerous. Even with the space between us, his inviting scent reaches me. I wonder if all fae men are as gorgeous as he is, then I mentally slap myself for allowing my head to go there.

I attempt to make myself leave—to force my feet to carry me out the door—but fail. "Did you follow me?" My eyes travel across his face and drop to his chest where a landscape of hard muscle pulls at his shirt.

"An interesting idea, but no. I received a phone call from one of my contacts—the gentleman who owns this bar—who tipped me off that the young woman I'm looking for was here."

Allison's cousin sold her out? What the hell could she have done to warrant that?

"I hope I'm not hindering another kidnap attempt." My voice is soft, laced with false sweetness. "Maybe you should find another career?" My chest rises and falls rapidly as I stand there, knowing I should leave.

His lips twist into an arrogant smile. "You're posing a bit of a challenge. It's amusing."

"Go to hell," I spit.

He chuckles. "Oh, I've been. Several times. I happen to be good friends with the Prince."

I roll my eyes. "I have no idea what you're saying."

He reaches forward, quick and graceful, and cups my chin. "I understand you found who I'm looking for. You seem to have misplaced her, yes?"

"I'm not going to let you hurt her."

"It sounds like you know this girl," he muses.

I close my eyes, unable to look at him anymore. "She's my best friend."

"Of course you want to protect her. You're loyal to her. That's admirable." Tristan's thumb brushes across my cheek, and my eyes fly open as my jaw clenches. "I'll offer you a deal. Our previous one didn't work out as I'd hoped, but I'm willing to give this another chance. I'm in the mood for some entertainment."

"You're twisted," I growl.

His smirk is a flash of perfect white teeth. "You find your friend first, and she's free to go. However, if *I* find her before you do, she's mine."

"What—"

"I'm not done," he interrupts, his eyes glimmering like a child's on Christmas morning. "Not only is *she* mine. You agree to have dinner with me. You're still a bit of a puzzle." His eyes flick between mine.

I manage to smack his hand away from my face with an exasperated laugh. "No way in hell is that happening." My tone is firm, and yet, the image of sitting across from Tristan at a restaurant flashes through my mind.

"Are you doubting yourself?" He's mocking me, and I want to slap the smug grin off his face.

"I'm going to find her," I vow. "I don't need to make a deal with you."

"Accept what I've offered and your friend could have the chance at immediate freedom. Her indiscretions will be forgiven, and she may remain where she wishes."

"You think I'm going to agree to something like this? On the off chance you find her before I do, I've not only sealed her fate to whatever you choose but my own as well? You're insane."

"And yet you've made a deal with me once before."

"I didn't have a choice," I remind him in a sharp tone.

"Look at it this way. You can accept this, or I can use you to get to her."

"Why does it matter so much?" I snap. "What did she do?"

"Consider it privileged information."

"You don't think spending time with you makes me privileged? I'm shocked."

"I do enjoy your wit," he says, "but you have a choice to make."

I scowl. "Unbelievable. You want me to entertain you."

"Immortality can get a little dull at times. I like to keep things interesting."

The way I see it, my options are limited. If I don't take his deal, I can't be sure what will happen to me, but if I do and he finds Allison before I can . . . I am *not* having dinner with him.

"I'm going to find her," I repeat.

His eyes hold a challenge in their dark blue depths as he watches me. "So, we have a deal?"

"Fine," I say through gritted teeth. "Now back off."

He raises his hands in front of him in mock surrender and steps back a few paces. I'm out the door in a second without looking back as I race toward the dance floor. I have to find Allison. I need to make sure she's safe. That, and if I don't find her before Tristan does, my future—everything I've worked for—will be for nothing.

I'm less polite this time as I make my way through the crowd of gyrating bodies. More than once, I think I see her, but when I approach, it's always a stranger. My heart is pounding so hard I can feel it in my throat. My palms sweat, and the fact that so much is at stake makes me frantic.

I catch the top of a blond head walking toward the back door, and I follow. My feet surge forward when I recognize the clothing on the girl. *It's her.* I grab the back of her shirt, and she whips around with wide eyes.

"Aurora?" she shouts to be heard over the music.

"We have to go!" I yell. I may have found her first, but I'm not taking any chances. I'm not trusting Tristan to keep his word.

"How did you find me?" she asks.

"It doesn't matter right now! He's here. We need to go!"

She nods and reaches for my hand, pulling me through a mass of writhing dancers. I manage to squeeze between two people, cringing at the damp warmth of their bodies and push a few more out of my way. Finally, we make it out the door and stand in the parking lot around the back of the bar.

"Why did you come here?" I ask, trying to catch my breath.

"I was hoping my cousin could help. When I got here, he wouldn't see me."

"If he wouldn't help, why are you still here?"

"I thought he'd come around. I tried to talk to him and get him to understand, but he wouldn't listen. He's too loyal to Tristan. After that, I figured it would be a good place to hide out until I could come up with a plan."

"And did you?"

She sighs and slumps against the building. "I'm barely hanging on, Aurora." She puts her hand to her head and groans. "I'm so scared. I didn't think this would happen."

"I understand, but we have to keep moving. Where's your phone? Call Oliver."

Her head snaps up, and she sways on her feet. "Oliver is

here?"

I reach out and grab her, steadying her, and nod.

Allison swears loudly, her hands shaking at her sides. Her wide eyes are slightly bloodshot, as though she's been crying. I've never seen her so frightened. *Why is she so afraid of Tristan? What did she do?*

"Breathe, okay? We're going to figure this out."

She shakes her head. "I can't . . ." She closes her eyes and licks her lips.

"You can't what? Come on. We need to go."

Her eyes fly open, and she grips my arms.

"Easy, Allison. You're okay." Her grip is tight. She's hurting me, but I grit my teeth and force a passive expression.

"I'm so sorry," she whimpers.

"You ran because you were scared. It's okay. We're going to get through this." I say it more for my benefit, to reassure myself I'll figure out how to discredit Tristan's idea that I have fae in my family tree.

She shakes her head again. "I'm so sorry."

I'm about to question her incessant apologizing when she whips us around and pushes me against the cold brick of the building. I don't have time to open my mouth to speak.

Allison's expression shifts to a distant, unfamiliar look as she cuts off my oxygen, gripping my throat. Panic clamps down on my chest. Dizziness floods in, and I can't move. Black spots dot my vision, but I can't fight her off. I can't make a sound.

The back door swings open with a loud smack against the brick, and Allison wrenches her hand away as if she's been burned. She looks terrified at her own actions. As fast as she went all fae on my ass, she vanishes.

With Allison no longer holding me by my throat, I sway

on my feet. The pavement rushes to meet me like we're old friends. I close my eyes in preparation for the impact, but it doesn't come. It takes me a few long seconds to realize someone is holding me. I pry my eyes open to find Tristan. He's glaring at me, his unfairly gorgeous features dark and sharp in the moonlight. Every one of his eyelashes casts a dark shadow on his cheeks.

I hear him snarl, a beast in a pretty package, and then I pass out.

chapter Five

I BLINK SEVERAL TIMES BEFORE I REALIZE I'M LOOKING AT the familiar ceiling above my bed. I'm back in my dorm room with no idea how I got here. I sit up in a panic and wince at the lingering dizziness. Swinging my legs over the side of the bed, I use the nightstand to help me to my feet. I'm surprised to find my cell phone sitting on the table, but I grab it, scrolling through my contacts until I find Oliver's name.

"Aurora? Hey, what's up?"

"Where are you?"

"I'm in my room. Are you okay?"

"When did you get home?"

"What?" He laughs. "I didn't go out last night."

The clock in my room reads just after noon. "You were home? The whole night?"

"Yeah . . ." he says, sounding worried. "You okay?"

"I'm fine." I lie without a thought. "Have you heard from Allison today?"

Twisted Fate

"She's fine," he says in a casual tone.

I press my lips together. "You talked to her?"

"She's fine," he repeats in the same tone.

What the hell? "I'll talk to you later, Oliver." I hang up before he has a chance to say anything else. As I change out of last night's clothes, the rage of being manipulated fills me. I didn't ask for any of this. I have no idea what's going on, no idea what happened last night after I passed out, but I have a good idea where to look for answers.

I'm on my way to the Westbrook Hotel before I can talk myself out of it.

I charge up the marble stairs that lead to the building and fly through the open door. My footsteps echo on the ornate lobby floor as I approach the reception desk where I slam my fist against the dark wood counter.

"I need to see Mr. Westbrook," I demand.

The young, blond receptionist offers a polite smile. "My apologies, Mr. Westbrook is in a meeting. Would you like to wait?"

"No," I snap.

Her eyes widen. "Oh."

"I need to see him. Now."

"I'm sorry, that's not possible."

I roll my eyes. "I don't have time for this. You seem like a lovely person, and I bet he's not paying you enough to deal with people like me, so I'm sorry for what I'm about to do." Before she can open her mouth, I sprint toward the elevator. Jamming the button as if my life depends on it, I look over my shoulder in time to see her lift the phone to call security.

Once inside, I press the button for the penthouse and blow out a breath. I lean back against the wall and watch the numbers tick by as the elevator ascends. About halfway up, it stops, and the door opens.

"You came back?" The woman Tristan made disappear—Skylar—steps into the elevator and presses the button for another floor. Today her knee-high dress is bright red, matching the stain on her lips.

I open my mouth to answer as I survey her from head to toe. She's very much not dead. A dead body couldn't pull off heels like that. "I had to," I whisper.

Her laugh is a tinkling sound, like raindrops on a window. "What for? To make sure it was real?"

I shake my head. "To make sure he doesn't hurt my best friend." Even though she tried to make a meal out of me, she was scared, cornered. Maybe she hadn't fed in a long time. There are so many possibilities. She wouldn't hurt me on purpose.

Skylar flicks her tongue over her lower lip. "Ah, you figured out who he was looking for."

My jaw clenches. "He sent me to look for her."

"And you found her. Obviously."

I nod.

"She's your best friend, huh?" Her lips curl. "You didn't know your best friend was fae?" she taunts.

I hold back a scowl. "I didn't know the fae existed until a few days ago, so no, I didn't know my best friend was one. How many of you are there?"

Skylar shrugs, and even *that* looks graceful. "Close to ten percent of the population. Ever since our world was destroyed, we've been here." The elevator stops, and Skylar steps toward the door as it opens. "Coming back here was stupid. He let you go once. I don't see him doing it again."

I stuff my trembling hands into my pockets. "She's my best friend."

Skylar sighs, as if my decision to put myself in danger irritates her. "Humans," she mutters before the door shuts, and I'm alone.

I tap my hands against my thighs, thinking over what Skylar said about their world being destroyed. Now I understand Tristan's less than pleasant response when it came up the day we met.

My heart hammers in my chest, and my nerves sing with coiled energy as the elevator reaches the penthouse level. I'm ready for a fight if it means getting Allison back. I step off the elevator and through the small foyer to his door and bang my fist against it several times. As I'm getting ready to kick the damn thing in, it opens to reveal an annoyed looking Tristan.

My eyes widen a fraction as I take in Tristan's casual attire. *In a meeting, my ass.* "Where the hell is she?" I growl, pushing my way inside.

He glances between the empty hallway and where I'm standing inside his suite. "Lovely afternoon, isn't it?" He offers an amused expression and then closes the door as if he's confronted by angry business majors every day.

"Cut the bullshit. Where is Allison?"

"You mean the young woman who almost killed you?"

My eyes narrow. "She didn't almost kill me. She stopped." I cross my arms over my chest and refuse to back down.

"Thanks to me."

I let out a shaky breath and rake my fingers through my hair. "She stopped," I repeat to myself. "Now tell me where she is."

"She's here. Awaiting my orders."

"What the hell does that mean?" I bark.

Tristan pushes away from the door and closes the distance between us in a few strides. "Fae laws are much like your own. Actions have consequences, and Allison must accept the punishment for her misconduct."

"What misconduct?"

He says nothing.

"What did she do?" I say louder. His silence makes it apparent that he isn't going to tell me why she's being kept here or what she did. I lift my gaze until our eyes meet. There's a moment of silence before I say, "please don't hurt her."

"I'll treat the situation as I see fit." His voice is firm and unforgiving.

"What—?"

"It's time for you to leave." Tristan dismisses me with a wave of his hand.

"You think I'm going to leave without Allison? You lost our deal. I found her first."

"Then you lost her when she almost killed you." Tristan glances toward the door as Max walks into the suite. My entire body stiffens as his eyes focus on me. A potent mixture of fear and disgust go to war inside of me.

"Back for more fun, blondie?" he taunts. "Let me show you to my room. I promise I'll be gentle."

I recoil, revulsion twisting my expression.

"Miss Marshall was on her way out," Tristan interrupts smoothly.

"You're letting the human go? Again?" Max questions. "She could open her mouth and put us all in danger. Wipe her memory. We've got the girl we were after."

I look between them and take a couple of steps back, my

heart rate kicking up as they turn to watch me.

"I'm handling it," Tristan says in a firm tone, flicking his eyes over to me. Evidently he isn't going to tell Max he tried and *couldn't* wipe my memories.

"Fine," Max mutters, his teeth flashing in a snarl when he glances at me.

"Obviously I can't tell people the truth, so what do you want me to say? You don't think people will wonder where Allison is? She has friends and a boyfriend. People will question her whereabouts."

Tristan sighs. "She will return to her life soon enough."

I try not to let my relief show on my face. At least he said he'll let her go. "When is 'soon enough'? After you're done with her? Because she answers to you?" I say in a tight voice.

"Yes. Just as you do. That's how this works."

"I do *not* answer to *you*," I snap.

Max whistles and leans against the wall.

Tristan appears in front of me faster than my eyes can register the movement. "I saved your life. Twice."

"My life was in danger twice *because* of you!" I wait for him to respond with some high-handed remark, but he stands there with a stoic expression. I notice Max leaving the room out of the corner of my eye before my gaze focuses on the fae in front of me.

"How unusual," he says thoughtfully, licking his bottom lip.

"*What?*"

"You're so responsive. It's refreshing. Most people I encounter have a healthy fear of me or a high level of respect. It's clear you have neither."

I stifle my laugh and arch a brow instead. "You want me to fear you? Too bad. I don't. As for the respect? That's earned. You don't magically get it because you're some supernatural leader."

"How do you think I became a leader?" he challenges.

"I'm guessing some seriously dodgy politics."

His laugh is a deep, rich sound that makes him seem dangerously human.

"I'm not going to stand here and pretend I understand anything about your world, Tristan, but I will say this: Allison is twenty years old. Fae or not, she's young. Whatever she did, allow her a chance to make up for it, and she will."

He regards me with an odd, almost confused look. "I don't understand."

I nod. "That's two of us."

"You're so protective of someone who—"

"Could have killed me. I get it. But she didn't, and she's my best friend. I'd do anything for her. She's probably scared out of her damn mind right now. All I'm asking is that you consider that when you deal with her."

He tips his head back slightly. "What makes you think that matters to me?"

I open my mouth, but nothing comes out.

"I don't care that she's your friend, nor do I care how she feels. Our deal has reached its completion. You're free to leave. Unless you'd like to take me up on that dinner I proposed? It's not quite dinnertime, but I'd be willing to dine early this evening."

My jaw clenches, and I fight the urge to punch him, knowing it won't do any good. "You're a real ass."

"I believe you established that already," he says without interest.

"Thought I'd repeat it," I mutter.

He chuckles. "Anything else I can do for you, Aurora?"

I scowl. "So, I'm assuming you wiped Oliver's memory, and that's why he doesn't think he went out last night."

"He was a loose end." He shrugs. "I could've killed him instead." He lowers his face, and his eyes meet mine. "You're welcome."

"So you made him forget last night altogether?"

"Precisely." He smirks. "You look nervous, Aurora."

I stand straighter. I keep a neutral face as my heart pounds crazily; I'm sure he can hear it. My confidence might be a false bravado, but I'm holding on to it with everything I have.

"I'm not nervous," I snap.

"Keep fighting it. It makes for wonderful entertainment," Tristan quips. "So, dinner?"

"Are you kidding?"

He regards me with an amused expression. "You're not hungry?"

"I'm not having dinner with you, Tristan."

"Perhaps another time."

I smile sweetly. "Yeah, perhaps not." With that, I head for the door. Nothing about this situation is ideal, especially my lack of control. Allison means the world to me, but it's clear there's nothing I can do right now. I need another plan.

When I get back to campus, I spend an hour moving from one spot to another—from my bed to my desk chair and then to Allison's bed and back to mine. Not knowing what she's going through at the hands of Tristan Westbrook is making it impossible to sit still. My hair is a tangled mess from swiping my fingers through it so many times, so I pull it back into a bun. Every time I try to think of a plan to get Allison back, the rational part of my brain shoots the idea down, knowing it won't work. The fae are too new to me. I don't have a chance at besting them. Not yet.

I make the mistake of searching fae lore online. After combing through so many different legends, I doubt any of them will do me much good. One piece of information I read multiple times is one that Tristan confirmed himself: iron is poisonous to fae. I tuck that away for future reference because if I'm going to fight Tristan again, I want to be prepared. Nothing else I come across gives me a better idea of what I'm up against. I also make several notes on things to look through the next time I have an opportunity to go home. Family photo albums, heirlooms, anything that has a chance of tying any of my ancestors to the fae.

There's a light knock at the door before it opens, and Oliver walks in. I shut my laptop, and my heart sinks. What am I supposed to tell him? He can't know the truth. It's too dangerous.

"Hey." He walks over to Allison's bed and drops onto it.

I smile, glancing over at him. "What's up?"

"I'm looking for Allison." He scans the room. "I tried calling her. I thought she'd be here."

I swallow the lump in my throat before I say, "I'm not sure where she is."

"Hmm, okay." He shoots me a goofy grin. I want to scream at him for dropping it so easily, but it's not his fault. "Want to grab some dinner?" he asks.

I catch my lower lip between my teeth and nod. I haven't eaten since, well, I can't remember, and despite the worry that swirls in my chest, I'm hungry. The constant upset in my stomach is only made worse by its emptiness. I need a break from all of the crazy. At least for a little while. "Let's go."

We walk to Taylor's Brew and are seated at a booth near the back. I've been here a handful of times with friends, but Allison never wants to come, saying they're too overpriced. While the prices *are* a little high, their deep-fried pickles are the best I've ever had. The amazing food makes up for the lack of interior decorating. Nothing hangs on the wood-paneled walls, and the bar stools and booths look as if they haven't been reupholstered in years. There's a stage at the front of the room where people perform on occasion. I play piano and have been writing my own songs for years, but I have yet to make it up there.

Turning my attention back to our booth, Oliver pores over the menu, and I bite my tongue several times to keep from saying something that won't make any sense to him.

"Aurora?"

Oliver glances up, and I turn my head when I hear my name. Grant stands a few feet away with a couple of other guys.

"Hey," I say with a polite grin before turning to Oliver. "This is Grant. He's in my elective class. Grant, this is Oliver." Grant's friends wave and head over to the bar.

When he sticks his hand out, Oliver leans over and shakes it. "Nice to meet you."

"Likewise," Oliver says.

Grant's gaze swings back to me. "Have you started that research paper?"

I laugh. "Not even a little bit." I've been a bit preoccupied.

He chuckles. "Sounds about right." He looks over at the bar. "I should get over there, but it was nice to meet you, Oliver. And don't worry about the bill. It's on me."

"No way, I'm not letting you buy our food," I say.

He shrugs. "I own the place, Aurora. It's no big deal."

"Are you kidding? That's crazy."

"It was passed through the family, and now it's my turn."

"We're not going to argue over free food," Oliver chimes in.

He grins. "I'll see you guys around," he says before rejoining his friends.

Oliver and I order our food and talk about school. For the most part, I offer one-word answers and struggle to keep up. My thoughts keep going back to Allison and what's happening at the Westbrook Hotel. I've decided to give it three days. If she's not back by then, I'm going to strap iron stakes to every inconspicuous part of my body, and I'm going to charge that fucking building. I have to. Even though I still don't understand why she lost her shit and attacked me, I have no doubt that Allison would do the same for me.

Chapter Six

IT'S BEEN TWO DAYS, AND ALLISON ISN'T BACK. TO SAY I'M a mess is an understatement.

I leave class an hour before the lecture ends and sit in my room, where I go over what I know about the situation. I've made several lists, all of which would make any outsider think I'm a lunatic. I fist my hair, groaning as I shuffle over to my bed and flop onto it.

"You okay there?"

I sit up in a flash, barely escaping a wicked case of whiplash, and see Allison standing in the open doorway. She looks fine, not a hair out of place, no wrinkles in her clothes. Her face is free of makeup, which is unusual for her, but aside from that, she looks normal. "Are you really here?" I ask.

It takes her a moment to smile. "Yeah, I'm here."

I launch myself off the bed and throw my arms around her.

She pulls back and stares at me for a moment and then hugs me back, tighter. "I'm so sorry," she murmurs. "I never meant to hurt you. I was so scared. I don't know what came over me. I'm never like that. I shouldn't have left you, especially after everything you went through."

"It's okay," I say, rubbing her back. "You're not going to disappear on me again, are you? What the hell was that?"

"I'm not going anywhere," she promises with a small laugh. "The disappearing is a fae thing. Shifting, we call it. Like teleportation, but calling it that makes it sound weird to me."

"That's because it *is* weird. Whatever, I'm just glad you're here. Are you okay?" I pull away enough to look at her. "What happened? What did he do? Did he hurt you? I swear to—"

"Hold on," she cuts in. "Slow down and breathe, Aurora. I'm okay."

My eyes narrow as I look her over again. She appears to be unharmed, but that doesn't mean she wasn't hurt. "What happened?"

"Nothing that you're thinking. He didn't hurt me, I swear."

The tension in my muscles doesn't relax any. "I came looking for you, but he wouldn't let me see you."

"You went back there?" she asks. "Are you insane? You could've been hurt."

"It was you, Al. I had to do *something*. But now, everything is going to be fine."

"How can you say that?" She sniffles. "With the news about your fae lineage, he isn't going to let this mistake go, which means he isn't finished with you."

The panic that's been living at the surface rears its unforgiving head.

He isn't finished with you.

Life settles into a comfortable routine over the following days, and I'm able to focus on my studies. It's almost as if I were never kidnapped, never told my family could be fae, never introduced to the insufferable Tristan Westbrook.

The morning of my work placement interview, I open my eyes to bright sunlight streaming in through my window. I roll over and reach for my phone. I'm still shocked that Tristan returned it, given he *did* kidnap me, but I'm in no place to question his kindness.

I squint at the backlight of the screen and my heart races when I read the time.

It's almost eight thirty.

I throw myself out of bed and into the bathroom to put myself together as fast as I can. Once my hair looks decent, twisted into a quick French braid, I apply a few swipes of light makeup so I look alive. I get dressed in a formal black jumpsuit and shrug on a matching blazer. Grabbing my bag off the dresser, I shove my portfolio inside before I pull on my heels and rush out the door.

I spend the entire cab ride to the conference center tapping my hands on my knees and chewing my lower lip. My stomach is swirling with nerves, and my pulse is so erratic I'm sweating. I can't remember ever being this anxious about something. If I'd had time for breakfast, I'm not sure I would've been able to stomach anything.

When the cab pulls up out front, I exit in a hurry after handing the driver some money. I burst through the front doors and speed-walk to the reception desk where an older looking man checks my ID.

"Aurora Marshall, you're the last student to arrive. Please follow me."

I almost scowl. Of course, I'm the last one here, did my frantic entrance not tip him off?

We walk down a wide hallway that opens into another lobby where a man sits behind a table.

"Register here, and you're all set," the receptionist says and walks away before I can thank him.

I step forward. "I'm Aurora Marshall."

"Degree program?" the man asks without looking up from the stack of papers he's looking through.

"Business," I say.

He lifts his gaze and hands me a lanyard with a visitor pass attached. "Your interview will be held in conference room E." He stands and points down the hallway. "Last door on your right."

"Great, thank you." I rush toward the room, but when I reach the door, my hand freezes halfway to the doorknob. Closing my eyes, I take a deep breath, letting it out slowly. *I've got this.* Straightening, I knock before walking into the conference room.

We all have moments in our lives where we reflect on every bad thing we've done in an attempt to comprehend why a terrible thing is happening to us. To determine why we deserve something so awful. As I approach the conference room table and lock eyes with Tristan Westbrook, I'm sucked into one of those moments. *What did I do to deserve this?*

He rises from his seat at the head of the table and buttons his black suit jacket. "Good morning, Miss Marshall," he says, and I stand there, screaming profanities in my head.

There's no one else in the room, no one to defuse the tangible tension or to look to for help.

"This isn't . . . you can't . . . what the *hell* are *you* doing here?"

His lips twitch. "An interesting way to introduce yourself to a potential boss."

My jaw clenches. "I'd sooner work under the manager of a Taco Bell," I seethe. "This is not happening." I move back a few steps. "There must be some mistake. I'll interview for someone—*anyone*—else."

"I figured you might say that. Unfortunately for you, I'm the last mentor available. You see, that's what happens when you sleep in and arrive late for an interview."

"My apologies. I haven't exactly been sleeping well."

"That's concerning to hear," he says, but the look on his face tells me he's far from concerned. If anything, he's amused. Bastard.

I stand there in silence for several beats before sighing. "This is my only option. Of freaking course." I approach the table that separates us. "This is serious. My education is the most important thing to me. I don't know why god hates me so much as to drop this in my lap, but here I am—and here you are."

He nods, remaining silent.

"For the duration of this interview, you are not you. You're a successful business owner and mentor that I'm meant to learn from, and I'm, well, I get to be me."

He presses his lips together against a smile, and I scowl.

"Quit it," I snap.

He arches a brow. "What am I doing?"

"You're looking at me like this is funny, and it's not. This is my future, and I'm pissed that you're screwing with it, so I'm telling you how this is going to go."

"Are you?" he asks. "Please continue."

"You ask questions, and I answer them. You're impressed with my answers, and then I leave. Simple as that. Got it?"

"I thought I was supposed to ask the questions."

"Tristan!" I shout without thinking. It's unprofessional, sure, but nothing about this situation is normal, and he has been nothing close to professional either.

"Relax, Aurora. Why don't we start?"

I huff out a breath and force a nod. "Fine."

He sticks his hand out. "Good morning. I'm Tristan Westbrook."

I hesitate but place my hand in his and shake it. "Aurora Marshall."

"Come on. You can do better than that. Do I make you that nervous?" His eyes dance with amusement.

I snatch my hand back. "No." My response is a bit too quick. "Let's just do this."

"Very well." He gestures to the chair across from him where I'm standing. "Please," he says before he returns to his seat.

I sit and pull my portfolio out of my bag. Opening it, I slide my resume out and set it on the table. I flick a glance up to find him watching me, and I push the paper toward him.

He picks it up and reads it over before setting it back down. "Your volunteer work is impressive."

"Thank you."

He meets my gaze. "What are you hoping to gain from this work placement?"

I take a deep breath. "Experience, of course. That's what anyone in my position would say. This isn't for me to get a taste of what my career might be to see whether I like it. I'm in my fourth and final year of this program. I don't have time to change my mind. Before walking into this interview, I would've said this might lead to full-time employment after I impressed my mentor, but alas, circumstances shape my answers. I'm going to go ahead and say experience—that's the safest answer."

"You choose to play it safe?"

"It depends," I say.

"On?" he counters.

"Circumstances." My voice has a bit of an edge to it.

"Have you been in positions of power in the past?"

"Yes. As listed under my volunteer experience, I led several teams during school events, and over the past few years, I've been one of the head members of the student union during the winter semester."

"Do you seek out these positions of power?"

"If you're asking me whether I like control, I think you—" I stop. "Yes, I do."

"You seem like a driven young woman."

"I like to think so," I say. "I know what I want, and I plan to do whatever it takes to achieve that."

He clicks the pen in his hand. "That doesn't surprise me."

"Any more questions?"

"Do you have a copy of your class schedule?"

I nod and hand it to him from my portfolio, cringing at the way my hand shakes. I knew this interview would make me nervous, regardless of the mentor, but Tristan sitting across from me is heightening that tenfold. *I just need to get through this.* I fold my hands in my lap and sit straighter, breathing in through my nose and out through my mouth to try to calm my uneven pulse.

"Excellent. So you have Mondays off?"

"Yes," I say.

"That works for me. You'll start this coming Monday, nine o'clock sharp."

My stomach flips at the burst of anxious excitement in my

chest. "I . . . wait, hold on. That's it?"

He leans back in his chair. "That's it."

"What if I don't want to work under you?"

"I don't think I've ever had a woman say that to me," he says with a twist of his lips.

"First of all, gross. Off to a great start with the sexual harassment." I shoot him a sarcastic thumbs up.

"Like I said, I'm the last mentor available, so it's me or nothing. Your choice. But as I recall, you need this to graduate. Like you said, your education is the most important thing to you."

"You did this," I accuse in a low voice as I stand, Allison's warning running through my mind. *He isn't finished with you.*

He shrugs. "That doesn't change anything."

"I'm going to—"

"What? Tell your program coordinator that the leader of the fae manipulated her mind to ensure that you were placed with his company?"

"You can't—"

"Yet I did," he says, an arrogant quality to his voice.

I step away from the table, turning my back on this fucked-up interview, and head for the door. I'm reaching for the handle when I make a snap decision. I turn around quickly, only to find myself face to chest with Tristan. His presence overwhelms me all at once. Heat radiates from him, warming my cheeks as I fight to not inhale his scent. I need to keep my thoughts clear, sharp. I can't have my head spinning right now.

"What?" I breathe.

He steals my gaze. "You turned around," he says, a challenge in his tone.

"You were following me," I counter, unable to force my eyes away from his.

"And soon you'll be the one following me." He flashes a grin. "Lighten up, Aurora. Your negative energy is ruining this moment. Try to see it as a unique learning opportunity."

I glare at him. "Are you kidding me?"

He raises a brow. "What would you like me to say?" He tips his face closer sightly, and I have to remind myself to breathe. "You're not making this little situation of ours any easier."

"You're the one who waltzed into my life all tall, dark, and . . . *you*." I want to kick myself for letting his proximity cloud my head for even a second. Damn him and his distracting blue eyes and crisp, alluring scent. *Fucking hell, I need to get out of here.*

He leans forward, and I step back until I'm against the door. "I'm almost glad my manipulation doesn't work on you," he says in a voice so quiet I barely catch it. "I think that would eliminate all the fun we have."

I shove him back, and he concedes a few inches with a nod, because there's no way my actual shove did anything. "What part of this do you think is *fun* for me?" I bark out a laugh. "You think I go home at the end of the day laughing to myself at how much *fun* I've had dealing with an arrogant, egocentric, fae leader who could ruin my entire life if he chooses?" My hands are still pressed against his chest. *Why* are my hands still pressed against his chest?

Tristan tilts his head to the side, watching me with interest. My chest swirls with nervous energy as my eyes flick across his face.

"I'm not afraid of you, as stupid as that is. I'm concerned as to why you're paying me so much attention. Max was right." I pause. "You better not tell him I said that. If only you could make me forget. Then I wouldn't have the knowledge of your race, regardless of whatever creepy connection my family has to the fae."

Tristan seems to consider this for a moment before he says, "If it were possible, would you really want me to make you forget?"

"That's not what I'm saying," I mutter, finally finding the will to pull my hands away and let them fall to my sides.

"I realize that. I'm asking you."

"I don't see that it matters now," I say.

"Answer the question."

"Why?" I snap.

He's quick in sliding a finger under my chin and tilting it up until our eyes meet, and my heart slams against my chest. His eyes flit back and forth across my face as I stand there, frozen. The wildness of his irises calms for a moment. There's a shift, almost too insignificant to notice, but I catch it. For a split second, a pained expression darkens his features. It's gone before I can understand what it means, and he steps away, giving me room to breathe.

His hands fall to his sides. "I think that answers my question."

My throat is too dry to speak; my voice will crack if I try, so I stay silent. This interview is over. I reach for the door and step into the hallway, feeling Tristan's gaze on my back. My feet carry me toward the lobby, but my mind is elsewhere. I'm almost far enough away to let myself relax when I hear his send-off.

"Good to meet you, Miss Marshall. I'll see you on Monday."

chapter
Seven

ALLISON JUMPS WHEN I RETURN TO OUR ROOM AND SLAM
the door shut, throwing my bag onto my bed. My mind
is still going a million miles an hour with no end in sight.

"We have to talk about the fae. Now." I need answers, or I'm
going to unhinge. My life has been uprooted and flipped upside
down, but knowing there's so much I *don't* know is making my
anxiety dig its claws in deep.

She sits up on her bed and turns her attention to me.

"Especially since I went for my interview . . ." She nods
along, but she has no idea where I'm going with this. "Tristan
is my mentor."

She stiffens. "What the hell? *How?*"

"How? He screwed with my program coordinator's head,
Al. He made her put me with his company, and now my life is
ruined." It sounds melodramatic, but it's true.

"We'll figure this out, Aurora. I promise."

"There's nothing we can do. I'm stuck with this. I need a

placement to graduate, so I'm going to have to bite the bullet and show up on Monday." It's days away, but I'm already wound up tight, my mind running through the possible ways it could go.

"Are you sure there isn't a way to get a new mentor?"

If I weren't so freaked, I'd hug her. Allison always tries to come up with a positive solution. Her suggestion might've worked, except Tristan was the last mentor available. "I don't have a choice." Damn that arrogant fae for screwing with me like this.

"I wish there was something I could do," she says, her voice filled with worry.

"I know," I say. "You know him better than I do. What can you tell me?"

She sighs. "You're sure you want me to tell you about him?"

"Unfortunately, yes." There's something about him, something that tells me he won't hurt me. He's had plenty of opportunities to and hasn't yet. There's a chance my fae lineage—as insane as that whole story is—will keep me safe when it comes to Tristan. That doesn't mean I trust him, far from it, but if I'm going to deal with him to complete this part of my degree, I'm going to need every piece of information Allison can give me.

She pats the spot beside her, and I walk over and sit. "I'll tell you what I've heard. First off, Tristan is a man of his word. This can be a good thing or a bad thing depending on the situation. He's big into respect—"

I laugh, cutting her off. "I find that a little hard to believe."

She frowns. "He has a small circle of people he trusts."

"He doesn't have many friends. Shocking," I remark dryly.

"Aurora, this is serious. You could be in danger every moment you're at that hotel. Other fae might not accept his decision to let you go."

"That's comforting. Thank you." I'm fidgeting with my hands in my lap. The more we talk about Tristan, the more I want to hop on a train and get the hell out of Dodge.

"I'm telling you what you need to know. Stay quiet. Don't be witty or smart or—"

"Or *me*?" I shake my head. "I'm not going to cower in the corner and be his bitch. He's screwing with my life, so I'm going to make this a living hell for him."

"*Aurora.*" She clasps her hands together in front of her as if she's about to pray. A girl who's never set foot in a church or said grace in the years I've known her. "Please don't put yourself in unnecessary danger."

I roll my eyes. "Relax. I'm not going to be stupid."

She eyes me with a look of concern. "Tristan can be very charming, and he's a good leader. As much as the guy freaks me out, I can't deny that. Do what you can to stay on his good side. He already seems to like you, which is odd for him. It's either going to help keep you safe or put a target on your back."

"Awesome. Like there was a target on *your* back? I still don't know why," I say, prompting her to explain it to me.

She scratches the back of her neck. "I broke one of his rules. Fae living in the human world are required to follow certain rules. One of which has to do with who we associate with romantically."

My forehead creases. "Are you kidding me? Fae aren't allowed to be with humans? That's the most ridiculous thing I've heard since I found out about the fae."

"Tristan is kind of—"

"A complete sociopath," I offer. He went after Allison because of her relationship with Oliver? The leader of the fae had nothing more important to do than track one fae who's dating a human? It doesn't make sense. I remind myself that not much about Tristan *does*.

She cringes. "You should be careful how you speak about him, or to him for that matter."

"I'm not going to walk on eggshells around him."

"I'm just saying, the guy can be intense. And he's fae—the leader—which makes him incredibly powerful. Like, more powerful than the average fae."

I sigh. *Of course he is.* "Why's that?"

"Generations of magic passed down to him. We all have the same abilities he does, but his are magnified because he's the leader. The power from each of his ancestors now lives inside him, making him stronger than me or Max, for example."

I blow out a breath. "Thanks for the info. I'll be sure to keep that in mind the next time he does something to piss me off." I'd bet good money that'll be sooner rather than later.

"Tristan has taken an interest in you," she says.

A faint flutter in my stomach makes the tops of my ears burn. "Why do you say that? Because he's stuck? Because I was kidnapped by mistake, and now I'm an obligation?"

She presses her lips together. "He doesn't usually pay attention to humans outside of his business."

"That doesn't make me feel better. I don't want his attention." The slight shift in my pulse tries to make a liar out of me.

"I know that, and I understand. My advice is to lie low and keep your head down as much as possible."

I arch a brow at her. "Does that sound like me?"

"Aurora, I'm serious. This is for your own safety."

"You think he's going to hurt me?" A faint voice in my head says *no*. It holds no merit, and yet, I want to believe it.

She hesitates. "No, I don't, but he's not who I'm worried about. Tristan has enemies, Aurora."

"Now *that* I believe."

"You stumbled into this world at potentially the worst possible moment."

I arch a brow. "As if there would've been a good time?"

"No, of course not, I just mean that . . ." she pauses, and her brows tug close as if she's trying to decide how to say something. "I think you should know all of the facts before you walk into work on Monday."

"Okay," I say hesitantly. "I'm all ears."

She blows out a breath. "This is going to be a lot, but try not to freak out, okay?"

"You're really not making me want to hear this anymore."

She laughs, but it's forced and awkward. "Right, okay. People like me and Tristan, we aren't the only type of fae." She gives me a minute to absorb that. "There are light and dark fae. Tristan and the rest of us are dark, and then there are others who are light."

All this time, I was under the impression there were just fae. Now there are different types? I can't keep up with this shit. "There's a difference?"

She taps her fingers against her thighs. "No, we're all the same. We have identical abilities. We're one race, divided because of politics—much like the humans. It's all boring history."

"I want to know," I say without a thought.

She nods. "It all started with our ancestors many years ago. I'm talking the beginning of humankind. Since there were humans, there have been fae. Some are born that way, and some are transformed—either intentionally or by accident. This didn't really start happening until the fae were forced to inhabit

Earth after our world was destroyed during the last war. That was before my time. But it's why some of the fae—from both sides—don't look on the humans in the most flattering way. They're jealous. The humans get to live in their own world, while the fae—we're stuck here."

I blink a few times, unable to form a coherent response. This is . . . a lot.

"Do you want me to stop?" she checks.

I shake my head. As overwhelming as this information is, it'll give me a better understanding of this world I'm trying to wrap my head around.

"We used to be a single race of supernatural creatures," she continues. "There were no light or dark, just fae. For the longest time, there were no leaders, but there were always a few who showed leadership qualities when conflicts needed to be handled. The fae, as one group, decided to elect several of these individuals to be the decision-makers of our race. There were four or five of them in the beginning, from what I remember reading. These fae were in charge of making laws and deciding the consequences for those who broke them.

"That was all well and good until the leaders started disagreeing with each other on things I don't know about. Two, in particular, seemed to butt heads often. In fact, it got to the point where the other leaders started choosing which one they stood with, and alas, one race with several leaders split into those who followed one—the light fae—and those who followed the other—the dark fae."

"Why light and dark?" I ask.

"Because after the fae had split into two groups, there was an agreement signed by the leaders from each side. The light fae were permitted to walk the human world during the day, and the dark at night."

"Obviously that rule is no longer in place."

Allison frowns. "Tristan's great-great-grandfather, the dark leader at one time, decided he and his people were tired of living in the human world at night. The fae world was much like New York City. Always awake. The human world, it closes at night. And so, the dark fae fell into poverty. So Tristan's grandfather breached the contract his ancestor created with the first light fae leader and started a territory war. If the dark fae were going to walk the human world during the day, there was going to be some pushback. Now, Tristan refuses to throw his people back into that life of not being able to attend school or hold whatever kind of job they want. It was a quality of life consideration."

"That's what the war is about? Sharing the human world?"

She nods but doesn't add anything else.

"Can't they come to a new agreement? Both sides are breaking the same rule now anyway, so doesn't that make it irrelevant?"

"You would think so." She pulls at a loose thread on her shirt. "I'm not actively involved with the politics. All I know is what I've told you."

I let out a breath. "This war, the rules and responsibility, that's a lot to put on one person."

Allison raises a brow at me, her eyes widening slightly.

The tops of my ears burn once again. "I just mean, I couldn't imagine being in that position, that's all."

"Well, the position you *are* in isn't exactly ideal, either." She presses her lips together. You're sure there's no way around it?"

My chest feels tight. "Without this placement, I'll fall behind and won't be able to look for a job until next semester ends." My voice increases in pitch. Graduating late is *not* an option. It will shred my plan for the future into pieces. I'm in no position to take my time finding work after next semester is over. I need to start paying my parents back as soon as possible. Shortly before Adam got sick, they took out a second mortgage on the house to pay my steep tuition bill. I wasn't all that involved with the process at the time, but the seriousness of the situation weighs on me now.

When my phone chimes from my desk, I slide off the bed and walk over to grab it. "Adam, what's going on? Shouldn't you be at school?"

"Yeah," he mumbles. "I wasn't feeling well, so Mom and Dad let me stay home."

I bite my lower lip. "What's wrong?"

"I'm not dying," he says with a laugh. "I have a headache, and my stomach is sick. I've been puking all morning." Adam doesn't mind making jokes about dying, considering he's survived cancer and isn't even thirteen.

"Why didn't they take you to the hospital?"

"Because it's nothing. Probably just a bug. You know my immune system sucks. Don't worry about it, Roar."

His nickname for me makes my chest swell with warmth. He's been calling me that since he was old enough to talk. In the beginning, he couldn't say my whole name but managed to learn part of it, and it stuck. "Get some rest, okay? If you're not feeling better later, ask Mom and Dad to take you to the hospital, okay? Please?"

"Yeah, okay. Can I ask you something?"

"Of course." I've been biting the inside of my cheek so hard it's bleeding.

"Can you come home this weekend?"

I finally let out a breath and laugh. "Miss me already?" I

tease. I've only been away from home for a few weeks.

"No," he grumbles. "I'm just bored, that's all. Whatever."

I muffle a giggle with my hand. I won't embarrass my twelve-year-old brother over the phone. No, I'll save that for when I can see his face get all red. "I'll see what I can do." I wouldn't mind taking some time away from the city before Monday. A trip home might be good for me.

I spend the rest of the week locked in my room when I'm not in class, drowning in homework while trying to mentally prepare for Monday morning. When Friday afternoon rolls around, I'm on a train, heading to Mapleville. I want to believe I'm doing this for Adam, but the truth is: I miss home. That, and going home means I'll get the answers I've been terrified to search for since Tristan told me about my ties to the fae.

I get a cab to the house with the intention of dropping my bag off before I meet Adam after school. I walk up the empty driveway and notice the front lawn needs to be cut. The rest of the house looks in order. The dull red brick and giant bay window in the front still make me smile, a lightness in my chest that only blossoms when I'm home.

I unlock the door and let myself in, setting my bag on the bench inside the foyer. I slip my shoes off, my feet padding against the hardwood as I walk into the living room where I'm surprised to find Adam curled up asleep on the couch. He's home from school again? Frowning at the washed-out color of his face, covered slightly with messy brown curls, I pull a blanket over him. I tiptoe out of the room and into the kitchen.

Our kitchen has gone through many renovations, but the one we have now is my favorite, with faux marble countertops and dark wood cabinets, a stark contrast against the stainless steel appliances. The breakfast bar where I always liked to sit while I was doing homework in high school was added at Dad's request. He wanted somewhere to eat that wasn't as formal as the table in the attached dining room.

Adam is still asleep when Mom and Dad get home shortly after six o'clock.

"Aurora? What are you doing home?" Dad asks when he walks into the room. He's dressed in his normal teaching attire: a suit and tie, and his salt and pepper hair is neatly combed to one side. Our eyes meet, and I'm reminded of how much I wish I had inherited his bright blue ones like Adam had instead of Mom's hazel ones.

"Nice to see you, too, Dad."

"You know that's not what your father meant, honey. We weren't expecting you, is all," Mom says with a smile, wrapping her arm around my shoulders. My mom and I share many features. I have her long, wavy blond hair. We're both a little over five feet and a bit curvy in the hip area. If she were a few years younger, we would look more like sisters than mother and daughter.

I smile back at her. "Adam asked me to come home this weekend, and I wanted to, so here I am."

She nods, glancing at my dad before she says to me, "Have you talked to him?"

I shake my head. "He was asleep when I got here, but I know he hasn't been feeling well, so I didn't want to wake him."

"I'll get him," Dad offers. "He should eat something." He walks toward the living room, and I turn to my mom.

"Did you take him to the hospital?"

Mom presses her lips together, nodding. "He collapsed at

school earlier this week." Her throat bobs when she swallows, and her hands are gripping the counter so tight her knuckles have gone white.

My pulse races and nausea rolls through me. Adam hadn't told me that. "Mom, is Adam sick again?"

She squeezes her eyes shut, nodding again before she opens them. "An MRI showed Adam's cancer came back and spread to his brain."

My mouth goes dry as my chest tightens. "His brain?" I force out, tears stinging my eyes. *No.* No way. This isn't . . . Adam is *not* sick again.

She nods. "He has an excellent doctor, and he starts chemotherapy next week."

I bite back several profanities. She waited to tell me Adam was sick until I showed up at home, and she didn't have a choice. I want to scream. "What—?" I'm about to ask why the *hell* no one thought to pick up the phone and call me when Adam's groggy voice makes my stomach drop.

"Hey, Roar."

I look past Mom to see him standing in the doorway with Dad behind him. I swallow the lump in my throat. "Hey there, buddy. How are you feeling?"

He frowns, shifting his gaze to Mom, and pushes the mess of curls away from his face. "You told her?"

Mom smiles, but it doesn't reach her eyes. "We're going to get through this as a family."

Adam looks at me again. "Quit looking at me like that, okay? It's freaking me out."

I blink a few times. "Sorry." How am I supposed to act around him? I shouldn't treat him like he's sick, that's what the doctors told us when he was first diagnosed a few years ago, but all I want to do is wrap my arms around him and never let go.

"Why don't we order a pizza?" Dad suggests, most likely in an attempt to break the sudden tension that's hanging in the room.

We sit around the dining room table, eating together for the first time since summer break.

Dad breaks the silence. "You had your work placement interview this week, right?"

The slice of pizza I have in my hand stops halfway to my mouth. "Uh, yeah." With what was thrown at me when I got here, I hadn't thought about Tristan for a while. *It was nice while it lasted.*

"How'd it go? Did you get the company you wanted?"

"I didn't get to choose. My program coordinator matched the students with mentors from local businesses," I explain.

"Okay, so where did you get placed?" Mom cuts in.

"At a hotel in the downtown core," I say.

"That's wonderful," she praises. "Congratulations, honey."

I clench my teeth together for a second and smile. "Thank you."

"When do you start?" Dad asks.

"Monday," I say. "Nine o'clock sharp." Using Tristan's words makes it difficult not to cringe.

After dinner, Adam offers to clean up what little mess we made, so I join in to keep him company. I could've used this opportunity to do some digging and find out what Mom and Dad might know about our lineage, but I'm still unsure how to bring it up in a way that won't have them worry that something's going on, and now doesn't seem like the time to be concerned about it. The last thing I need is for them to get suspicious and ask questions I can't answer.

We finish the dishes and meet Mom and Dad in the living room to watch a movie. I'm struggling to keep my eyes open for the first half, and by the second half, I'm dozing in and out before I fall asleep. After the week I've had, it doesn't surprise me in the slightest.

I open my eyes, blinking until they focus.

"Is this the part where you start freaking out?"

I gasp at the familiar voice and sit straight up in a flash. My eyes scan what appears to be one fancy-ass bedroom, landing on where Tristan leans in the doorway.

He steps inside, closing the door behind him.

I scramble off the bed, almost slipping off the black silk sheets. "What the hell is going on?" I demand, my heart pounding in my chest.

"Nothing," he answers in a calm voice.

I gesture around the room. "What is *this*?"

"My bedroom," he says.

I glance back at the bed I was in. *Oh god.* "Your bedroom . . ."

He chuckles. "You're asleep, Aurora. This is a dream."

My eyes snap to his. If it's a dream, why do his blue eyes look so real? So damn captivating? I shake my head, pushing the thought away. "You're in my head? In my *dream*?"

"That's right. You're dreaming about me."

"Why? How?"

"Because I want you to," he explains. "Another perk of being me: dreamwalking."

I shoot him a dark look. I'm not in the mood to learn what other fae tricks he has up his sleeve. This is pretty close to the *last* thing I need right now.

"Would you like me to leave?" His question throws me off. He's giving me a choice.

"I want you to tell me what you're doing in my dream. Don't tell me you want to spend more time with me," I remark. "I'm already stuck with you one day of the week. Isn't that enough?"

He offers a charming smile, and it occurs to me that dream Tristan is just as dangerously attractive as reality Tristan. "You're fiery tonight," he says.

"And you're annoying. Can I have my dream back now?"

"You don't like me, do you?" What a loaded question.

I gape at him. "Is that . . . Seriously? Do you want to be my best friend or something, Tristan? Because I'm pretty sure medical professionals have a name for that. It's called Stockholm Syndrome."

He huffs out a frustrated sigh. "You left town," he says. "Or did you run away?" He knows I left. Was he looking for me?

"I went looking for answers about my ancestors. Instead, I found out that my brother is sick." I sigh. "You can't scare me away. I'll be there on Monday. I know what's at stake here, so not even the idea of you being there could stop me from showing up."

"I'm sorry to hear about your brother," he says, and the sudden softness in his expression makes my chest ache.

"Thanks," I say after a stretch of silence. I stare at him for what feels like far too long. I'm still trying to decide whether this is real. "So, you did this to creep me out?"

"I was hoping to learn something," he admits.

"Learn what? How I'd react to you being invasive as hell?" I counter, resting my hands on my hips.

He offers a bemused smile. "I'm trying to figure you out. Humans are supposed to be simple creatures. They have impulses and fears. Considering what I am and my position in both the human and fae worlds, humans are intimidated by me. And then there's you. The elusive human with fae lineage. You're . . . everything I can't control."

My breath hitches as it becomes harder to hold his gaze. "Control is overrated," I say in a shaky voice. "At least that's what I've heard."

"An interesting concept. One I'd guess was created by someone unable to grasp control."

I shrug, pushing the hair out of my face. For me, control is necessary. As long as I have it, for the most part, I can keep my anxiety at bay. Dealing with a sick brother and an intense degree, I don't have time to allow anxiety to suffocate me.

"I expected you to run," he says. "Even more so when you found out about your family's involvement in the fae world."

"Figures." I sigh. "What would've happened if I had? I wouldn't have gotten far; I know that. I don't have the energy or desire to fight this. So long as it doesn't affect my life any more than it already does, I'll accept it. I think you can agree there are more important things. You have your world, and I have mine. Sometimes they overlap, but when they do, we'll just have to deal with it. I mean, preferably without the two of us having to interact, but I suppose some sacrifices must be made." Perhaps this is the wrong moment to be snarky and make jokes.

He stands there, staring at me with what I can only interpret as a look of wonder on his annoyingly attractive face as the scene slips away.

chapter Eight

I WAKE UP ON THE COUCH WITH A KNITTED BLANKET draped over me and a cushion under my head. The TV is off, and the room is dark except for a crack of light coming from the kitchen.

I stare out into the darkness. Tristan can waltz into my dreams. Great. Now not only do I have to deal with him during the day, but I also can't escape him at night, either. Can't escape the way he makes my heart race and my stomach flip. *I'm so screwed.*

Exhausted as I am, this is the perfect opportunity to look through the house for some answers. I have to be quiet; I don't want to wake anyone and have to lie about why I'm searching through old family things.

I tiptoe into the office, a small room with a couch, a desk, and chair. One wall is lined with bookshelves filled with old textbooks, some of my parents' books, and our family albums. I cross the room, flicking on the lamp on the desk as I pass, and run my finger along the spines. I crouch and pull out an album.

I flip through the pages. Nothing. This one is far too recent to hold any answers.

I sigh, glancing at the shelf full of matching binders. They're all too new. If I weren't half asleep, I'd have realized that before I wasted my time in here. If I crawled into the attic, I might be able to find something that dates back far enough, but I can't do that when I'm trying to stay quiet. I'm not going to get any answers tonight.

With a yawn, I drag myself to my bedroom and fall onto my bed, hoping Tristan will leave me alone for the rest of the night.

When I find myself in another dreamscape, anger swiftly rises, and I grit my teeth. My eyes focus on the ground beneath my feet. Cracked pavement. I frown as I lift my head, and gasp sharply when realization knocks the air out of me.

I'm not in my dream anymore. I'm in *Tristan's*.

He's standing atop a mess of rubble, staring right at me, but doesn't see me. He doesn't know I'm in his dream. *How am I here?*

I shiver, coughing on the smoke that's heavy in the air, and blink until my vision is as clear as it's going to get in this war-torn environment. There's nothing left for as far as the eye can see. Buildings are gone, nothing left but piles of concrete and metal, and leafless trees are fallen, scattered in the mess. It looks like a scene out of a dystopian movie.

My eyes shift back to Tristan. He's a mess. His dark clothing is torn, all but shredded in some places along his midsection, and his hair is darkened with dirt and ash. I walk closer, careful where I step, and watch his face pale. His eye are bloodshot and wide, rimmed by dark circles underneath. They're bouncing all over the place, never stopping in one spot too long, but growing more and more frantic by the second. His chest rises and falls quickly, and his hands are balled into fists at his sides.

"Tristan," I whisper, my voice cracking, and suddenly I'm fighting this all-consuming urge to comfort him. The pain in his expression is hurting *me*.

I say his name again, louder this time, but he still doesn't hear me.

My eyes burn as I watch the dark fae leader fall to his knees and stare at the ruins with an utterly hopeless expression that makes my blood run cold.

Tristan wasn't alive during this fae war, during the destruction of his people's homeland, but he's forced to experience it in his nightmares.

My eyes fly open, and daylight streams into my room. I stretch my arms and legs, taking a few minutes to shake the scene I just witnessed. Once my heart slows to a normal rate and I stop sweating, I try to enjoy the fact I'm waking up in my own bedroom.

There's nothing like sleeping in your own bed at home. Compared to the old, twin mattress I sleep on at school, this bed feels like a cloud of comfort and warmth. Everything about my room makes me want to stay here: the Polaroid photos I have hung on one wall, the desk that's covered with books on business and marketing, the window seat my dad built me the first summer I got into reading when I was thirteen. The giant bookshelves are the best thing about the room, though. They hold so many books that I'll probably never read them all. I glance longingly at the keyboard set up across the room. If I could somehow make it fit in my room at school, I'd have it there. I've been playing piano since I was little. Playing always makes me feel in control and at ease. It helps make life less chaotic.

With all of my belongings unchanged, my bedroom is one of the things I miss the most when I'm at school.

I head down to the kitchen to grab a cup of coffee and find Mom sitting at the breakfast bar. "Morning," I keep quiet in case Dad and Adam are still asleep.

"Morning, honey. How'd you sleep?" She ties the belt on her soft blue robe and yawns.

I shudder. "I slept okay." I don't want to think about the vividness of that dream. My stomach is still in knots.

She takes a sip of her coffee. "Adam is happy you're home."

My chest tightens at the mention of his name. I'd give anything to have yesterday be a nightmare, to wake up and find out Adam isn't sick again. I pour some coffee into my mug and smile. "Yeah, I'm happy, too." I take a drink. "I'm guessing they aren't awake yet?"

Mom's soft laugh lightens her eyes. "You know Adam is a monster to get out of bed before noon, and your father went out to run some errands."

I glance at the clock on the stove; it's just after eleven. "Gotcha," I say. "So, in class the other day, we were talking about things running in families . . ." *Nice segue, Aurora.* "Businesses and traditions and such," I add. "Do you know if our family had anything like that, maybe a long time ago?" What a time to be completely *not* subtle. I don't know how else to search for what I'm looking for. Hell, I don't really know what I'm looking for. Maybe bringing this up was a bad idea. Maybe it's best I don't know.

She glances at me. "That sounds interesting. I can't think of any on my side," she pauses, biting her bottom lip. "Your dad's family was always more . . . eclectic than mine. Maybe you could ask him?"

My lips part as if I'm going to respond, but no words come out. "Yeah," I finally say. The back of my neck tingles, the hairs standing straight, and my arms break out in goosebumps. *Was Tristan right?* The thought invites too many questions, so I push it away and say, "What's your plan for the day?"

She sighs. "Grading, grading, and more grading."

"Oh." I frown. "I was hoping we could all go out and do something fun if Adam is feeling up to it."

"I would love to, but I'm on a pretty strict deadline. Maybe the two of you can spend some time together. You can have the car when Dad gets home. He shouldn't be too long now. He's been gone for over an hour." *Does he know about the fae?* I doubt it, considering Tristan said the fae in my family were hundreds of years old. My stomach drops. How could I not have thought about it until now? If my ancestors were fae, does that mean they're still alive?

I blink a few times. "Yeah, sure," I answer.

Mom was right. It's almost one in the afternoon when Adam shows his face in the living room. At least he's brushed his hair and gotten dressed. It's hard to imagine him being sick again. He looks like the Adam I knew before he got sick the first time.

"Good afternoon, sleeping beauty," I tease.

He sticks his tongue out at me. "You're hilarious, Roar."

"Looks like it's you and me today, kiddo. Do you want to do something?"

He shrugs, yawning. "We can walk around the mall or go see a movie."

"Sure. Whatever you want."

When Dad gets back an hour later, he gives us the keys, and we head to the mall. It's nothing special—not an ideal hangout place, even when I was in high school, but it's something to do.

Mapleville is tiny compared to Rockdale, but I have fond memories of hanging out with friends at the Purple Cat café down the street from my high school.

My phone chimes with a text from Oliver, pulling me out of a memory as Adam and I walk out of his favorite clothing store.

I'm in your room waiting for Allison and some dude was here looking for you.

I frown. I'd told Grant I was going home this weekend when he asked to get together to work on our research papers. I hit reply and type, *Grant was there?*

This guy said his name was Max.

My throat goes dry, and I glance over at Adam. He's looking at me with raised brows. *Did he say why he was there?* I send back.

No, just that he was looking for you. Is everything okay?

Everything is fine. I'll see you and Allison when I get back.

Talk to you later.

I pocket my phone. "Sorry about that."

Adam shrugs. "Want to get some fro-yo while we're here?"

"You bet I do. Lead the way."

While standing in line at the fro-yo place, I send Allison a message to tell her Max was creeping around. I don't know why he was there, but I figure it's best to let her know about it. As far as I know, she still isn't on great terms with Tristan, so I want to make sure she's safe.

"Hello, Adam," a pleasant female voice says.

He turns toward the voice and smiles. "Oh, hi, Dr. Collins. Aurora, this is my new doctor."

I glance at the woman standing in line behind us. She looks to be in her mid-forties and wears a slightly wrinkled casual sweater and mom jeans.

Her eyes flick to me, and she smiles. "You must be Adam's sister. I'm Richelle Collins."

We shake hands, moving up a bit as the line moves. "Nice to meet you," I say. The timing is an odd coincidence. Yesterday, I found out about Adam being sick again, and today we run into his doctor at the mall of all places. A shiver shoots up my spine. No. I'm overthinking this. Had I not been recently kidnapped by the fae, I wouldn't automatically be so suspicious of everything that seems a tiny bit off. I force the feeling down and smile.

"You too," she says.

"What are you doing here?" Adam asks.

"My daughter wanted to come look for some new video game she's been saving up for." She laughs. "I left her scouring the electronic store. She could spend all day there, so I thought I'd walk around a bit."

"Cool," Adam says with a grin. The kid beams at the mention of video games. We step up to the counter and order our fro-yo, Adam picking his favorite cookie dough flavor, and I go for a tart green apple.

Adam waves goodbye to Dr. Collins, and she says, "See you next week."

I haven't asked him how he's feeling about the treatment yet, and I'm not sure how to bring it up or whether I should, but I imagine he's scared. Anyone would be.

"Do you want to talk about it?" I ask him as we enjoy our frozen treat.

He pokes at the fro-yo with his spoon. "Not really."

"We don't have to, but I want you to know that I'm here if you ever change your mind."

He finally smiles, which loosens the knot in my stomach a

bit. "Thanks, Roar."

Adam and I spend the rest of the day together, popping in and out of stores, chatting about my classes and his friends. We grab dinner on the way home—Chinese food from Mom and Dad's favorite place downtown—and we all eat together in the dining room.

I sit there, enjoying a chicken ball drenched in sweet-and-sour sauce, and smile at my family. My thoughts trickle back to Tristan and the mess that I'm going back to at school. I didn't get any answers from coming home like I'd hoped. I can't say anything about it, which makes it harder to bear. I doubt Tristan would take kindly to more humans knowing about the fae, not that I think my parents would believe me, even though my dad apparently has fae ancestors. They'd blame it on stress and sign me up for therapy. Adam would believe me, though. The kid has a killer imagination. He believes in almost everything.

Looking at them now is making me want to stay. I wasn't homesick much in the past, but I feel it now, even more so considering Adam's new diagnosis. The urge to stay is strong, but the growing need for answers is slowly overpowering it. I don't want to think about it, but it's looking more and more like there's only one person I can go to for those answers.

"What time do you have to leave tomorrow?" Adam asks between giant mouthfuls of fried rice. Man, that kid can eat. He's already on his second plate, and it doesn't look like he's going to stop anytime soon. I'm glad he hasn't lost his appetite.

"Early afternoon. I have some things I need to deal with before my week starts." Things like figuring out why the hell Max was looking for me and how he knows where I live on campus.

"Your sister is going to be busy over the next couple of months," Mom says with a smile. "We're all so proud."

"Thanks, Mom."

Dad cleans up after dinner, and Adam follows me to my room to hang out while I pack the few things I brought home with me.

"I wish you didn't have to leave," he says.

"I know. I don't want to go back, either." I peek over at him and smile. "But don't worry, I'll be home to visit as soon as I can."

If I survive this week.

chapter Nine

MONDAY MORNINGS SUCK. OKAY, MONDAYS IN general suck, but this morning specifically sucks harder than usual. I didn't get much sleep last night, and it isn't because Tristan showed up—because he didn't. Which is a good thing, considering there's a high chance I would've punched his stupid, perfect face for invading my unconscious thoughts. Dealing with him when I'm awake is enough.

Every time I came close to falling asleep, I would remember what was waiting for me this morning, and I would be wide awake again, filled with dread and nerves.

When my alarm goes off at six o'clock, I open my eyes and stare at the ceiling. Should I drop out of school? If there were any other way to get this credit to graduate, I would be all over it, but *my mentor is a dangerously charming, yet infuriatingly arrogant fae leader* isn't exactly a believable excuse to be exempt.

I swing my legs over the side of the bed and stand, followed by my regular morning routine of showering and blow drying my hair before getting ready the rest of the way.

Our door opens, and Allison walks in, holding a tray with two cups of coffee and a bag in her hand. "Morning," she says, setting the tray on my desk. "I brought coffee and muffins. Today is a big deal for you, so I wanted to start it off right."

Despite the slight nausea in my stomach, I smile. "You didn't have to do that."

"Of course I did." She hands me a coffee. "I have class in . . . five hours anyway." She presses her lips together against a smile.

I take a small sip, hoping my stomach won't reject it. "Thank you. I appreciate it."

"Whatever I can do to make today a little less difficult for you."

I wrap her in a one-armed hug and squeeze her shoulders. "You're the best."

She's proven that many times. When I got back to campus yesterday and told her about Adam, she held me while I cried about it much like the first time. I don't know what kept the tears at bay while I was home, maybe wanting to be strong for my family, but the thought of Adam enduring cancer treatments again makes my heart feel like someone is slicing it to shreds with razors.

When it's time to leave, my stomach twists, and my hands dampen as they shake at my sides. *Get a grip.* I clench my hands into fists, take a deep breath, and grab my bag before I head for the door.

"You've got this, Aurora." Allison shoots me a thumbs-up from her desk.

My lips manage to form a smile as my chest loosens a

fraction. "I'll see you later."

The streetcar ride to the Westbrook Hotel feels like hours when in reality it takes fifteen minutes. Both the hotel and campus are in the downtown core, but traffic is a bitch in the morning.

I step off with a crowd of people and shoulder my bag before I head for the building. The sound of my heels echoes against the concrete, and I focus on the repetitive *click, click, click* to keep myself from spiraling.

The hotel lobby is as extravagant and posh as I remember it. My gaze bounces around the room. A few employees and guests walk around, chatting or watching the morning news on one of the many flat screens attached to the walls.

Someone brushes past me, scowling. "Watch it, human," the man says.

My body tenses as I fight back a snide remark. He's in a building full of humans. What the hell is his problem with me? How many of the fae know I'm working for Tristan? *Working for Tristan.* That's a dark idea; it fries my nerves.

I straighten, gripping my bag until my knuckles turn white, put on my best pleasant-yet-professional face, and walk to the reception desk. I smile at the familiar face. It's the same girl as the day I stormed in, demanding to see Tristan. Marisa, her name tag says. "Hi there. I'm sorry if you remember me."

Her expression is bright, friendly. "Miss Marshall, welcome back to the Westbrook Hotel."

"Thanks. Again, sorry about last time. Tristan, er, Mr. Westbrook, can be . . ."

"Don't worry about it. I've worked here for almost five years. I know what you're talking about. Mr. Westbrook instructed me to send you to the office upon your arrival."

I nod. "Right, okay."

"Head over to the elevators. The office is on the twentieth floor," she says.

I glance at the clock behind her and sigh. I guess it would be too childish to whine about how I don't want to go. Pretty unprofessional, at least. "I'd better make my way there. Don't want to be late on my first day."

"I doubt you wanted to come at all," she says with a little grin.

I offer a tight-lipped smile. "Is it that obvious?"

"Well, you look like you'd prefer to swim in a pool of rattle-snakes than spend your day here."

I grimace. "Perfect," I say before walking away. How much does Marisa know about the man she works for?

I tap my fingers against my thighs the entire ride, glancing at myself in the mirror that covers the back wall. At the twentieth floor, I approach the office reception desk.

"Hi," I say in the most cheerful voice I can muster.

A black-haired man in an expensive-looking suit, who can't be much older than me, lifts his head and nods. "Good morning. Miss Marshall, I presume."

"You presume correctly." I try to stay pleasant.

"Wonderful," he says, but something in his voice makes me think he feels the opposite.

I offer another smile. *Keep smiling*, I chant over and over in my head.

"Good morning, Miss Marshall."

The smile drops right off my face.

I square my shoulders before turning toward the smooth, commanding sound of Tristan's voice. Seeing him so clean and put together only reminds me of how broken he looked in that nightmare.

"You're prompt. I appreciate that."

I nod. My jaw is clenched so tight I couldn't speak if I wanted to. This is a terrible mistake. I can't do this.

"Why don't you follow me, and I'll show you to my office?" he suggests in a level tone. He's strictly business right now, and I'm all for it.

We walk side by side down a long hallway with clear glass doors lining each side.

"Are you not going to speak?"

"You haven't asked me a question."

He arches a brow at me. "You don't strike me as an 'only speaks when spoken to' type of woman." He knows my personality already, and it makes my stomach flip. Tristan seems like the kind of man that demands attention and whose attention is craved. My body becomes almost hyperaware when he's watching me, as if it doesn't know whether it likes it or not. Maybe it's a fae thing.

I almost laugh. "You're perceptive. I'm sure that's useful in your position."

He nods. "Indeed."

I jerk my thumb back toward the guy sitting behind the desk in the entrance. "Your receptionist is lovely, by the way," I say with a touch of a smile.

He shrugs. "He's not a morning person." We have that in common.

"What are we doing today?" I shift the conversation as we continue down the hall to a set of glass double doors.

"*We* won't be doing anything. I'm handing you off to my chief of staff for the day."

"My first day, and you're already rewarding me," I say sweetly.

He smirks. "Good to know you're smart-mouthed during

all hours of the day." He pushes the door open, holding it for me until I enter his office, and follows me inside.

The far wall is made of windows, letting in the natural light and giving the room an incredible view of downtown. Near the windows, there's a massive oak desk, covered with papers and a computer. Off to one side, a couple of couches and arm chairs surround a coffee table that matches the desk and the book-shelves lining the opposite wall. A flat screen is mounted above the seating area, and under it is a huge fireplace.

Tristan walks over to the desk and sits before pressing a button on his phone. "Miss Chen, our business student has arrived. Would you be so kind as to come collect her from my office?"

There's a brief pause. "You're seriously making me do this?"

Tristan says nothing, just sits there with a ghost of a smile on his lips.

"Fine," the female voice snaps. "I'll be right there."

I stand by the door, tapping my thighs until it flies open and the fae woman I met when I was kidnapped waltzes through, looking like she's on her way to the Met Gala.

Tristan stands, fastening the button on his dark suit jacket. "Skylar, you remember Aurora. She's a fourth year business student here to learn from my company. I would like you to mentor her."

Skylar sighs before glancing at me. "You can't stay away, can you, little human?"

I swallow. "I don't have a choice. I need this to graduate."

She looks me over, her eyes narrowed with judgment. "Lucky me."

"Play nice, ladies." Tristan chuckles from behind his desk.

We both shoot him dark looks.

"Follow me," she growls and walks back out the door.

I walk quickly, worried she might leave me behind in hopes of getting rid of me. I catch up to her halfway down the hall. "Look, I know this isn't ideal for you. I get that you don't like me, and that's fine. All I ask is that you don't make this hell for me. To be honest, I'm relieved I don't have to work with Tristan."

Skylar stops dead and whirls to face me, forcing me back a couple of steps. "You think I'm going to make this easy for you?" She barks out a laugh. "Think again, Aurora. You might think you got off easy when Tristan stuck you with me, but you're wrong. Piss me off once, and you will regret it. Is that clear?"

I nod. "Do you hate all humans?" I ask in a low voice.

She actually smiles. "Yes."

"Okay." I'm not surprised, but her response makes the dread in my chest weigh heavier.

"Now let's go." She pushes open one of the doors Tristan and I passed on our way in, and I follow her inside, letting the door close behind us. "I have meetings back to back until this afternoon. You can either stay here and do photocopying, or you can sit in on the meetings. I don't care."

I try to hide my shock that she's giving me the option. "I'll sit in on the meetings." I pull out a notebook and pen from my bag.

"Fine." She gives me a once over. "Let's go."

I spend the entire morning and most of the afternoon in meetings, scribbling notes as fast as I can with one fifteen minute break for lunch. Skylar leads a lot of the meetings, standing at the head of the long table. I keep my head down, my hair curtaining most of my face while I try to keep up from my spot at the far end of the table. I estimate at least half of the attendees are fae, several looking less than pleased to see me sitting with them.

I'm still writing a few things about social media marketing as the room empties.

"I'm surprised your hand still works."

My pen stops moving, and I look over at Skylar. "You gave valuable information," I say. "I want to remember it."

She blinks at me, then opens the folder in her hand and drops some papers in front of me. "Don't waste your time writing everything. Listen to what everyone is saying. Next time, I want you to offer an idea, comment, or opinion. Got it?"

"I . . . okay." I flick a glance at the paper. She's given me her meeting notes.

"See you next week, human," Skylar says.

"Yeah. Thanks for—"

"Don't," she cuts in on her way out the door.

"Right," I mumble to the empty room.

Leaning back in the chair, I sigh, tossing my notebook and pen onto the table. My eyes close, and I rest my head against the chair back for a couple of minutes.

When I open my eyes, I find Tristan leaning in the doorway with a faint grin, and my cheeks flare with heat.

"Long day?" he asks, pushing off the wall to walk into the room.

"Yes. Not that I expected anything less."

He perches on the edge of the table a few feet away from me. "Did you learn anything?"

"Yes," I repeat.

He nods. "My job is done."

I laugh. "*Your* job? You didn't do anything."

"Are you disappointed you didn't get to spend the day with me, Aurora?"

I roll my eyes. "Oh man, was I that obvious?" I shoot back.

He chuckles, tilting his head to the side.

"You're being creepy," I say. "Speaking of, why was Max at my place?"

His back stiffens. "I wasn't aware that he had been. When was this?"

"While I was home for the weekend."

His mouth is set in a tight line. "I'll deal with it."

"Good. I don't want him coming around. Ever." I put as much force behind my words as possible. "And speaking of *that*, what the hell was that dream invasion thing you pulled the other night?"

His lips pull up. "It gets a bit boring around here on the weekend."

My jaw locks. For once, I consider my response before I open my mouth. "Don't do it again," I say, forcing my gaze to hold his.

"Did it bother you?"

It didn't bother me as much as it should've, but I'm not about to tell him that. "It's unnecessary. You want to talk to me, pick up the phone."

"Are you asking me to call you?" The twinkle of amusement in his eyes makes my eyes narrow. "Aurora, you're so forward."

"Seriously?" I want to throw my pen at him. "Stay out of my dreams." I decide not to tell him about what I experienced after he left *my* dream. I can't see him reacting well to the idea of me seeing him like that. Vulnerable.

He inclines his face in acknowledgment and stands. "How

was your trip home? You must be concerned about your brother."

I try to keep the shock off my face. The last thing I expected was for him to ask about Adam. "Yeah," I say. "He's the strongest person I know, but no one should have to fight a battle like that." *Or like the one from your dream.* I quickly push the thought away.

"If he's anything like his sister, I have a feeling he's good at putting up a strong front."

I swallow the lump in my throat. "He is."

Tristan steps closer. "And the rest of your time away from the city? Was it enlightening?"

Shooting him a look, I say, "I couldn't come out and ask my parents if they knew of any relatives that had freaky powers and never aged."

He licks his lips. "That would've been amusing to watch."

I struggle to hold back an eye roll. "The day we met, you said I wasn't fae. So why do you care?"

"Consider it a mild interest." He shoves his hands in his pockets. "I've not come across a human like you with such ties to my kind."

"I'm not some thing for you to ogle or study. I refuse to allow this to affect my life anymore, so unless you're going to give me some answers, don't bring it up again."

"I'm not sure what answers you'd like me to give you."

I massage my temples with my fingers, squeezing my eyes shut for a brief moment. "Anything that would help me make sense of this."

"Whatever fae ran in the Marshall line were alive before my time, Aurora. The extent of my knowledge ends with knowing that fae magic touches you and where it comes from."

I sigh. "That's it? You're the leader of the fae. You should know more."

His eyes glimmer with amusement. "My apologies. I didn't expect I'd have an outspoken human to answer to when it came to the history of my kind in relation to her family."

So much for answers.

"I can see you're disappointed. For what it's worth, I'll look into it and see what information I can find that might put you at ease. Quite frankly, it might help my people feel more comfortable with your knowledge of them if they can hear about your connection from one of your fae relatives."

My gaze lifts to meet his. "Really?" The optimism in my voice makes me cringe. I shouldn't be asking him for anything, but there's no one else I *can* ask.

He nods curtly. "You should get going. Not all my employees are human, and not all of them will be as tolerant as Skylar was today."

I collect my things and stand, heading toward the door. I pause in front of Tristan. "Why do you all hate humans so much? Your kind are the ones who chose to live with us. I don't care that you're fae, Tristan. That doesn't make you more or less of an ass—which you are—I'm saying that I don't think it's fair that you all look upon us as some lesser race because we aren't like you. Evidently, your kind aren't fans of diversity." I remember what Allison told me—about the fae being jealous of the humans—I guess I thought there was more to it.

His gaze is unwavering as he says, "I don't hate humans. I wouldn't own a business that interacts so closely with them on a daily basis if I hated them."

"I'm not talking about you, specifically. Not everything is about you. Shocking, I know."

His lips twitch, but his eyes look tired. "You're brave."

"I'm sharing my opinion. If you think that's brave—if you think I should be intimidated by you—you think too highly of yourself." I lift my bag onto my shoulder and step around him. "Goodnight, Mr. Westbrook. I'll see you next Monday."

chapter Ten

A FEW WEEKS PASS, AND THE SEMESTER PICKS UP, ENSURING I have plenty to keep my mind busy. I've gone home each weekend since I found out Adam's cancer came back. They moved him into a hospital room shortly after I left, which made me want to turn around and go back, but Mom and Dad insisted he was doing fine. During my last visit, I sat with him during treatment. It was hard on me, so I can't imagine how Adam felt. He's been so strong through all of this. He seems to be responding well, according to Dr. Collins. I'm not sure whether it was the strange way we met that threw me off with her, but when I was in the room with Adam, I kept feeling her eyes on me. It made the skin at the back of my neck tingle. I tried to ignore it the best I could; I knew she was there to help Adam, but the unease stuck around after she left.

Back on campus at the end of another week, I'm sitting in the uncomfortable plastic seat, rereading the chapter for today's class.

Grant sets up the lecture for the professor and takes the seat next to me again, tossing me an easy smile. "Hey, how was your week?" He pulls out his textbook and clicks his pen against the desk.

I smile. If he only knew. "Busy," I say. "Never a dull moment."

"How's your research paper going?"

I purse my lips. "Not bad. Want to read it over for me?" I'd managed to get a rough draft of it done on the train ride from Mapleville.

"Sure, if you'll read mine."

Laughing, I say, "Sure thing. Hand it over."

We swap papers and read through them, marking suggested edits on each other's work. I hand his back before the lecture starts and peek at the notes he made on mine.

"You're officially my editor," he teases.

My lips curl upward. "Only if you'll be mine."

He sticks his hand out, and I shake it. "Deal."

We spend the rest of the lecture taking notes and delving into a class discussion that I tune out of, yawning every so often as I fight to stay awake.

I take the long way back to my dorm and go to the Mexican grill off campus to grab dinner. I haven't had a chance to hit this place up since the semester started, and with the stress of midterms looming, I decide to treat myself to some tacos and chips with guac tonight.

After successfully stuffing my face with food, I head out, tucking my phone in my back pocket so I can zip up my sweater.

A short distance away, I hear muffled shouting. Figuring it's normal Friday evening pre-partying, I keep walking until I pick up some of what is being said.

"You're a disgrace to *all* fae," a delicate female voice says.

I freeze at the end of a brick storefront. There's a walkway separating the two buildings that leads to more parking for the local businesses, and from the sounds of it, a couple of fae are having an argument. I doubt they'll take kindly to me interrupting them.

A deep, male laugh reverberates against the exterior walls, echoing down the alley. "You're one to talk, considering you left us." His voice is unfamiliar, but he sounds pissed.

The female growls viciously, and the building shudders. The male grunts. "You know, I'm surprised they sent you. You were never much of a fighter."

"Yet they knew I'd kick your pathetic ass without a problem."

He grunts again. She must've hit him. I want to look, but I can't bring myself to peek around the corner for fear I'll get caught. They're too wrapped up in whatever is happening between them to notice my heart pounding in my chest, but I get the feeling they'll react the second they see me.

A firm hand grabs my wrist and pulls me hard, away from the building. My mouth opens to scream, but it's quickly covered. Panic surges through me before my eyes connect with Skylar's. She lets me go once it's clear I'm not going to make a sound.

"What the hell do you think you're doing?" she hisses.

"I was walking home." I look past her. "Why are they fighting?" I leave out the part where I know about the light and dark fae. I can't help but think that's what's going on—that the fight I overheard was caused by the fae war.

Her eyes narrow. "That's what you're concerned about?" She scowls. "Typical human. You realize if they'd seen you, you'd probably be dead right now or being fed on." She cocks her head. "Unless that's what you wanted."

My brows inch closer. "Of course not," I snap. "What are *you* doing here?"

"I was a few blocks over when I heard them and then your annoying little heartbeat."

"And you came to make sure I didn't get hurt?" I almost smile.

She rolls her eyes. "Yes, Aurora. I live to ensure your safety from my kind. Why else would I be here?" The sarcastic tone of her voice makes it impossible not to grin this time.

Whatever I was going to say is cut off by the sight of the male fae flying through the air. He lands with a *thud* on the sidewalk and jumps up, brushing off his black denim jacket. His eyes swing to where Skylar and I stand, and I bite my lip. This isn't good.

"What the fuck, Sky? Thanks for the backup." His eyes slide to me. "Hi."

I offer an awkward wave.

Skyler scowls. "I was coming. I got a little caught up." She nods at me.

"Well, don't next time. She got away, along with our answers." *Answers?* What is he talking about? My eyes flick back and forth between the guy and Skylar, waiting for one of them to explain the situation.

She shrugs. "We'll deal with it."

He rolls his eyes and then shifts away without another word, leaving Skylar and I alone on the sidewalk.

I arch a brow at her. "Care to explain what *that* was about?"

She gives me a look.

"Right. Didn't think so."

When I get back to our room, Allison is sprawled on her bed, already in sweatpants and a hoodie. I tell her about the fae attack I overheard, and she frowns.

"They're happening closer together," she murmurs, concern weighing heavy in her voice. "The light fae continue to orchestrate attacks on our side."

I scratch the back of my neck. "You're not making me feel any better."

"I don't think you have to worry about the light fae."

"Of course I do. They're attacking dark fae. *You* are dark fae. And I'm . . . I don't know, but either way, most of the dark fae hate me."

She sighs. "That's only because Tristan didn't deal with you the way they wanted him to. They don't trust you."

"How's that my fault?" I grumble.

"It's not. Maybe they'd feel differently if they knew about your lineage. If we can prove you have a connection, it could help keep you safe." She pulls on the string of her hoodie. "Have you found out any more about your ancestors?"

I sit at the end of my bed and sigh. Allison has the same idea as Tristan when it comes to using my lineage to protect me. "Not much, other than, whoever they are, they were on my dad's side."

"You don't know if they're still alive?"

I shake my head. "I'm not sure I *want* to know." Even with the chance that could help in convincing the fae I'm not a threat, I really don't know. "Does that make me terrible?"

She sits up and looks over at me. "Absolutely not, Aurora. You *just* found out you have fae in your family tree. If any of them are still around, you shouldn't feel obligated to know them. None of this has been easy on you. You deserve to do whatever is going to make you feel okay. Don't let anyone make you think otherwise."

Despite the pit in my stomach, I smile. "Thanks, Al."

She blows me a kiss. "You betcha."

With a heavy sigh, I stand and walk over to my desk. I open my laptop and frown at the unread email from Skylar.

Aurora,

I'll be away from the office Monday. I'm sure you'll find something to do. There are always files to put away, and there is coffee to fetch. Enjoy.

Skylar Chen

Westbrook Hotel Chief of Staff

My loud groan fills the small room as I delete the email.

"What's up?" Allison asks, eyeing me from behind her textbook.

"I don't have a mentor on Monday, which means I'm going to be stuck doing coffee runs for people who hate my guts."

"Oh. I'm sure they don't all hate you. Tristan has *some* humans working for him."

I roll my eyes. "Yeah, that's helpful, Al. Thanks."

"Other than the shitty coworkers, how's your placement going?"

I purse my lips. "Not as bad as I was expecting. Skylar can be a bitch, but she's a surprisingly good teacher. And I think I've only seen Tristan a few times the whole month I've been there."

Allison laughs. "Well, that's good. Hopefully it will continue that way." She says it with a nervous smile. We both know full well I'm not lucky enough for it to continue.

I head to Mapleville for the weekend to spend time with Adam and make sure everything is still okay, or at least as okay as it can be right now. We've been keeping in contact regularly over text and video chat when he's up for it, but nothing beats being able to give him a real hug.

Dr. Collins is chatting with my parents when I walk into his hospital room. "Hello, Aurora." She smiles. "I was just updating your parents on Adam's treatment."

"How's it going?" I walk over to him and kiss the top of his head, and, wrapping my arm around his shoulders, I sit on the edge of his bed.

"Pretty good, I guess," he grumbles. "Dr. Collins says the meds are working, so that's cool."

I smile. "Very cool." I fight the urge to jump up and dance because this is the good news I've been hoping for since his cancer came back.

Dr. Collins checks Adam's chart before saying goodbye to us. I watch her walk away, and my pulse spikes when she turns her head at the doorway, her eyes meeting mine for no more than a few seconds before she disappears down the hall. I work to shake the unsettled feeling in my stomach after she's gone. This is getting ridiculous. Being so focused on the fae and the people I care about being in danger makes everyone a suspect. Anyone could be fae at this point, but I can't let myself obsess over that when I'm here to support my family. This isn't about the fae; it's about Adam and his recovery.

chapter Eleven

STARBUCKS IS A NECESSARY PIT STOP ON MY WAY TO THE Westbrook Hotel Monday morning. I grab coffee for myself and Marisa. She's been nothing but kind to me since my placement started, so I like to bring her little treats every week to express my thanks.

"Where'd you get that dress? You look amazing," she says after I hand her a coffee.

I smile, glancing down at the knee-length, navy dress I'm wearing. "Thanks. Honestly, I can't remember. A thrift store, maybe? I needed business attire for this placement and didn't have a lot to spend, so I went hunting."

"You hit the jackpot. Teach me your ways. I'm getting tired of the same variation of pantsuits every day." She laughs and takes a sip of her coffee.

"For sure." We exchange numbers so we can set up a day to go shopping together before I glance at the time and cringe. It's a few minutes after nine. "I'd better get upstairs."

"Have a good one, and thanks for the coffee."

I muster a smile. "I'll try my best."

I'm almost halfway to the office when the elevator stops and a man and woman in business wear step on. After the door slides shut, the woman looks over at me, tossing her long, dark red hair over her shoulder. "I cannot believe Tristan let you live," she seethes.

I should ignore her, but my lips move before I can press them together. "I can't believe he puts up with people as ignorant as you. Welcome to the *human* world. Where *humans* live."

Her lips twist into a cruel smile in the same moment the man pulls the emergency stop, halting the elevator.

Shit.

My free hand curls into a fist when they corner me, and my pulse skyrockets, fear raging through me as I assess the situation. I knew working here would have some hazards, but I was hoping an altercation like this wasn't going to happen. I suppose I should've known better.

The man runs a hand through his black hair and flicks a glance at the woman. "I'm dying to taste her. You know nervous energy is my favorite, but ladies first."

My mouth goes dry. This is *not* happening.

The woman laughs. "She's not so mouthy now." She steps toward me, the tips of her high heels almost touching mine.

"Don't you dare touch me," I growl. I'm about two seconds away from throwing my coffee in her face.

She rolls her eyes. "Well, now she's annoying." She shoves me hard, narrowing her eyes at me. "What the hell makes you so special?"

I grit my teeth, my shoulder blades throbbing from being pinned against the wall. "What's it to you? God, don't tell me you're jealous?" If I'm being harassed in an elevator because this chick has the hots for Tristan, I swear to—

The woman grabs my face, digging her fingers into my skin. "Say another word, and I'll steal every living emotion you've got."

My head starts spinning, the woman's voice echoing around me. This bitch is feeding on me, and I can't move a muscle to do anything about it.

"Easy there," the man says. "If Tristan is keeping her around, I doubt he'll take too kindly to you killing her."

Dying in an elevator isn't something I had planned for today.

"Whatever," she snaps, finally backing off. She slams her fist against the emergency stop again, making the elevator continue its ascent, and I stand there frozen until they get off a couple of floors later without another word. When the door slides shut, I let out a breath and tip my head back against the wall. I spend the rest of the ride trying to shake off the odd, forced calmness in my muscles.

Arriving at the twentieth floor, I step off the elevator and freeze when I see Max sitting behind the reception desk.

He glances up as I approach and smirks. "Morning, blond-ie. Is that coffee for me?"

"Not a chance. What are you doing out here? Boss man got you working the phones today?"

His eyes narrow. "Boss man? I'm sure he'd love you calling him that."

Shaking my head, I blow out a breath as I turn away and step toward the office doors. I drop my things at my temporary spot and make my way to Tristan's office. I knock a few times before letting myself in.

Tristan is sitting behind his desk having an animated conversation with someone on his phone. I take a seat on the couch while I drink my coffee and wait for him to finish. I tap my fingers against the side of my cup and stare at the unlit fireplace, debating whether I should tell him what happened on my way up here. I'm quick to decide against it, noting the dark look on his face. I try not to eavesdrop, but the tone of his voice is sharp and agitated. The Tristan I'm used to is the image of self-control, so hearing him this way is unsettling. His hair looks as if he's run his fingers through it about ten times too many, and his tie is pulled away from his collar.

Tristan is sitting across the room, but I feel him everywhere. How could I have forgotten what that was like? That constant presence . . . it's not all that unpleasant anymore, which makes my head spin.

I glance away when he catches me watching him.

He joins me once he's off the phone and sits on the couch across from me. "Good morning," he says in his normal, smooth voice.

"Morning." I look over at him and bite my lip.

"What is that?" he asks, a sharpness latching onto his tone. It makes my pulse jump.

My forehead creases in confusion. "What?"

Before I can shift away, his hand is tilting my face to the side, his fingers brushing along my jaw. I wince at the stabbing pain that follows his touch. He drops his hand and pins me with a dark stare. "What happened?"

I bite the inside of my cheek. "Nothing. It's fine."

"You want to play this game, Aurora? Really?"

I scowl. "I'm not playing any game. I just know it's not worth talking about. I can take care of myself."

"Clearly," he remarks, his brows tugged closer as if he's disappointed that I'm not confiding in him.

I huff out a breath and grab his hand, lifting it to my face until his fingertips are pressed against the spot where the fae woman dug her nails into my skin. "Heal it so we can move on, will you?"

"Now you're asking—?"

"Yes," I cut in, still holding his hand against my face.

He shifts closer, which is unnecessary, sending my heart racing. "Tell me what happened, and I'll be happy to help."

My eyes snap to his. "Are you kidding me?"

He holds my gaze. "I need to know what goes on in my hotel, Aurora, so you can tell me, or I can find out on my own."

I clench my jaw until my teeth ache. "A couple of fae ambushed me in the elevator on my way up here." I swallow, casting my gaze down as embarrassment floods through me. "The woman started feeding on me."

Tristan tilts my head back up as the familiar warmth of his healing magic shimmers across my cheek. His gentle touch is a stark contrast to the hard, violent expression darkening his features.

"Can you chill?" I don't want to look at him anymore.

He pulls his hand away from my face. "You'd like me to allow my people to threaten you?"

"That's not what I'm saying. I just don't want to make a bigger issue."

He chuckles. "Since when?"

I scowl. "This is exactly why I wasn't going to bring it up."

The smile fades from his lips. "I'll make sure it doesn't happen again."

"Okay." I tug at a tiny loose thread on my dress for no

reason other than to have something to do with my hands. "Thanks for the healing," I mumble.

He nods.

"Is everything okay? I mean, apart from what I just told you."

"Why do you ask?" He clasps his hands together and pins me with his intense gaze. You'd think I'd be used to it by now, but the endless blue makes it hard to look away.

"When I came in, the tension in the air was enough to suffocate a person, human or otherwise."

His lips twitch. "You're worried?"

I blink, ignoring the dip my stomach does when I look at his mouth. "Well, yeah."

"That's interesting," he muses.

I ignore his comment. "What's going on?" I can't help but wonder whether it's related to those fae I saw fighting the other day.

"Nothing you need to worry about."

Images of Tristan's nightmare scene flash through my mind. Yeah, I *am* worried.

I set my cup on the coffee table and cross my arms. "Skylar isn't here to boss me around, so I've got nothing else to do but sit here until you talk." I shoot him a fake smile.

He laughs like what I've said is humorous.

"What?" I snap.

"I find it amusing that you think you have control here." He points at the door. "The moment you stepped into this office you lost it."

My pulse races as anger bubbles in me. Every time I think we're making progress, that he's going to treat me like something more than a toy for his amusement, he goes and ruins it with a line like that. "Were you not validated as a child?"

He tilts his head to the side.

"I'm curious," I say. "You couldn't have been born an asshole, so I'm wondering when you picked it up."

"Ah, Aurora, you're as charming as ever." He stands and walks back to his desk.

I follow, leaving my coffee behind. "Should I go ask Max why you have an entire tree up your ass?" I push.

His eyes snap to mine as he walks around the desk to stand opposite me. He towers over me, but I don't back down. "Enough," he growls. "I don't want to talk about this. End of discussion."

"There was never any discussion. You upended my life, and now you won't tell me anything," I shoot back, my voice rising with each word. I shouldn't care, and I had no right to ask, but something inside of me—maybe my concern for Allison and my curiosity about the light and dark fae—made me ask anyway.

He blows out a breath, shaking his head. "Why do you want to know what's going on?"

"Because something tells me I'm missing information. I know more about the fae world than I'd ever wish to, but not everything. Call me crazy, but I don't make a habit of putting a book down halfway through the story."

"What about the ones you don't enjoy?"

I shrug. "Sometimes I need to remind myself to give them a chance."

"You're right. You don't know the whole story," he says.

"I know about the whole dark and light thing," I say. Maybe now is when I'll get some real answers.

He nods, but he doesn't look surprised. "We've been at war

with them for as long as history can remember. They've been killing ours for centuries."

The idea of Allison being in danger surfaces. Even looking at Tristan, a pang of concern passes through me—something I was *not* expecting.

I swallow, but the lump in my throat remains. "Why?"

"You know what a war means. I think you can figure it out."

I nod. "Wait. Were my ancestors light or dark?"

He tilts his head, looking at me through his lashes. "Do you have a preference?" I found out about the different sides a couple of days ago. Of course, I don't have a preference, but I would still like to know.

My brows shift closer together. "Which were they?" I push.

"They were dark."

"Were?" I ask in a low voice.

He frowns. "I don't know if they're still around."

My stomach drops. I'm not sure why knowing that makes my chest ache. I never met them, but they're still family. "Oh."

"I'm still looking into it," he says.

I nod. "What was that phone call about?" I ask, shifting the conversation.

"It's been calm for the most part on both sides until recent weeks. We're losing numbers. Lucky for us, they can't kill too many at once out in the open. It would attract too much human attention." He sighs, rubbing his jaw. "I'm trying to figure out a solution that results in the least number of tragedies when it comes to my people."

"What's your solution?"

"I'd rather not kill anyone, but I will if it comes to that. I refuse to allow my people to continue living in fear."

"Have you considered talking about it instead of retaliating physically? Words are powerful weapons."

"No," he says. "The time for talking was before the light fae started killing."

"So, you want to add to the bloodshed?"

A muscle ticks along his sharp jaw. "This isn't your fight."

"You're right. Forgive me for losing my head and forgetting my place." I'm not sure why I'm so upset, or why I offered my opinion. There's nothing I can do to protect Allison that she can't do herself, but with this new information I've learned, it makes me feel like a caged animal.

"Hmm," he murmurs, and I take a healthy step back as the corner of his mouth lifts. "You seem concerned."

I glare at him. "I *am* concerned. My best friend could be in danger. I don't want her to get hurt. And you—" I bite the inside of my cheek. "It's dangerous," I mutter.

"I will protect my people, Aurora."

"Who protects you?" I blurt. If my concern for *him* wasn't clear by the energy I've been giving off, he knows about it now. It's funny, it doesn't bother me as much as I thought it would.

He's silent for a few beats. "You never fail to surprise me."

"Why do you say that?"

He pins me with a focused gaze that turns the temperature of my body way up. "You spend your time trying to hate me for what happened when we met, which is fair, but you don't, do you?"

The muscles in my jaw tighten. "Are you kidding?"

"Your cheeks flush when I'm around, and I make your pulse race. I can hear your heartbeat right now."

"An excellent observation," I remark dryly despite the dampness on my palms.

"I affect you."

My pulse jumps, and he smirks as if to say *told you*. "That's ridiculous," I say.

"Is that why your heart is trying to beat its way out of your chest right now?"

"No," I grumble. "You're wrong."

Tristan cocks his head. "I don't think I am." His eyes glimmer with heat, and my throat goes dry. "Now you look afraid," he muses.

"Why are you doing this?"

"I'm used to you being upfront with your feelings, so this is new."

My eyes narrow. "Are you expecting me to say I'm head over heels for you and will worship at your feet?" I laugh. "Just because I don't hate you anymore, just because I care if you're in danger, doesn't mean—"

"What? That you feel something for me?"

My heart stutters, and at this point, I don't care that he heard it. Maybe I do feel something for Tristan, but I'll be damned if I let myself admit it out loud. I cast my gaze away from him. "You're busy enough with fae politics today. You don't need to deal with me." His words play over in my head on a loop. *You feel something for me.* I need to get out of this room, away from his presence that makes my head spin. "Staying here isn't going to help anything, so I might as well go back to my dorm and prep for my study group tonight."

"Be my guest," he replies.

I brush past him, grabbing my things from the couch. Then I head for the door and slam it shut behind me.

Marisa frowns at me when I walk through the lobby downstairs. "You're heading home already?"

I nod. "Yeah, I—"

"Get your ass back here, blondie." Max approaches us from the elevator. He wasn't sitting at the desk upstairs when I left, so I thought I'd gotten lucky.

I sigh. "Maybe not."

"Where do you think you're going?" he asks. He glances at Marisa and offers her a nod.

"Home," I say.

He shakes his head and grabs my arm before he walks away, dragging me with him. Because *that's* not an odd thing to do in a lobby full of people. Subtlety is lost on Max.

"What the hell, Max? Let go of me," I demand.

"Chill out, human." He releases his grip and faces me. "What did you do?"

"What are you talking about?" I counter.

"Tristan is up there snapping at people; he's *pissed*. So, I'll ask again. What did you do?"

"I tried to help."

He barks out a laugh. "Why would you want to help? We kidnapped you. We forced you into this world, and now you want to help? What do you think that says about you?"

It's my turn to laugh. "*You're* the one who kidnapped me. What do you think that says about *you*?"

He grins. "Fair point." He shrugs. "Do what you want, blondie, but try not to piss Tristan off. For some reason, he seems to care about you, but when he's moody we're the ones who have to deal with it."

"Then he needs to grow up and control his emotions."

His eyes flash with amusement. "You feel free to let him know. I would love to see where that gets you."

"I bet you would." I adjust the bag on my shoulder. "I'm going home. Skylar isn't here, and Tristan isn't in the mentoring mood. I'll be back next week."

"Your choice." He rakes his fingers through his hair. "How's that roommate of yours doing?"

"Allison? What do you mean? She's fine."

He tilts his head. "Really?" He draws out the word.

I scowl. "Yeah, *really*. Why?"

"I'm surprised she got off so easily with Tristan."

"What are you talking about? So she's dating Oliver. Big deal."

"She got in trouble for dating a human?" He laughs. "Is that what she told you?"

My eyes narrow. "Don't. I know what you're trying to do, and it's not going to work."

He holds up his hands. "Think whatever you want, blondie. There's no rule against fae dating humans. Your friend managed to sneak around the truth without lying. I'm sort of impressed."

I swallow, my chest tightening under the pressure of Max's words. "I have to go." I don't wait for him to say anything else.

While I wait for the streetcar, I pull out my phone and send a new message to Allison.

I'm coming home. We need to talk. Now.

chapter Twelve

ALLISON IS SITTING AT THE END OF HER BED WHEN I STORM into our dorm room less than fifteen minutes later. I throw my bag down and take a deep breath before facing her. Her eyes widen in what looks like apprehension.

"Why did you lie to me?" I ask in a calm tone. I'm trying to allow her a chance to explain before I get angry. I don't want to be mad at my best friend.

She shakes her head. "What?"

"Dating Oliver isn't against the rules. There isn't a rule about fae dating humans."

She looks away. "I didn't lie—I can't—I just didn't correct you when you assumed that Oliver was my indiscretion."

My eyes widen. "What the hell? Care to explain what *actually* happened?"

She sighs. "Okay. This is going to sound terrible, and you'll probably hate me, but please let me explain before you decide to never speak to me again."

I stare at her. "Tell me."

"I cheated on Oliver. Well, sort of. It was mutual."

I open and close my mouth twice before I can form words. And then I manage to say, "What?"

"Oliver doesn't love me." Her voice is light, as if she isn't upset by what she's telling me, whereas I'm freaking out on the inside. God, why did Max have to open his mouth and screw things up? Why did Allison keep this from me?

"Are you kidding? Of course he does."

"Not romantically. He loves me like he loves you. Platonically."

"But you guys have been together for years," I say. I'm more upset about this than she is.

"I know." She folds her hands in her lap. "We started off as a genuine couple, but since the beginning of the summer, we haven't been together."

I think about the dates I tagged along for over the years. I don't understand what she's saying. "You need to keep talking." There's an edge to my voice.

"We aren't together anymore," she repeats. "We're keeping up the ruse for Oliver's sake."

"Why?" I ask.

"Because he doesn't want to come out in college. He feels strongly that just because he likes guys it doesn't mean he should have to tell the world."

I understand what she's saying and why Oliver feels that way, and I agree. "It's his thing to share, but I talked to him about it. He said it was okay for me to tell you. We don't want you in the dark anymore, and now I can explain why I didn't tell you what's been going on." That makes it sound like she was planning on telling me the truth before Max sold her out to me.

123

Knowing that makes me feel a bit better, but the fact she kept it from me to begin with still stings.

"What does Oliver being gay have to do with the fae?"

"It doesn't, exactly. Oliver doesn't know, but he wasn't the only one using our relationship as a cover."

My brows tug together. "Are you telling me you're gay? Fae aren't allowed to be gay?"

She laughs, but it's uneven, different from her normal laugh. "No, I'm not gay. I don't think the fae care about that. Love is love."

"Okay. What did you need the relationship to hide?"

She hesitates. "The guy I *am* seeing," she says in a timid voice.

"Who are you seeing, Allison?" I press.

"His name is Evan. He's a fourth year, like us, and he's fae."

I'm missing something. So far, her explanation has yet to provide a real reason for her getting into trouble with Tristan.

"I still don't see the problem—other than the fact that the guy you loved realized he doesn't like girls. I can't imagine how that made you feel."

She shrugs. "It hurt at first, but I get it, and I don't blame him. He didn't do it to hurt me. He didn't know what he wanted at that point. We've gotten past the awkwardness, obviously, considering what we're doing for each other now."

"Now you're going to tell me what the problem is with you dating Evan, right?"

She wraps her arms around herself. "Well, Evan is light fae . . . and pretty close to their leader, Jules, who is Tristan's enemy."

A weight settles in my stomach. "This sounds more dangerous than you're making it out to be." I'm sure she can feel the concern pouring off of me by now.

She sighs. "We care about each other, Aurora. I tried to explain that to Tristan, but you know him well enough now to know how that went. There's a chance, if I refuse to walk away from Evan, that'll I'll be incarcerated for treason."

My stomach drops. Do the fae have their own type of prison in the human world? "What? No. I'm not going to let that happen to you."

She almost smiles. "Thanks, but there's not much you, or even I, can do. I understand the rules. They are in place to keep our people safe." She blinks a few times. "I don't know what to do," she whispers.

I run my fingers through my hair and let out a slow breath, trying to ground myself so I can think about this situation rationally. "Is it worth it?" She looks offended by the question. "I'm just saying, this could cause a lot of trouble for you. Tristan won't accept that you're—for lack of a better phrase—sleeping with the enemy. I don't know much about the whole thing, but I know that it's serious." Tristan's unease during the phone call this morning, and his responses during the conversation we had afterward tell me enough to make that statement.

"I know that," she mumbles. "I don't want to lose him."

"Tristan said light fae are killing dark fae. What if you become a target?" I grab her hands and squeeze them gently. "I can't stand the thought of you getting hurt."

"I . . ." She looks away. "I don't know what to say."

"Did you know he was light fae?"

"I did," she says. "And before you ask, yes, he knew I wasn't, but we decided that it didn't matter."

"I think it matters more than you want to admit." Everything I've heard about the light fae urges me to be wary of them.

Especially when my best friend is involved.

She scowls, pulling her hands from mine. "How the hell would you know?" My eyes widen at her sudden sharp tone. That went from zero to one hundred *way* too fast.

I stand there for several beats. Allison never snaps at me. I don't think I've ever heard her raise her voice at anyone. It's clear she's not about to apologize for it. "You're right, I don't know everything about the fae, but I will do whatever it takes to make sure you're okay. Even if you're pissed at me now, you'd do the same for me."

She blinks a few times, her expression softening. "I would and I love you for caring so much, I do, but I need to figure this one out on my own. I'll be careful, I promise, but please don't be mad at me for this."

I don't *want* to be angry, but it takes some effort to push those feelings down. Maybe I'll feel better about the situation once I've met the guy. I decide to reserve my judgment until then.

"Okay," I say. "I need a coffee. You want to join?"

Her shoulders easing, she smiles. "Thank you. I've got to head to class, but I'll catch you later?"

I nod, leaning over to hug her. "Sure."

At the cafeteria, I'm standing at the self-serve station putting a lid on my cup when Oliver walks over with his own. By the looks of his eyes and messy hair, it isn't his first. You can always tell when it's midterms around here. Hell, I'm surprised he's wearing jeans and a T-shirt instead of pajamas. I would be if I hadn't been at the hotel this morning.

Oliver blows out a breath. "It's just after noon, and I'm

ready for bed."

"Do you have time for a break?"

His eyes widen. "Break? You'll have to explain that foreign concept to me."

I giggle. "Well, we can sit and talk about something that has nothing to do with study cards or assignments. I've heard it's enjoyable."

"Let's give it a go," he says.

We pay for our coffee and find a quiet spot in the corner of the lounge attached to the cafeteria.

"Listen, there's something I've been wanting to tell you for a while now." He fidgets with his hands in his lap. "Did Allison talk to you?"

I smile. "She did. I understand why you guys kept it from me. I'm not mad." I'm a bit upset with the whole situation, but that's my issue to deal with.

He nods. "I'm sorry I didn't tell you. I've felt so terrible about it, especially for Allison. I never meant to hurt her. She's been so amazing about all of it."

"Don't apologize, Oliver. You shouldn't have to say anything. In my mind, you dating guys is no different than you dating girls."

His face relaxes. "Thanks for being cool about this."

"Of course." I give his shoulder a gentle punch. "So, are you seeing anyone?"

He scratches his head. "Not officially. I'm not broadcasting my relationship status publically, but I'm sort of hanging with someone on and off."

I press my lips together, hesitating before I ask, "Do your parents know?"

He offers a weak smile, and my chest tightens.

I reach across the table and squeeze his hand. "I'm sorry."

He drags a hand down his face before taking a sip of his coffee. "It's okay. There's a good chance I'm going to move into an apartment in Rockdale after graduation. I figure one day I'll bring my boyfriend to meet them without saying anything."

Oliver's parents are the perfect picture of conservatives. I can imagine how well that surprise would go over.

"We can get a place together," I say, only half joking. I'll most likely stick around Rockdale after graduation, and having a roommate *would* make rent easier to pay.

"Yeah?" The corner of his mouth quirks. "I'll keep that in mind. Unless, of course, I'm living with my theoretical super-hot boyfriend by then."

I laugh. "Right, of course."

Oliver gives me a bear hug before he heads upstairs. I grab my textbook and join a few of the girls from my program who are there with their books already open, chatting about the upcoming test. I hurry over and sit, cracking my book open to join in the discussion.

We're all scribbling away when Danielle walks in with drink trays in her hands.

"Hey, sorry I'm late." We set a meeting time in the group chat for a reason. "I brought caffeine!" Danielle sets the drinks down on the counter and throws her brown curls into a messy bun before passing them out. She sits next to me and hands me a cup before taking a sip from her own.

"Thanks," I say with a smile, and tip the cup to my lips.

"My pleasure." She returns the smile and opens her book, glancing over at mine to find her place. I've got respect for this girl. She can party, as she did at the first kegger of the semester, but when it counts, she can focus on school.

I take another sip before returning my attention to my textbook.

"So, are we all ready for this test?" Danielle asks.

A collective groan sounds around the room.

Hours later, I'm shuffling down the hallway, headed for bed with a unsettled stomach, an all too familiar sign I've consumed too much caffeine today. My eyes burn—it's a struggle to keep them open. A constant side effect of college life. I even missed the Halloween party one of Oliver's friends threw last week, needing to catch up on sleep instead.

Allison is asleep in our room when I close the door and drop my bag at my desk before crawling under the sheets. I can't be bothered to change out of my clothes; I imagine it's unnatural how fast sleep pulls me under.

I don't know how long I'm asleep before my eyes shoot open and an agony-filled scream tears its way up my throat. I clutch my chest as it burns with such a fierce pain I think I'm going to faint.

Allison is at my side in a second, having thrown herself out of bed when I started screaming.

"Aurora." She tries to grab my wrists and pry them away from my chest, but I hold strong, groaning in pain. "What's happening?" Her tone is frantic, but I can't do anything. I can't speak, not that it would matter—I have no idea what's wrong with me.

I cry out as the sharpness claws deeper, and Allison's eyes widen. I thrash against the sheets, and the moment my arms slip away from my chest, Allison pushes my shirt out of the way to look. When she curses, I know it's bad.

Panic clamps down on my burning chest as I squeeze my eyes shut.

"Aurora, this is bad." She shakes her head, her eyes flicking over my face. "I have to call him. I don't know what else to do."

"Don't," I bite out through clenched teeth. "I'm . . . fine."

"You're not fine," she snaps. "You have fae poison coursing through you." She grabs my hand and squeezes it. "I'll be right back."

My breaths are quick and short as I try to fight through the pain. My vision blurs, ebbing in and out, and I know that isn't a good sign. I should be freaking out, but I don't feel anything.

I close my eyes for a second; I think. They snap open when cool hands grip my shoulders, shaking gently. Tristan is kneeling at the side of my bed.

"Aurora." His voice is soft, urgent. "You need to keep your eyes open for me, sweetheart."

I think I manage to nod as my eyes drift shut again. *Did he call me sweetheart?* Maybe it's because I feel like I'm dying, but I like the sound of it.

"Aurora," he repeats, sharper this time, as he tilts my chin up.

Blinking a few times, I try to focus on his face. The pain in my chest is spreading.

"Are you going to help her?" I hear Allison ask.

I watch his face as his jaw tightens, and my heart sinks when he says, "I can't." He glances over his shoulder at her. "Not here."

"Tristan, please." She says in a small voice. "Whatever it takes. Please."

I try to swallow, but my throat is too dry. He drops his hands and scoops me into his arms without any effort. His eyes meet mine for a brief moment before the room around me shifts.

I'm still shivering when Tristan's bedroom materializes, and I grip his wrists, struggling to breathe as the weight of the situation tugs at me. He peers at me and frowns, his eyes wild and his mouth set in a thin line. He cradles me in his arms and walks over to the large four-poster bed I woke up on in my dream. When he sets me on the black silk sheets, I want to close my eyes.

Yeah, this isn't looking good.

"Do you remember what you told me when we met?" he asks.

His question surprises me, but I try to recall that day. After thinking about it, I lift my eyes to meet his and nod.

"Tell me."

My jaw is clenched against the pain; I don't think I can speak. If I open my mouth, I'm afraid I'll scream again.

"Aurora," he says. "Tell me."

I close my eyes and force my jaw to unclench. "I told you I wasn't going to die here," I say, the words slow to come out.

"And you're not."

My eyes open at the sound of his voice. "How?" I whisper, and my voice cracks. He sounds so sure, and yet I feel as though I'm breaking apart in front of him.

He lifts his hand and brushes the hair away from my face, tucking it behind my ear. "I'm going to fix this. I'm going to make it better."

I manage to nod. "Okay."

"Okay," he repeats.

His expression focuses as he lifts my shirt over my head. I try not to wince, but the pain is excruciating. I suck in a sharp breath when I see my chest. Black veins run under my skin, circling my stomach and disappearing under my bra, which

Tristan makes no move to take off.

He presses his palm flat against my skin above my belly button, and I hold my breath, my lips pressed together. "I need you to breathe, sweetheart," he murmurs.

Letting out a slow breath, I watch his hand shift upward. The pain fades eventually, and so do the shivers, but the black veins running under my skin remain.

"You can close your eyes now," Tristan says in a gentle tone as he stands. "I'll be right back."

I watch him leave the room and wait, eyes open, until he returns to my side.

He kneels and looks at me, his expression soft. "Close your eyes."

I shake my head. "What are you going to do?" It comes out as more of a whisper, but he hears me.

He leans forward and lifts my chin with two fingers. "I'm going to heal you. You don't need to watch."

My eyes narrow. "Tristan . . ."

He huffs out a breath. "Don't say I didn't warn you." He pulls out a syringe, and my entire body stiffens. "Relax. I'm saving your life."

I watch his every move as he shrugs off his jacket and uncaps the needle. I look away as he slips the needle into his arm and fills it with his own blood.

"Aurora."

I force myself to look at him and notice the needle is out of his arm. He holds it in his hand, waiting.

"This will cure you of the fae poison in your blood, but there could be unforeseen side effects."

"Like?" I whisper.

"I'm not going to list them for you right now. You need

this." His voice is firm; he isn't giving me a choice. Given the alternative involves me dying, I can't find the will to be annoyed by that.

I close my eyes briefly before nodding. "All right," I breathe.

He slips his free hand up my arm and grips it near my elbow. He turns it over so my palm is facing up, and when he lowers the needle, I look away again. As it pierces my skin, I flinch, and I swear I can feel his blood entering my system.

My entire body ignites with searing heat, but before I can react, the sensation is replaced by a calming, icy chill. Everything is too bright, so I close my eyes, and I shift as he withdraws the needle from my arm. Dizziness floods in, and I force my eyes open.

"It's okay." He sets the needle aside and faces me. "You can sleep now. This will take some time to work through your system." He helps me back into my shirt and pulls the blankets around me.

"You keep saving me," I mumble.

He chuckles, but it holds no amusement.

"It's annoying." I take a couple of deep breaths. "I don't want to need saving."

"Get some rest, sweetheart," he murmurs.

Closing my eyes, I curl onto my side to get comfortable. Sleep drags me under before I can feel weird about being snuggled into Tristan's bed.

chapter Thirteen

WHEN I OPEN MY EYES, IT'S STILL DARK OUTSIDE. It takes more effort than usual for me to slide into a sitting position. My entire body aches as if I ran a marathon without any preparation, but the unbearable pain in my chest is gone. Everything else I can handle.

My eyes scan the dark room as I swing my legs over the side of the bed and stand. After flicking on a lamp, I wander the perimeter of the room, never having had the chance outside of my dream to see what it looks like. I shouldn't care, but I'm curious. I squint and wobble over to the bookshelves lining one wall. I run my finger along the spines and glance out the windows that cover the far wall, looking out over the city from a magnificent height. Everything is neat and simple. There's nothing else that expresses Tristan's personality out in the open. A pang of sadness grows in my stomach. I wonder if he's this closed-off with Max and Skylar. I hope not. Everyone needs people to share things with, even a fae leader.

Once I've finished exploring, I grab the blanket off the bed. Wrapping it around myself to try to keep warm, I slip out of the room. The black silk trails behind me like a train as I pad down the hallway in search of Tristan. I stop at the only other door in the hallway, and poke my head inside to find him sitting behind a desk.

He glances up the moment I open the door and watches me walk into the room. "You should be sleeping," he says in a hushed tone.

"I woke up." I approach his desk. He changed out of his formal attire into a black T-shirt and slacks. I rub at my temples, wanting to close my eyes against the light beside him.

Tristan rises and walks around the desk, making me turn so I continue to face him. "Are you in pain?" The concern is so clear on his face, I'm shocked. It looks like he cares. *He does*, a voice at the back of my mind sings.

I shrug. "A little. Nothing compared to earlier, though. I'm fine."

"Will you let me help you?"

My forehead creases. "Okay." Apprehension rings loud in my voice.

"Don't worry, sweetheart. No more needles." The unease in my chest lets up.

He lifts his hand, and I find myself stepping toward him. He cups the side of my face, and my skin tingles with a familiar warmth as the aching in my body melts away under his touch. My eyes travel over his face—his soft, focused eyes; his strong jaw and the stubble that shadows it; his lips . . . My gaze gets stuck there too long. I watch the corner of his mouth twitch, and I realize he's no longer touching my cheek.

"How's that?" His voice makes me shift my eyes upward.

Clearing my throat, I say, "Better. Thank you."

He nods, and the weirdest part is, I can *feel* the relief shimmer through him. He's glad I'm okay. I don't know how I know that, but—

. . . there could be unforeseen side effects . . .

My hand flies to my mouth as my wide eyes meet Tristan's blazing gaze. He's realized what just happened.

"Holy shit," I breathe, my hand falling to my side.

He licks his lips. "I suppose this evens the playing field a bit," he muses, his brows shifting closer together.

"I can *feel* you."

He nods. "A gift from your fae ancestors, I'd guess. I wasn't sure what my blood would do, but it seems to have stirred a bit of magic in you."

"Magic? Hold the hell up. Am I fae now?" He looks like he's trying not to laugh, and I smack his arm. "Well, I don't know!"

"You can relax. You're not fae."

I can still feel the light amusement coursing through him. My eyes flicker across his face as his emotions become more subdued.

His eyes narrow a fraction. "I think that's enough for now."

I arch a brow. "Says the guy that's been able to read my emotions since day one. Sucks to be on the other side, doesn't it?"

He chuckles. "If you'd like to know what I'm feeling, Aurora, I have no problem sharing that with you."

I shake my head. "This is too weird."

"Does the connection bother you?"

"Not right now." I purse my lips. "How long is this going to last?"

He shrugs. "This isn't something I've experienced before. A human being able to feel what I'm feeling. It's as new to me as it is to you, I'm afraid."

I release a breath and shoot him a smile. "Lucky us."

He tweaks my chin. "Look at it this way. At least you're not stuck feeling Max's emotions. He tends to keep them locked up tight, but depending on the day, when he makes them known, it's no fun for anyone."

I groan. The thought of being connected to Max makes me shudder. "Ugh, I hate when you're right."

His laugh is a deep sound that booms throughout the room. It's genuine. I know that with a fresh certainty I feel in my chest. This reading emotions thing could get dangerous.

I glance over at his desk. "What are you doing up so late?"

His eyes flicker across my face in the dim light. "I spoke to Allison while you were asleep. She knows you're okay. I don't take what happened tonight lightly. I will find out who is behind this, and there will be consequences." The tang of anger radiating from him makes me frown. I miss the light emotions he was giving off a few minutes ago.

"You think it was one of your fae?" I ask, masking my surprise at his reaction to the situation. I'm not fae—not his to protect.

"No, I know it wasn't."

"Then I'm not sure why you think—"

His anger rises, but his calm and collected expression holds. If I weren't privy to his emotions, I wouldn't notice the shift. "They won't get away with harming you, Aurora. Whoever ordered this action knows you're significant. That's why it happened."

I swallow. "I don't understand why."

"Don't be naive." His breath tickles my cheek, a reminder of how close he is. "You know I care about you." The worry and attraction swirling inside him become muddled, making my head spin. I need to figure out a way to turn this off.

Swallowing, I say, "I'm not naive. I knew there was something, or you would've figured out another way to approach the situation after you couldn't wipe my memories." I shrug, still pretty drowsy. "And I—" I clamp my mouth shut before I say anything. I'm not sure what I was going to say, considering my mind is still caught on the whole *I care about you* thing. "I understand," I say. If I can feel *his* emotions right now, he can feel mine. I don't have to to say it back.

"Good."

I shake my head. "Not good." My throat tingles as if I'm going to hurl. My stomach feels heavy, and my pulse is uneven. "Someone wants me dead." The words have to fight to make it through the chattering of my teeth. Clenching my jaw to try to make it stop, I watch Tristan's eyes focus on my face.

"Aurora, you're okay."

My eyes sting as I hold back tears, gripping the blanket around me tighter. It's all too much. I can feel my heartbeat in my throat as black spots dance across my line of sight, and my ears ring. The light fae want to kill me; Tristan is acting . . . not like the Tristan I've come to tolerate; Allison is putting herself in danger; my brother has cancer again, and I can't even think about school.

"Hey." His smooth, certain voice brings me back from the edge. His hand is on my shoulder. "Breathe."

I stare at him, and he nods.

"Take a deep breath for me, Rory."

Rory. I say it over in my head. That's new.

I inhale, and all I can smell is *him*. Fresh, warm . . . comforting.

"Good girl," he praises. "Now again."

I hold his gaze, standing so close I can count his eyelashes. The pressure in my chest eases, and my throat isn't so tight I can't breathe. My grip on the blanket loosens as I exhale again, and my pulse returns to a normal pace.

His eyes flick back and forth across my face. "Okay?"

I swallow the lump in my throat. "I'm good," I say, placing my hand over where his still rests on my shoulder. "Thank you."

His lips curl into the most genuine smile I've ever seen from him when he lets his hand fall back to his side. "How are you feeling now? Are you up for a late dinner?"

"What were you thinking? I don't eat, uh, emotions."

"Though you seem to be enjoying the fact you can sense mine." He licks his bottom lip. "Anything you want, name it. I don't *have* to feed on emotions all the time, just enough to keep me alive. I can feed once a week, and it's plenty. That's to say, I eat human food, too."

I catch my lower lip between my teeth. "You never talk about it."

"About what?"

"Feeding. Being fae."

His forehead creases. "I wasn't aware you wanted to hear about it."

My cheeks heat. "I'm saying you *can* talk about it. It's not going to freak me out." I need to stop talking.

His eyes lighten as pleasant surprise flares through the new bond we share. "I'll keep that in mind."

"Oh-kay." The word comes out more like two words.

He tilts his head. "You're quite the human."

There goes my pulse again. "Did you *just* meet me?"

He chuckles. "It feels like I've known you much longer."

That brings an unexpected smile to my lips. "Yeah, I guess

you're not so terrible yourself."

"All right, smart mouth. Let's see what we can find in the kitchen."

I drape the blanket over a chair and follow him out of the office.

Tonight is *not* going how I thought it would.

It's been a week and a half since Tristan saved my life and showed me a different side to the fae leader I've been dealing with. I still think about it every day. I go to class and think about him. I sit in my room doing homework and think about him; there aren't many times I'm *not* thinking about him. I have no idea what to do, so I've decided to avoid it—and by *it*, I mean Tristan. As much as possible. He's respected me and stayed out of my dreams, but when I'm awake, I'm never sure when I'm going to see him.

As the days pass, fewer and fewer of his emotions seep through. The ones that do are a mixture of worry, anger, and uncertainty, as if maybe he's trying to figure something out. It's rare he feels anything light or warm. Considering the constant pressure he's under, it's understandable.

One day, I can't sense his emotions at all. Part of me is relieved, but hell, it was interesting knowing I had a leg up on at least one of his fae abilities for a handful of days. Oh, well. I'll take being human over being able to read emotions any day. Even with the absence of his emotions, I still think about him way too much.

At the hotel on Monday, I almost kiss Skylar when she tells me Tristan is out of the office all day. I don't because I value my life, but the heavy sense of relief that pours over me is borderline embarrassing.

"Tristan wanted to talk to you about something," she says.

I hesitate before asking, "What . . . uh, what did he want to talk to me about?"

"Westbrook Inc. hosts a charity gala every year, and he wants you to spearhead the planning of the event."

"Are you serious?" Excitement bubbles through me. An event like this would look amazing on my resume.

She gives me a look.

"Wow. I mean, this is awesome. I would love to." I make a mental note to text Allison when I get a break. We're going out for drinks tonight to celebrate. Our friendship has been somewhat strained lately with the whole Evan thing, but there's no one I'd rather toast to this new opportunity with.

"Great." She feigns enthusiasm. "You'll be working with me. Max is also on the gala committee along with several other employees, but I'm sure that won't be a problem, right?"

"Right," I answer, my voice more uptight than normal. "When do we start?"

"Now, and it's going to take more than your one day a week here. Can you make that work?"

"Of course. My Friday class finishes at noon, so I'll come here right after, and I can do some evenings and weekends, too."

"Good," she says before handing me a list. "This is everything we have to do."

I scan the paper until the words blur. "Sure. When is the event?"

"A month tomorrow," she answers.

"That's soon."

"You can read a calendar. Good for you. Let's get to work."

After a couple of hours, Skylar announces she's leaving

for the day, and Max takes her place on the other side of the table. He's dressed in more casual attire than I'm used to seeing around here. He's wearing a navy blue collared shirt with a loosely knotted tie and black jeans.

"You're still alive, I see," he says after sitting across from me.

I force a smile. "Looks like it."

"What's keeping you around, blondie?" he asks, raking a hand through the mop of hair on his head.

"Uh, my education," I answer. "I need this to graduate."

"You don't need the dozens of extra hours this charity event will give you."

"Maybe I enjoy doing something for a good cause. Or maybe I like working here."

"Really?" he inquires with an amused expression.

I shrug. "Yeah. Do you hate me or something? Are you still mad you didn't get to kill me?"

Max laughs. "I don't get to have a lot of fun around here, so I find entertainment in screwing with you. You're such an easy target."

I stare at him, scowling. "You're such a child. I've been working my ass off around here for a while now, and you've treated me like shit since the beginning." I stand and walk out of the room, leaving my belongings behind. I need some air—I need to take a break so I don't attack Max and get my ass handed to me. Stepping off the elevator into the lobby, I offer Marisa a quick wave on my way to the door.

"Aurora, come here," she calls after me, so I turn and walk to the reception desk.

"What's up?" I ask.

"You look pissed. I didn't think Mr. Westbrook was in the

office today."

I laugh. As agitated as I am, Marisa is good at making me feel better. "Yeah, he's not." Which is making avoiding him a bit easier. "It's Max."

"Ugh, he's a major dick. All the time."

"Tell me about it." I sigh.

"Remember when you told me you play piano?"

I nod.

She glances around as if to make sure no one is overhearing our exchange. "I saw some movers bring a piano into the ballroom." She points to a hallway off of the lobby. "The double doors at the end of the hall. You can't miss it."

"You can't be serious," I say, my fingers already itching to play.

She grins. "It'll make you feel better." She drops a key on the counter. "No one else is in there. Go take a break and relax."

"Thank you." I grab the key and head for the ballroom before I can talk myself out of it. I hurry down the hallway as if I'm about to be caught doing something I shouldn't.

After unlocking the door and closing it behind me, I take in the room. It's elegant: gold walls, high ceilings, over-the-top chandeliers. The marble floor is so smooth it makes me want to lie on it and stare at the twinkling lights. My eyes land on the piano, and I suck in a breath as I walk over to it. It's the most amazing piano I've ever seen. I can see my reflection in the glossy black finish. I lift the lid that covers the keys; they look as if they've never been touched. I run my fingers along them without pressing any and then sit on the bench. With a breath, forcing the tension out of my system, I put my fingers to the keys again. I can lose myself in the music. That's what convinced me to come in here. A part of me is worried I'll get

143

caught, but the other part doesn't care.

I wrote a song the last time I went home for a weekend. I don't know where it came from, but the lyrics flew through me. As my fingers graze the keys, I sing, keeping in tune with the soft, deep key of the song that matches the lyrics.

He's an unstable bomb
He makes me feel wrong
He makes me feel right
But that's not for tonight

By the middle of the song, I'm belting it out with thick emotion laced in every word.

I hate that I wrote this damn song, but even more, I hate that it's about *him*.

He shows his soft side
And will start to confide
But then makes a huge mess
Of the life I have left

The song comes to a close. Eyes shut and my hands in my lap, I sit there, taking several deep breaths before I open them again.

Clapping sounds behind me, shooting a wicked shiver up my spine, and I freeze.

"Boundaries mean nothing to you, do they?" Tristan's amused voice carries through the empty room and latches onto my heart, sending it racing.

I scowl and turn to look at him. "You're one to talk."

He approaches at the same time I stand from the bench. Leaning against the side of the piano, I try to pull off a casual stance that fails epically. Damn. I need to get better at this shit.

"I own this hotel, Aurora, therefore nowhere is out of bounds for me."

I roll my eyes. "Because that's what I meant," I respond dryly.

"I didn't know you could play," he comments, glancing at the piano.

"There's a lot you don't know about me."

"Duly noted. That song you were playing, did you write it?"

My cheeks flush, and I want to look away. By the smug grin tugging at his lips, I can tell he already knows. "Yeah."

"I like it."

I rock back on my heels, wishing I could use that fae shifting trick to get the hell out of this room, away from his gaze. "Uh, thanks."

"Max said you took off. What happened?"

I shake my head. "It doesn't matter now. I don't want to talk about it."

"Do I need to be concerned?"

"If there were reason to be concerned, you would know. What are you doing here? Skylar said you'd be gone all day."

"All right," he concedes. "I had business to attend to this morning, but my afternoon meetings got canceled, so I came back. Care to join me for lunch?"

I sigh, shaking my head because hell *yes* I want to, but I shouldn't. "Tristan."

"Aurora," he levels.

"I'm not sure what you think you're doing when it comes to me, but—"

He closes the distance between us in a second, stopping just before he presses me against the piano. "Neither do I," he says on an exhale.

When I don't balk, he takes another step and creates a cage with his arms. "But when we're close, your heartbeat kicks up, your cheeks flush, and best of all, you get this look in your eyes, and I never know if you're going to smack me or let me closer."

"Depends on the day," I say without thinking.

He chuckles. "How's today looking?"

My eyes narrow. "Not great." I've gotten good at saying the exact opposite of what the voice in my head is screaming. She wants me to wrap myself around him and never let go, which is why I shove that voice away and force out the safe answer.

"Is that so?" he inquires.

I tilt my head back so I can look him in the eyes. "You want to get closer to me?"

His eyes darken. "Hmm."

"Okay, then tell me what's going on. Was that meeting this morning about the light fae?"

"You've been avoiding me," he says, ignoring what I asked.

I shoot him a look. "I have not. Quit evading my questions."

"Quit evading *me*," he counters.

Crossing my arms over my chest, I look away. "I've been busy."

"You're spiraling, Rory," he murmurs. "I don't want you to worry about the light fae. Nothing is going to happen to you."

My mouth goes dry. If I could speak, I have no idea what I'd say. I'd rather know I can protect myself, but his reassurance that my safety means something makes it hard to keep convincing myself he's the bad guy. Maybe he's not the bad guy anymore . . .

"During the meeting this morning, I was informed that a female by the name of Danielle was the light fae who poisoned you."

I have to swallow more than once before I say, "*What*? No. She's in my program. We study together. Hell, she bought me—"

Oh my god. *The coffee.* "She poisoned my coffee," I whisper.

He nods. "She confessed. I'm sorry." I can't feel his emotions anymore, but the furrow of his brows and downturn of his lips tells me enough. He's upset that I'm upset.

"But why?" I ask in a small voice.

"I had Max spend some time with her to see whether he could find out. All he gathered is that she felt bitter toward you because of something her leader said. Jules is always screwing with people, so I'm not surprised."

"Max?" The idea of him doing something to help me—it's almost unfathomable. "What would Jules have to say about me?"

"We don't know. Danielle stopped talking after she told Max about Jules, so she's been dealt with." I knew what that meant. I wouldn't see Danielle in class anymore.

Tears gather in my eyes. "Max killed her." It isn't a question.

Tristan nods, his back straight, as if my being upset is making him uncomfortable. "Would you have liked me to spare her?"

My whole body tenses. "I couldn't make that call."

"I wouldn't ask you to. I told you—I will protect my people."

My eyes widen, and heat rises in my cheeks. "If your blood activated some weird magic inside of me, why didn't the fae poison she tried to kill me with do anything like that?" I'm almost pissed at myself for not thinking about it sooner, but in my defense, I've been doing my best to try to forget that night.

He presses his lips together. "You remember the black veins under your skin? From what I found out, those appeared as your body tried to fight the poison off, but because you're human, it didn't work."

I sigh. "This is so messed up. Do you think the light fae are going to come after me again?"

"I'm handling this." He lowers his voice. "I'm not going to let you get hurt." His fiery gaze burns into me, making my pulse race as his words terrify me and bring me comfort at the same time. Nothing makes sense right now.

"I told Skylar I would work on the charity gala with her and Max," I say, looking away. "I should get back to work." I drop my gaze to his arm, and he lets it fall to his side. Then I hurry out of the room before he can say anything else.

Chapter Fourteen

I'VE BEEN STAYING ON CAMPUS SINCE SPENDING THE night at Tristan's when I was poisoned, and Allison has been looking out for me. She hasn't mentioned seeing Evan since Danielle tried to kill me, and I haven't asked. If she thinks seeing him in secret is safe, I have to trust her. I need my best friend.

I use the rest of the day to work on readings and get started on a couple of assignments. I'm stuffing my face with cold pizza when someone knocks on the door. I holler at them to come in, but when the door doesn't open, I get up and open it myself. On the other side stands a tall guy with sharp green eyes and cropped dark brown hair. He's dressed casually in T-shirt with a black leather jacket and jeans.

"Uh, can I help you?" I ask, holding onto the door.

The guy wrinkles his nose as his eyes flicker across my face. "Is Allison around?"

I offer a smile. "You must be Evan," I say in lieu of an answer.

He nods, pulling his hand out of his pocket and sticking it out to me. "You're the roommate, right?"

I glance at it, then shake it gingerly. "Aurora," I say. "Allison isn't here."

"That's too bad." He lets his hand fall back to his side. "Maybe I could come in and wait for her?"

I grip the door a little tighter. "I don't think so. I'll let her know you stopped by. I'm sure she'll call you." Unease slithers its way up my spine, and considering the last interaction I had with a light fae, it's not unwarranted. My mind goes to the bottom drawer of my desk where the iron stakes I'd picked up weeks ago are hidden. Maybe I should have one on me all the time now.

He glances at where my knuckles have turned white. "Relax, I'm not here to hurt anyone."

"Forgive me for not trusting you. The last light fae I knew tried to kill me."

He frowns. "I wasn't aware. I'm sorry."

I blink at him. "Allison's in class," I say, ignoring his apology. I start to close the door, but he raises his hand.

"Can I come in?" His eyes flick between mine. "Please?"

My pulse kicks up. "No," I say in a firm, unwavering voice.

"Look, I need to talk to you. There are things you need to know, and I can't talk about them in the hallway."

I glare at him for a moment and then exhale harshly. "Fine." I step back, opening the door so he can come in. Once he's inside, I leave the door ajar.

I turn to face him. "Speak."

"I care about Allison. A lot. Not all of us want to be involved in the war, Aurora."

I cross my arms over my chest. "She is going to get in a lot more trouble if whatever the two of you are doing continues. Does that not matter to you?"

His eyes narrow. "Of course it matters." He shakes his head. "What am I supposed to do? Walk away from her?"

"That would help."

"No. It would hurt her."

"Temporarily." I sigh heavily. "The last thing I want is for my best friend to get hurt, but I'd rather she be heartbroken for a little while than have to spend god knows how long in prison for sleeping with the enemy."

"I'm not the enemy!" He glances to the door and frowns briefly. "I'm sorry, but I'm no threat to you, her, or Tristan."

"Okay, fine. I don't know what you want me to do."

"You can get Tristan to meet with me," he offers.

I scowl. "Do you think I'm his secretary or something?"

"No, but I know you have influence over him."

I press my lips together to keep from bursting into laughter. "Um, we are talking about the same fae leader here, right?"

He arches a brow. "He'll listen to you."

What has Allison told him about me? About Tristan?

I lean against the side of my desk. "Say I could get him to agree to meet with you. Why should he want to? So you can plead your case to stay with Allison?"

"Would that be enough for you to agree to try?" he asks.

"If it'll make my best friend happy, I'll do it. But that's me. I doubt it'll be enough for Tristan to listen to you."

"But there's a chance, so I have to try."

"Look, maybe the two of you should just take some time away from each other. At least until things get—"

"Better?" he cuts in with a sharp laugh. "We're close to war, Aurora. Things are going to get a hell of a lot worse before there's even a chance of them getting better."

"What happens if Tristan says no? Are you going to stop seeing Allison, or are you going to take the chance of her getting punished?" It occurs to me that I don't know whether Evan would get punished by Jules, or whether the light leader even cares that he's with one of the dark fae.

"Then we'll figure something else out." He meets my gaze. "Tell me you'll try. Please."

I inhale slowly through my nose, and let the air out through my mouth. "I'll try."

He nods. "Thank you."

I drop my gaze. "You should go."

He steps back, heading for the door. "It was lovely to meet you, Aurora. Your reputation precedes you, and I must say, it's remarkably accurate." His lips curve upward. "I'll see you around," he says and leaves.

I stare at the back of the door, my mind reeling with what Evan said, and what I agreed to do.

I make a point never to be late for class. I consider it practice for the real world. If I'm late for work, that says I'm not dedicated to my job. This morning would be no different except I sleep through all three of my alarms. I've been in a state of exhaustion since being poisoned. I don't know whether it's remnants of fae magic running through my veins that makes it difficult to keep my eyes open all day, but I'm sleeping more often and longer than usual.

When I do wake up, I grab my phone to check the time. My loud groan fills the empty room. Allison didn't wake me before she left; that's *if* she slept here last night.

Throwing my comforter off, I force myself out of bed. I pull a comb through my tangled waves and brush my teeth while trying to throw together a presentable outfit. I'm out the door with a breakfast bar and my bag in less than fifteen minutes and all but sprint across campus. I'm still half an hour late. Of course, today's class is held in the largest lecture hall, and my professor has a guest speaker scheduled.

As I approach the double doors, I pray for an open seat along the back row that I can sneak into without interrupting. I silence my phone and slip it into my bag before I hold my breath and open the door. I tiptoe in and scan the room. A couple of heads turn when the door shuts. I hurry to an empty seat, three rows from the front of the room, which means everyone watches as I make my way to it.

Once I'm seated and have my laptop on the small fold-out desk in front of me, I let out a slow breath.

"Glad you could join us, Aurora," Richard, my business finance professor says.

"I'm so—" Words stop forming the moment my eyes shift to the guest speaker. *Fuck*. "Sorry."

Tristan stands at the podium, front and center, grinning like a cat in his usual business attire. "As I was saying . . ."

Sliding down in my seat as if my laptop could hide me, I pray to anyone who will listen that this lecture ends early.

It becomes apparent that no one is listening to me when over an hour passes before Richard announces a break before the second half of the presentation. I groan and whip out my phone to occupy myself. Now would be the time to gather my things and get the hell out of here, but if I leave, I'll never hear the end of it from Tristan.

"He's so young looking, so attractive—it's unfair," the girl beside me squeals to the girl next to her.

"Unfair? It's inhuman. Jesus, if he was our professor, I wouldn't miss a single lecture. In fact, I'd apply for extra credit assignments"—she pauses—"with lots of after-hours work."

"Mmm, me too," the first girl gushes.

The sudden urge to rip my hair out makes annoyance simmer in me. I sit lower in my seat and press my lips together so I don't respond.

"Oh my gosh, he's looking at me," the one beside me whispers and slaps the other girl's arm.

"Uh, no he's not, babe. He's looking at *her*."

I don't have to look up to know the *her* they're referring to is me. Keeping my head down, I stare hard at my phone screen.

Students who left for the break file back in, and the second half of the lecture gets underway. With Tristan's focus on the lecture and addressing the room, I use the opportunity to look at him. He's dressed how I'm used to seeing him at the office, and today it looks like he skipped shaving. It's a look I could get behind.

He speaks passionately about how he grew his business from the ground up, starting with an idea and a goal. Admiration floods through me as I listen to the story. His eyes pause on me, and recognition flashes in them. Something tells me my emotions are on display. He smiles at me as if we're sharing a moment, as if we're the only two people in the lecture hall, and then his gaze shifts across the room as he continues to speak.

My phone vibrates, and I glance down at the screen. I have a new message from my mom, giving me an update on Adam's chemo treatment. She says, "So far so good." Adam is taking it like a champ, which I knew he would. Still, an ache blossoms in my chest. I wish I were there with him through this. My parents are doing the best they can while still working full-time, and I visit as often as my course load will allow. Adam doesn't want me to fall behind by staying in Mapleville too long. He's always trying to put everyone else before himself. He's the most compassionate twelve-year-old I've met.

I'm still typing my mom a reply when I notice people leaving. The room empties, and I attempt to throw my things into my bag to follow them out. Only a few others remain in the room. If I'm going to get out without—

"Miss Marshall, a moment, please."

I glance up and lock eyes with Tristan and hesitate before I offer a curt nod. Leaving my bag at my seat, I make my way to the front while Richard and the remaining students chat on their way out of the room.

Tristan is packing his things, appearing to be in no rush to leave.

I slide onto the large desk off to the side and let my legs dangle over the front, swinging them back and forth.

"What was this morning about?" he asks, zipping up his fancy leather bag.

I look over at him and shrug. "I was late." I should tell him about Evan stopping by and what he said, but here doesn't seem like the place to talk about it.

He leaves his bag at the podium and approaches me. "I know that, Aurora. I'm asking you why. You're never late for work. I imagined school would be the same."

I sigh, rubbing my hands over my face as I recall I didn't have time to put on any makeup before I sprinted to class. "I'm tired. It's no big deal."

He steps in front of me and grips my wrists, pulling my hands away from my face and setting them in my lap. "It's been over a week since—"

"I know," I cut in. I don't want him to say what went down the night Danielle poisoned me, or the day in the ballroom. It all felt too intimate. "It's fine. I just need to grab a coffee."

"Have you spoken to Skylar?"

"About *this*?" I ask in a sharp tone.

He chuckles. "No. About the charity event."

"Oh," I mumble. "I was going to head over and meet with her now."

"I'm going there, too. Why don't you ride with me?"

I catch my lower lip between my teeth. The idea of riding in a car alone with Tristan sets me on edge.

"Aurora," he says in an amused tone.

"Yeah, okay," I say. "Before we go, why didn't you tell me you were coming today?"

"And miss the look on your face when you saw me? No way."

I narrow my eyes. "For an all-powerful fae leader, you sure can act like a twelve-year-old."

He chuckles, arching a brow. "All-powerful, huh?"

I push him back a few steps and slide off the desk. "Why are you here? You wouldn't waste your time teaching humans without your own agenda. You won't teach me."

"You must be upset about that, considering this isn't the first time you've mentioned it," he points out with an arrogant smirk.

"Whatever. Stop avoiding my question."

"I was here to monitor a situation."

"A light fae situation?"

"I want to make sure you're safe." His eyes meet mine and soften. "I don't want you targeted because of me."

"Screw that. Who I spend my time with is no freaking concern of the light fae."

Tristan smiles as if he's trying not to laugh.

"What?" I snap.

"Nothing. Just you." His tone is confusing.

"Yeah, go ahead, laugh at the human who can't protect herself from the supernatural. I'm hilarious." I roll my eyes. "Mark my words, if I catch wind of more light fae targeting me, you can bet your ass I'm going to cut a bitch."

"Take a breath, sweetheart. It won't come to that."

"Danielle tried to kill me. What makes you think someone else won't try?"

"I won't let anyone hurt you," he vows in a deep voice.

I glance away before nodding. "We should go."

Never did I think I'd be walking out of class with Tristan beside me. While I've gotten used to his presence, I'm not used to the eyes that follow us the entire way to the parking lot.

Tristan goes through the Starbucks drive-thru on the way back to the hotel and orders himself a coffee. As I'm about to tell him what I want, he orders my usual iced caramel macchiato and drives to the window. He's paid attention to the coffee I drink at the office. Something so minimal shouldn't stick out to me so much, but it does.

Max pulls Tristan into a meeting the minute we get back to the office, so I drop my stuff and find Skylar in the conference room, poring over a stack of papers.

"Hey," I say.

"You're late," she snaps.

"By three minutes," I toss back, ignoring her defensive tone, and sit across from her. "What are you working on?"

"I'm going over the donors for the event. We've got more

than enough, and I'm still waiting on a few companies to get back to me."

"That's great. Is the guest list finalized?"

Skylar pushes a sheet of paper across the table, and I scan it. "This looks good to me," I offer.

"I don't care what it looks like to you, human. I need you to take it to Tristan and get his approval." She doesn't spare me a glance.

I bite back my retort. It won't do me any good. Pushing the rolling chair away from the table to stand, I grab the guest list and head for Tristan's office. I knock and wait this time, knowing he was pulled into a meeting. One of his employees answers, and I hold out the list. "I need Mr. Westbrook to sign off on this."

"Sure. Wait here," he instructs, taking the paper from me.

I stand in the hall and wait for him to return.

"That's not what I'm saying," Max growls from inside the room.

I bite the inside of my cheek. Whatever the meeting is about, he's unhappy with it.

"What *are* you saying?" a female voice asks.

"We can't keep letting them attack. Our numbers are dwindling as it is. We have to take action. Fight back. *Now.*"

Someone slams their fist on the table, and I suck in a breath from behind the door. There's a pause in conversation when the employee returns to the door and hands me back the list.

"Thanks," I say. He closes the door in my face without a word as if he's worried I've already heard too much. I return to the conference room and give Skylar the list. "All good."

"Fine. I need you to call the bartender to confirm what they're bringing."

"Sure." I glance at my hands then back at her. "Can I ask you something?"

"If you must," she answers.

"When I went to Tristan's office, he seemed to be in a pretty important meeting about the issues that have been going on with the light fae."

"That's not a question."

"Right. I was wondering why you're sitting here working on this human event and not in there offering your opinion. I'm sure you have one."

She laughs, stapling some pages together. "I chose to sit out of that meeting. I sit in enough meetings for Westbrook Inc. as it is. I lead the physical training. Teaching fae how to protect themselves and each other. Max gets to sit in there and take notes, which I'll be briefed on later. This power struggle between the two sides has been going on for a long time. Too many of ours have died. We're going to retaliate soon, and we're going to make sure we have the resources and power behind us to win. That takes time, training, and planning."

"When is this going to happen?" I'm not sure I want an answer.

"Don't worry about it," she grumbles, and with that, she goes back to work as though I'm not there.

All I can do after that is worry about it. What will happen once the dark fae launch their retaliation? How many innocent humans will get killed in the crossfire? What will happen when Allison finds out the dark fae—her people—are going to kill the light fae, including her boyfriend? What the hell is going to happen to *me*?

chapter Fifteen

I T'S DARK OUTSIDE WHEN I COLLECT MY THINGS. SKYLAR left hours ago, but I wanted to keep working. The charity gala is fast approaching, and being given the opportunity to spearhead it makes me want to ensure it's a smashing success. It'll look good on my resume, and it's a great opportunity to gain some contacts in the business world. So I'm all for the extra work, even if it means juggling my responsibilities.

I flip the light off on my way out and peek down the hall to see Tristan's light still on. I walk to his office, my flats not making much sound, and knock on his door before I slip inside, letting the door close behind me. "Can I talk to you?"

He glances up from the paperwork on his desk.

I take that as my cue to speak. "I had a conversation with Allison's—uh, Evan the other day."

His eyes narrow. "He approached you?" A muscle ticks along Tristan's jaw. "What did he say?"

"He wants to meet with you. Something about wanting to prove he's not a threat."

He arches a brow. "He and Allison are still seeing each other." It's not a question.

"My loyalty lies with my best friend, Tristan. I understand why the rule is in place, but shouldn't you be willing to at least hear him out? Listen to what he has to say. Not all of the light fae have to be enemies." I shrug. "But hey, that's just one human's opinion."

Tristan chuckles. "You say that like your opinion doesn't mean anything. It does."

I nod. "Okay, then while were on the relative topic, I think you need to put on your big boy pants—you have an unfairly huge closet full of them—sit down with their leader and call for a freaking ceasefire. Why do fae have to keep dying?"

"While your idea is decent in theory, it's more complicated than that."

"From my experience, which some would say is minimal, there's nothing about the fae world that isn't. Stop using that as an excuse. You have a solution right in front of you, but you won't consider it because it's not complicated enough."

"You came here to talk to me about how I should lead my people? You want to talk fae politics? I've been the leader long enough to know what I'm doing."

"What's your point? This war is proof that you don't have all of the answers."

"I'm handling it, Aurora," he says in a deep, tight voice— one that isn't friendly and one I don't hear often.

"Fine," I grumble, shrugging.

His features smooth. "It's interesting that you seem to care so much."

"No, it's not." I'm not in the mood for where this conversation is going.

He chuckles again. "Okay, sweetheart." His tone is borderline mocking.

I scowl. "Don't do that."

He rises from his chair and walks around the desk, closing the space between us. He stops a mere foot away, so close I could lean in and feel his breath on my face. "It seems we both have things we don't want to talk about."

"I . . ." Blood rushes to my cheeks. "There's nothing to talk about."

He reaches forward and twirls a strand of my hair between his fingers. "You'd rather not talk, then?" he murmurs.

My heart lurches in my chest. This scenario could go a few different ways. I know which way my *body* wants it to go, but my *mind* is screaming at me to run away.

"I know we got off to a bad start, Rory, but I think you can agree things have changed since then," he says in a hushed tone before dropping his hand back to his side.

I open my mouth to—what? Dispute his claim? He's right. I just don't want to admit it.

He wets his lips and backs away a few steps. "Tell me you don't want me. Say it, and I won't bring it up again." His eyes flick back and forth across my face as he waits for my response. He's giving me an out. All I have to do is say I don't want him.

I can't do it. I can't make the words form on my lips.

"This is ridiculous," I mutter instead.

"I'm not asking for much," he says.

"You know what you're doing. I'm not going to do this with you. We work together. I have to see you at least twice a week on top of the times you pop up out of nowhere, including when

I'm asleep—"

"That happened one time," he cuts in.

I run my fingers through my hair. "It's late, and I'm exhausted. I should go home."

"If only you were in a hotel full of beds," he says with a wry grin.

I sigh. "You are insufferable."

"Thank you," he replies.

I turn my back on him and walk to the door, opening it quickly. I need to get out of here and clear my head.

"When you're ready to admit what you want," he calls after me in that deep voice I can feel all over, "you know where I am."

I pause for half a second at the door, and then I hurry out of the room, grabbing my things before leaving the building.

I stay in bed for over an hour after I wake up. It's Saturday; I have no assignments due right away—no responsibilities I need to rush out of bed for. I pull my computer onto my lap and answer emails from classmates about group assignments and scroll through my social media feeds. When I've wasted as much time in bed as I can stand, I throw the sheets off and shuffle into the bathroom to take a shower. I shampoo my hair, humming a new song I've been working on. By the time I rinse out the conditioner, I'm singing the lyrics and enjoying the sound echoing around the tiny bathroom.

I towel dry my hair and wrap another around my body, my fingers and toes pruned and my skin radiating heat. Still humming, I open the bathroom door to grab some clothes from my closet.

I stop dead when I find Tristan and Allison standing in our room.

"Hey." She presses her lips together as if she's trying not to smile. "Nice singing."

Tristan chuckles.

I stand there, staring at them both. Aware of my lack of clothing, I grip the towel tighter around me and look between them. "Do I even want to know?" I ask.

Tristan looks like he's about to pounce on me. The dark, intense focus in his eyes makes my heart pound and the heat between my thighs pulse.

"Tristan told me that Evan came here and talked to you."

I force my eyes to shift over to Allison. "Yeah."

"Sorry I wasn't here." She keeps her eyes on me, as if she's too scared to look at Tristan now that we're talking about Evan. "Look, I know no one trusts him, but *I* do."

Tristan chuckles again, but his jaw is hard.

"Like you've never wanted something you shouldn't? Something your people don't agree with?" Allison's cheeks flush quickly, and her eyes widen, knowing she said something she shouldn't have.

Tristan's eyes shift to me, and I shake my head.

Knowing she's made a mistake, Allison grabs her bag off the end of her bed and hurries out of our room, leaving me standing before Tristan in nothing but a towel.

Chapter Sixteen

TRISTAN SITS ON THE END OF MY BED AND WAITS FOR ME to come back out of the bathroom, this time with clothes on. I comb my fingers through my hair while he sits there, watching me without a word. I'm not sure why he's here, but it's clear that he has no plans to leave yet.

I walk around the small room in quick, unmeasured strides, tidying things here and there.

"You're pacing," Tristan comments in a calm voice.

I ignore him, busying myself in case that might keep me from having to talk to the fae leader still sitting on my bed. I guess I should be grateful he let Allison leave, especially after she snapped at him, clearly defying his position—and fae law.

Tristan catches my wrist as I pass by him and holds it in a gentle grip, stopping me from whizzing around. "Aurora, come sit for a minute, please. You're making me dizzy."

I peer down at his fingers wrapped around my wrist, where my pulse is humming with the energy of being so close to him.

"She's not going to stop seeing him, no matter what you say. She could get hurt, and there's not a damn thing I can do."

Tristan lets go of my wrist and slips his fingers through mine. "This isn't your fight, and she's not your responsibility."

I sit beside him. "She's my best friend. You guys are going to war, and I have no idea what's going to happen. It seems like she's not even concerned about the consequences of her relationship. Why would she risk that for one person?"

"You'd be surprised what some people would do for one person."

I sigh. "Are you really going to throw her in prison?"

He turns toward me and our eyes meet. "Are you asking me to let her break one of our laws?" He regards me with a thoughtful expression. "I can't do that, Aurora. I'm sorry."

I nod, understanding he's looking at the bigger picture. He has the responsibility to take care of his people, and until proven otherwise, Evan is a threat.

Thrusting my fingers through my still-damp hair, I blow out a breath. "You haven't told me why you're here."

He wets his lips. "I've been looking into your family history."

"As most stalkers do," I quip, trying to lighten the mood in hopes that will ease the tendrils of anxiety wrapping around me.

His eyes glimmer. "You wanted more information, so I did some research."

I bite the inside of my cheek. "You're saying you did this for me?"

"Yes, and because of my own interest in the matter."

"Okay." I glance at the floor, wiggling my toes. "What did you find?" I'm terrified to hear the answer. It seems crazy to think that I have fae ancestors, but after the way Tristan's blood affected me, it's hard to deny my family's past.

"I'm not sure what you're hoping to hear. I don't want to disappoint you."

My stomach drops. "Tell me, Tristan. Please."

He nods. "Your father's fae ancestor had her daughter's magic deactivated, which is why it didn't continue down the bloodline."

I frown, confusion coursing through me. "You said I'd been touched by fae magic, but it was dormant."

"You're right. Because the fae whose magic was repressed was female, it only affects females in the Marshall bloodline, and you're the first since that fae."

I scratch the back of my neck. "So I'm fae, but not?"

He shakes his head. "You are one hundred percent human, Aurora."

"Because some old witch or something took my family's magic?"

His brows draw closer. "That's right."

I wet my lips. "Okay. Are any of them . . . ?"

"There's no one left in your bloodline. They were lost when our world was destroyed."

My chest aches. "You're sure?"

"Yes. I would know if they were still alive, especially after meeting you and sensing their dormant magic."

"If *you* could sense it, what was to stop any other fae from doing the same? Were they not concerned about that when they screwed with magic?"

He shakes his head. "I wish I had more answers for you."

The darkness under his eyes and his tired expression makes me think he'd been hoping for more, too. If I have no fae ancestors left, there's little chance at getting the dark fae to accept me—for my lineage to protect me from those who are against my knowledge of the fae, and the freedom Tristan granted me even though he couldn't wipe my memories.

I bite the inside of my cheek. "At least now I know." I meet his gaze. "Thank you for looking into it for me."

The weather shifts as the daylight hours become shorter, and midterms pass in a whirlwind of studying and hand cramps from writing so much. I'm so sick of lectures and note-taking that my Friday afternoon at the office with Skylar is a reprieve from the chaos. We've been working nonstop for hours and have made progress on the charity gala.

Skylar goes to have the financial guy approve some things, leaving me to put the finishing touches on the menu to fax to the caterer.

I glance up from my laptop when Max pops his head into the office.

"Come on, blondie."

"Come on where?"

"It's almost ten o'clock." He takes a step forward and leans in the doorway. "You were done for the day hours ago."

"Okay . . ."

"We're going out. Grab your shit, and let's go."

"You want me to go out with you?" I arch a brow. "Did Skylar spike your coffee?"

He offers a little fake laugh and shoots me a pointed look. "No, but she told me to invite you, so I am. Plus, it'll make Oliver feel more comfortable."

I bark out a laugh. "Wait. You mean my Oliver?"

He rolls his eyes. "Uh, sure."

"Did Skylar invite him? She better not be screwing with him to get to me."

Max crosses his arms and sighs so softly I almost don't catch it. "Skylar didn't invite him. I did."

I stare at him for a few beats. "Oh," I say. "I didn't know you were—"

"Gay?" he cuts in with a slight smirk.

"Into humans," I say.

He shrugs. "Just because I don't like you most of the time doesn't mean I don't like humans. You don't represent them all, blondie."

I flip him off. "How do you know him?"

"He was fake-dating your fae bestie, and I met him on campus while I was looking into something for a friend."

My brows shoot up. The urge to make a joke about Max actually having friends is on the tip of my tongue, but instead, I say, "I know it's not against the rules to be with a human, but I'm still surprised." Oliver and Max? I try to picture it, but I can't.

He laughs, and I'm pretty sure it's the first time I've ever heard something so genuine come out of his mouth. "Exactly. There are rules to protect us from being exposed, but none that explicitly say 'don't fuck the humans,' so I think I'm safe."

I press my lips together against a smile. "All right. So you're saying Oliver doesn't know about the fae?"

He nods. "And I plan to keep it that way."

"Good," I concede. "Does Tristan know about you and him?"

"He does."

"Okay," I murmur. "Where are we going then?"

He grins, another thing that shocks me. "Grab your things.

The car is waiting out front."

I close my computer. "I can't believe I'm doing this."

Max rolls his eyes. "Relax, blondie. We're going to a bar, not skydiving." He backs out of the office, and I stare at the empty doorway.

Sitting around a small, round bar table with Max and Skylar isn't something I ever thought I would be doing, and yet, here I am, sipping on my virgin margarita. With work scheduled in the morning, I figured I'd better play it safe. Max and Skylar don't seem to care.

The music is loud, but not so loud that we can't hear each other speak. Not that any of us say much. The large room is lit with dim track lighting and spotlights from the stage at the front.

Skylar glances at her nails and frowns. "This is boring."

Max takes a long swig of his beer and rolls his eyes. "You're just cranky. Finish your drink, and you'll feel better."

She glares at him but doesn't disagree.

Oliver chooses that moment to arrive, which puts Max in a better mood. The way his whole face changes the moment Oliver gets here is incredible. It's something I've never seen before. It's nice. It makes him seem more human.

"Are you ready?" Max asks, turning to me.

I arch a brow. "Ready? For what?"

Skylar presses her lips together against a smile. "You didn't tell her?"

Oliver throws his arm around my shoulders and gives me a half hug, laughing.

Max shrugs, still looking at me. "It's karaoke night." He tilts his chin in the general direction of the stage. "Tristan mentioned you were a singer. Thought we should see for ourselves."

"Aurora can sing," Oliver assures him.

Glancing between Max and Oliver, I say, "I'll sing, but only if Skylar goes first."

She narrows her eyes at me. "I'm not going up there."

"Come on," I say. "I'm sure you're great. If you get up there, I'll buy your next round."

"Fine. Whatever." She downs the rest of her drink as an employee finishes getting the microphone ready. She gives him a song, and he nods, looking a bit starstruck as he walks away. She leans over the stage to where the bar is and grabs another beer. Max and I exchange amused glances when she walks back and taps on the mic.

"I'm doing this for the free drink. My coworkers are assholes." She lifts her beer in the air. "Cheers."

When the song ends, the entire room roars with whistles and claps. She smirks, tosses her hair back, and hops off the stage, coming back to our table.

She waves the bartender over, and he brings her another drink. "You're up, Aurora," she says, grinning like a cat.

I chew on my bottom lip, take another sip of my drink, and then head for the stage. When the music guy looks over at me, I lean away from the mic and pick a song before clearing my throat. Tapping my hand against my thigh to catch the beat, I start singing when the music comes on. My voice echoes through the room, getting louder as I go into the chorus, and the audience claps along. My eyes shut, and the lyrics flow through me. I grip the mic with both hands and sway with the music.

When I open my eyes, I almost stumble going into the last

chorus. My eyes lock with Tristan's where he stands with Max, Skylar, and Oliver. When the hell did he get here? *Why* the hell is he here?

The song ends, and the room gives me the same send-off as Skylar, hooting and hollering. I walk toward the stairs and trip over a cable on the stage. I'm heading for the floor—I'm going to fall right off the damn stage—but then Tristan's arms are there catching me. He hauls me up against him with an amused glint in his eyes.

"Shut up," I mutter.

"I think the words you're looking for are 'thank you,'" he murmurs.

"Not likely."

"You're feisty tonight." His arm tightens around my waist, and parts of me like that *way* too much. "I was surprised to hear you left the office with Sky and Max." His lips brush my ear when he speaks, making my skin tingle.

We shift to the side of the room as another person takes the stage to give karaoke a go, the crowd giving this guy the same attention Skylar and I received.

"They kidnapped me," I mumble. "That seems to happen a lot around you guys."

His breath tickles my skin when he chuckles. "That's because we like you," he says in a low voice. "Let me get you out of here." The idea that he's offering to save me from Max and Skylar makes me smile.

"I can't," I say. "Skylar wants me to work in the morning. We still have a lot to do for the gala."

"You're going to spend time with Skylar on a weekend?" The glint in his eyes makes it look as if he almost doesn't believe me. Playful Tristan makes me giddy as a freaking teenager.

Seeing him outside of the office, away from the constant fae issues he's forced to deal with, it's nice. Normal. Part of me is attracted to the mystery of him, but I find myself craving moments like these where I can look at him without seeing the leader of the dark fae and just see Tristan.

"I am."

"Stay at the hotel. You'll be an elevator ride away from the office in the morning." He squeezes my hip, making my breath catch.

"If I say yes . . ." My voice trails off. I don't know what to say next.

"Say yes," he whispers.

Part of me is nervous, but another part feels I owe it to myself—the constant thoughts of Tristan, the way my body responds to him—to explore what this might be. My cheek grazes his chest as I tilt my head up to meet his gaze. "Okay," I say.

He slips his arm from around my waist and grabs my hand, lacing his fingers through mine as we approach the table.

"You done feeling her up?" Skylar quips.

Tristan smirks at me. "Not nearly."

"I'm going to head out," I cut in. "Tonight was . . . fun." I pull out enough money to cover the drinks.

"Damn, blondie, you're packing the cash. We have to bring you out more often." Ha. I wish I were 'packing the cash.' I'd gotten lucky when my parents sent me some money for food, most of which I just spent on booze I didn't drink.

I laugh, giving Oliver a quick hug. "Goodnight, guys."

"You better be in the office by nine tomorrow morning," Skylar grumbles.

I mock salute her. "Yes, ma'am."

Tristan leads me away from the table. Once we're outside, I

pull away, needing room to breathe for a minute.

"Rory." His nickname for me sounds so smooth rolling off his tongue. "You need to relax. I can feel your anxiety. It's pouring off of you in waves."

Spinning around to face him, I cross my arms over my chest so he can't reach for my hands. "This isn't a good idea." I glance around the street to make sure we're alone.

He tilts his head, regarding me with a thoughtful expression. His eyes alone make me want to give in. "You're in control here. I won't do anything you don't want me to," he says.

My jaw clenches as my eyes flicker across his face. "You want me?" I whisper.

Taking a step toward me, he dips his face closer. "For some time now," he says as if he has no qualms about admitting it. "You have a fire in you. It's something I admire. While you tend to put yourself in unnecessary danger, sticking your nose into fae business as of late, your perspective on certain things is refreshing, to say the least."

My mind races. "I don't think . . . we can't."

"Why?"

"Because I'm terrified!" The words fall out before I can clamp my mouth shut. "I don't feel like I'm in control when I'm around you." It's not something I ever wanted to admit. This moment feels different, as if it's setting us on a new path.

He laughs. "You don't think I feel the same? You challenge my every word. You go against everything I know."

"You don't know enough about me," I say as if that might have the power to deter him while part of me hopes it won't.

"You're providing a weak argument." His dark-eyed look sets my body ablaze. "I can hear your heart," he murmurs.

"Good to know I'm still breathing," I mutter. Sarcasm, my

automatic defense against anxiety.

When he chuckles, a wicked shiver runs through me, and my mind goes places I wish I could say it hasn't before.

"There's that fire I told you about."

I uncross my arms and let them fall to my sides. "Can we not talk about this anymore?"

"Why? Because you know I'm right about what's going on between us?"

I shake my head.

"You're afraid because you can't control how you feel."

My eyes narrow. "You're talking like this isn't affecting you."

"I'm not the one fighting it," he says.

"Don't you wonder why I am? This isn't—I can't see any way for this to work out well. I don't understand why I feel whatever this is for you because I know I shouldn't. You would think that might deter me, that I might be able to walk away from this because of everything that's happened." My heart races while my chest rises and falls in quick successions.

"But you can't," he says.

"Shut up," I snap, breathless, grabbing his face in my hands. "Just . . . shut up." My lips collide with his in the same moment his hands drop to my hips and pull me closer. Eyes closed, I deepen the kiss, sliding my fingers into his hair, tugging at the ends. He growls, gripping my hips tighter as his mouth devours mine. My lips part in a moan, and his tongue slides in, brushing against mine and flicking across the roof of my mouth. My pulse pounds in my ears. My breasts tingle. Pressed flush against his body, a delicious warmth spreads through me, and the world fades away.

I spend the ride to the hotel in a daze. All I can think about is how everything feels so right after I've spent weeks trying to convince myself it's wrong.

It's silent between us from the time we get into the car until we reach the penthouse. I glance around the place. The simple, sleek, and modern elegance of it catches me off guard every time, even though I've been here before.

Tristan steps into my line of sight with dark eyes and a wicked curve on his lips. "What are you thinking about?"

I press my lips together, trying to form an answer. "A lot, to be honest."

"Can I help with that?" he purrs, slipping his arms around me, pulling me toward him.

A smile curls my lips, and I lean into him, sliding my arms around his neck. "This is weird to me," I say.

"What's that? Me touching you?"

I laugh. "Me *letting* you touch me."

"Any time you want me to stop, you say the word."

"Okay," I whisper, but I don't want him to. In fact, I'll be disappointed if he does.

"Do you trust me?" he asks, his eyes locked with mine.

I swallow, trying to alleviate the dryness in my throat. "I trust you," I answer, and I mean it. Had he asked me that a month ago, I would've laughed in his face, but now? Things are different between us, so yeah, I do trust him.

"Good," he says, and then his lips are on my skin, trailing up my neck. Kissing. Licking. Sucking.

I hold onto him, sighing softly, which encourages him. He kisses my jaw, my temple, and the corner of my mouth before his lips close over mine. I gasp into his mouth when his lower half presses against me, my mind swimming in a pleasant haze. My eyes close and my hips press into him, making him groan against my lips.

I jump when his phone goes off in his pocket, and we break apart. He pulls it out with a growl and swears. "I have to take this," he says. He swipes at the screen and barks into the phone. "What is it?"

There are several beats of silence, and then, "God dammit. I'll be right there." He shoves the phone back in his pocket. "I'm needed downstairs."

"What's going on?" I ask.

He thrusts a hand through his hair. "A group of light fae attacked Skylar after Max left with your friend."

Jules is attacking fae who mean something to Tristan, striking closer to home.

My eyes widen. "Is she . . . ?"

"She's alive. Barely."

"I'm so sorry, Tristan."

He nods, his posture stiff. "Stay here. I'll be back as soon as I can."

I stop him before he can turn away. "Be careful," I say in a firm voice and lean up to kiss him. He returns the kiss chastely, and he's gone.

Chapter Seventeen

THE WESTBROOK INC. ANNUAL CHARITY GALA IS HERE. Weeks of planning and overtime spent with people who used to hate me went into this event. I've been working my ass off. Every day for over a week, I've been putting on the finishing touches between lectures and homework, but it's ready. The gala is tonight, and my stomach is filled with nerves and excitement.

Skylar recovered from the attack well, considering she almost died. Despite our rocky start, I'm glad she's okay. The light fae attacking Skylar makes me more worried for Allison.

Tristan wanted me to stay over last night, but I declined. As much as that would've made this morning run smoother by already being at the hotel, I need to put a bit of distance between us. There's no more denying what we feel for each other, and I've accepted that—for the most part—but I need to keep a clear head. I haven't slept at the hotel since that night after the bar a week ago. I'm not sure Tristan slept at all with the uproar over the attack on Skylar. He and Max stayed with her while she healed. Meanwhile, I curled up on the couch in Tristan's living room in front of the fireplace—I couldn't bring myself to stay in his bed.

I wake up over an hour before my alarm is set to go off, but I can't get back to sleep. When I peek over and see Allison asleep on her bed, I breathe easier. When she's here, that means she isn't sleeping at Evan's. It's not that I don't want my best friend to be happy—that's all I want, but I can't stand knowing she could get hurt, or be prosecuted for blatantly disobeying fae law.

I toss back my comforter and stare at the ceiling before getting out of bed. I tiptoe into the bathroom and get into the shower. Today is going to be a long day.

After I've gone through the motions of washing and conditioning my hair, I let the hot water cascade over me until it loses its heat. I towel dry my hair and change into a sweater and leggings. I don't plan on putting on my dress until the last moment.

I peek my head back into the room to make sure Allison is still asleep and notice my phone ringing on my dresser.

"Hello?" I whisper.

"I wasn't sure you would be awake yet," Tristan says. "I wanted to make sure you were okay."

I step out into the hallway, closing the door behind me. "What are you talking about? I'm fine."

"Tonight is a big deal, Rory. You've put weeks of work into this event. I know what that means to you."

"Oh. Well, yeah," I mumble.

"Would you like to join me for breakfast?"

I catch my lower lip between my teeth and lean against the

wall, trying not to smile. "I don't know, Tristan."

"We can order room service. I know you love the chef's French toast."

Talking to this Tristan throws me off. It's different from having a conversation with the leader of the dark fae. Times like these, I can pretend that he's just a guy asking me to breakfast. Which makes it difficult to say no.

I sigh, a grin touching my lips. "You do know your audience."

"I'll see you soon," he murmurs.

I throw everything I'll need for tonight into a suitcase and head out.

I arrive at the Westbrook Hotel half an hour later and scan my ID card to get in the back door. Skylar hooked me up with it a couple of weeks ago so I wouldn't have to come in through the guest entrance and get let into the office. Now I can get into the building through any door.

I fidget with my phone on the ride to the office and step off the elevator to find Max sitting at the desk.

"You're here early, blondie," he says.

I nod. "Couldn't sleep."

"I see. I think Tristan's in his office."

"Great," I say. "What are you doing here this early?"

"I spent the night at Oliver's and didn't feel like going to my place when I knew I'd have to come here later on anyway."

I arch a brow. "You stayed at the dorm? Things seem to be getting pretty serious with you guys. You haven't known him that long."

His eyes narrow a fraction. "Say what you're thinking, Aurora."

I shrug. "I'm a bit concerned, is all. He's one of my closest friends. I'm looking out for him."

"Do you think I'm going to hurt him?"

I shake my head, recalling how he looked at Oliver the entire time we were at the bar. "No, I know you won't, but there are so many things he doesn't know about this world that could hurt him."

"We've barely hung out, blondie, so chill," he says with an edge to his voice.

"All right, I'm not trying to piss you off, Max, but you can't blame me for showing concern for my friend."

He rolls his eyes. "Whatever." He turns back to his computer, and I don't exist anymore.

I shake off the bad mood talking to Max for five minutes causes and walk down the hall to Tristan's office. I knock a few times and let myself in. "Tristan?" I call, glancing around.

"He's still upstairs," Skylar says as she walks in from the connecting conference room.

"Oh, hey. I'm, uh, glad you're okay."

She nods, her lips almost forming a smile. "Thanks. Tristan is waiting for you."

I nod and walk back to the elevator and ride up to the penthouse.

"I thought we said breakfast at the office, Tristan. I told you, I don't think—" My voice stops working when my eyes land on Tristan in the kitchen with nothing but a towel tied dangerously low on his hips. My mouth goes dry, and I have to swallow several times before I can speak again. "What . . . are you doing?"

He grins slowly, enjoying my reaction to his all but nakedness. "Making breakfast. Turns out I make better French toast than the chef downstairs."

I cross my arms, then panic. I didn't put on a bra this morning. Thank goodness I threw on a heavy sweatshirt before I left.

Heat rushes to my cheeks, and I turn my face to the side. "This isn't what we agreed on."

"I thought this might be better," he says.

I sigh. "Tristan—"

"I'm going to go put some clothes on so you can focus on something other than my body, and then we'll have a nice, *casual* breakfast before work."

My eyes snap back to his, and I gape at him.

He smirks before walking away, and damn it if I don't stare until he's out of sight.

Once Tristan returns, wearing a black T-shirt and dark jeans, I sit at the counter on one of the bar stools and watch him slice an orange. The whole scene is way too domestic, and it makes my chest ache with longing.

"Everything is set for tonight," I say.

He glances at me and shakes his head. "No work talk before breakfast."

"I . . . okay, what do you want to talk about?"

"Why don't you tell me about school?" He drops the orange slices onto a plate with strawberries and blueberries before he whisks the eggs and milk for the French toast.

I grab one of the strawberries and bite into it. "I've been working on my resume and portfolio since the beginning of the semester, so after graduation I can apply to positions right away. There are several businesses in Rockdale I have in mind, and a few out of town as well."

"Have you considered mine?"

I pause. "I wasn't aware there was a position open."

His lips twitch. "There isn't."

My brows inch closer before I shake my head. "I'm not going to work for you, Tristan."

He dips one slice of bread into the egg before laying it in a frying pan, then does the same with another. "I figured you'd say that."

"Good, then you won't bring it up again."

He bites into a strawberry. "I won't bring it up again."

I smile. "You have powdered sugar, right?"

"Top shelf in that cupboard behind you." He inclines his head toward the row of storage behind me, so I slip off the stool and open the door. I reach up on my tiptoes and can almost grab it. I jump a little and still can't manage. I hear a faint laugh behind me before an arm extends past mine and pulls it down, setting it on the counter in front of me.

"There you go," Tristan murmurs, his lips brushing my ear.

"Thanks," I mumble.

"Turn around," he instructs in a deep voice. I don't feel the mental pull I imagine would come with his mind manipulation if it worked on me, but hell if I don't want to do what he says anyway.

"No," I breathe, unable to keep my eyes from fluttering shut. "If I turn around, you're going to kiss me."

"Am I?" The amusement is clear in his voice.

"Tell me I'm wrong."

"Hmm . . ." His voice trails off to a light hum as his lips press against the side of my neck, just under my ear. "I can't do that."

"We should eat," I say.

He inhales. "I couldn't agree more." He nips my earlobe, and I gasp.

"That's not what I meant." I press my lips together, trying to ignore the pleasant warmth pooling in my stomach and between my thighs. My pulse thrums loud throughout my entire body, and I know he can feel his effect on me.

He slides an arm around my waist and guides me back against his chest. My cheeks flush when I feel him against me.

I hold my breath. "Tristan."

He spins me around, keeping a small distance between us. "You affect me too, Rory. I thought you should know."

I swallow, forcing a nod.

"And you were right," he murmurs, dipping his face closer.

"About?" My voice is strained, my senses overwhelmed by him, his arms on either side of me, his cologne tickling my nose, his closeness warming my skin.

He smirks. "I'm going to kiss you." He presses his lips against the corner of my mouth, and I turn my face enough that our lips meet full-on when he kisses me again. His hands slide from the counter to my hips where his fingers dig into my leggings as if he's fighting the urge to rip them off of me. *I wish he would.*

I drape my arms over his shoulders and lean into him, deepening the kiss and sliding my tongue along his lower lip. He lifts me onto the counter with ease, and I wrap my legs around his waist, pulling him as close as the counter will allow. I gasp when he nips my bottom lip, but the sound is swallowed by his mouth on mine.

After several minutes of the two of us battling for control, he leans back a bit and peppers kisses along my jaw before stepping away.

He walks back to the other side of the counter and plates the food. "Hungry?" he asks.

He has no freaking idea.

chapter Eighteen

I SPEND THE AFTERNOON PREPPING THE BALLROOM. Skylar and Max help here and there, but for the most part, it's up to me and a team of the hotel staff. This is my event . . . well, not *my* event, but it's my project, my responsibility, and to ensure it goes well, I like to know I have control over most of it. That's my type A personality rearing its insanely organized and control-freakish head.

Once the room is prepared and I've spoken to the bartender, the caterer, and the classical musician Skylar contacted, I take a breath and allow myself to get ready. There isn't much time before guests and donors arrive, so I sneak upstairs to Tristan's place to finish my hair, do my makeup, and put on my dress.

I'm surprised when Skylar comes in and grabs the curling iron while I'm trying to rush through doing my makeup. She goes to work on my hair, pulling part of it up and curling it into loose waves before braiding a portion of it, which gives me time to touch up my face. We don't talk, and when she's finished, I don't say thank you because she'll snap at me if I do.

I pace around the guest room until there's nothing left for me to do but put on my dress. I stare at where it hangs on the closet door. It's a floor-length, sleeveless, rose gold gown that glimmers with every movement. It has a sharp V-shaped neckline and an open back. It's the most gorgeous dress I've ever seen. The fact that I'm wearing it for a work event was my justification for the expense, but when Tristan insisted the company reimburse me for it after he found out how much it cost, I didn't argue.

I step into the dress, pulling it up until it falls into place, and slip on my heels. My breath catches when there's a soft knock at the door. "Come in," I say.

I watch the door open from the mirror in front of me as Tristan steps in and closes it behind him. The world slows. There's nothing but the two of us, and we can't stop looking at each other. I've seen Tristan in formal wear at the office for meetings, but I've never seen him like this. His hair is slicked back, none of the usual unruly pieces sticking out, and it looks darker than normal. It suits him. He's wearing a black tux with a bow tie, making me smile at the thought of watching him standing at a mirror tying it.

He walks over to where I'm standing and stops behind me. He stares at me in the giant mirror, a look of genuine admiration on his face.

"You look stunning," he says in a low voice, as if dozens of people fill the room, and his voice is meant for my ears only.

I meet his gaze in the mirror and smile. "Thank you. You look handsome."

He leans in and kisses my cheek. "This is your night. You've worked hard on this event, so I know you want it to be nothing short of perfect, but try to have a good time."

"It *will* be perfect," I assure him.

He chuckles. "Of course it will."

I nod. "I'll have a good time. Don't worry about me, Tris."

He tilts his head. "What did you call me?" he asks, his tone light with amusement.

"Sorry," I mumble. "I didn't mean to—"

"No. I liked it," he admits, making my belly swirl with warmth.

"Okay," I say after several beats.

His eyes travel the length of me, taking in every curve the material is hugging.

"I just put this dress on, and you're looking at me like you're about to tear it off." The idea isn't one I'm completely opposed to, but this dress *was* expensive, and I kind of need it for tonight.

He licks his lips, making heat rush to my cheeks and far lower. "It's a stunning dress, but I think what's underneath would interest me much more."

I swallow, my pulse kicking up as he slides his hand into mine and guides me around to face him. I grip the lapel of his jacket with my free hand as my heart pounds in my ears.

He dips his face closer until our noses brush before resting his forehead against mine. "You have no idea how badly I want you, Rory."

I suck in a breath, but before I can get a word in, his lips seal over mine, and whatever I was going to say is lost in the feel of his mouth. I slide my hand up his chest and grip the back of his neck, tugging him closer as I flick my tongue across his lower lip.

A soft growl rumbles in his throat, and he nips my lip before his tongue darts out to meet mine. His hands grip my waist, rubbing slow circles against the fabric of my dress that I'm suddenly wishing didn't exist. *Well, that escalated quickly.*

"How much time do we have?" I ask, kissing the corner of his mouth.

"Not enough," he murmurs against my lips. He leans away and brushes my hair back into place before adjusting his suit jacket. He offers me his arm. "Our guests will be arriving any minute. We'll have to pick this up later."

I press my lips together so I don't suggest something stupid like missing the beginning of the event. *No,* I silently scold myself. I'm going to be a responsible adult and ignore the delicious throbbing between my legs. Jesus. I need a cold shower.

Placing my hand on his arm, we walk to the elevator. Once we're on, I pull my hand back and stand against the wall opposite him. I need a clear head going into tonight, and whenever I'm too close to Tristan, it can prove difficult to think straight—or think about anything other than his hands on me.

Tristan says nothing, but the smirk on his lips is telling enough. He knows why I put distance between us—he thinks it's hilarious.

I roll my eyes and keep my gaze trained on the wall the rest of the ride to the main floor where the ballroom is.

Skylar and Max, along with several other Westbrook Hotel employees, are already downstairs when Tristan and I arrive. We walk into the room, and I feel eyes on me. Squaring my shoulders, I stand straight, refusing to look as nervous as I am.

"That's my girl," Tristan murmurs from beside me.

My girl. Oh boy. My chest swells. I like that statement *way* too much.

I take a deep breath and exhale. I'm ready for this.

Skylar and I stand at the entrance to the ballroom to greet

guests as they come in, while Tristan mingles with everyone in-side. Tonight is all about getting cheques out of these high-class attendees to donate to charity. Westbrook Inc. chooses a new charity each year, and this year the money is going to a popu-lar LGBTQ+ support for adolescents organization that Tristan handpicked from hundreds of applications. Most of the attend-ees of this event are businesspeople and friends of Tristan's, meaning they have the money we need to be donated.

I shake hands with an endless line of people entering the room. By the end of it, my mouth aches from smiling so much, but I feel good. Potential donors soon fill the entire room. While my job this evening is far from over, this is a decent start.

I spend most of the event chatting with some of the most successful businesspeople in Rockdale. It's a dream come true for any business major, and I'm taking full advantage of the net-working opportunity. Graduation is always on my mind, espe-cially as it inches closer.

Tristan makes his annual speech, discussing in detail the organization set to receive this year's charity, and wraps up by thanking guests for coming and donating generously.

I find him after he exits the stage and hand him a glass of champagne. "Nice speech," I say.

"I should've had you make it," he says, clinking his glass against mine before taking a sip. "You've put the most work into this event."

I shrug. "Tonight isn't about me. It's about the amazing people who are willing to give donations to make a real change."

"You're right. Tonight may not be about you," he says as he takes my champagne flute and sets it beside his on a banquet table, "but the next few minutes can be. Dance with me, Rory."

I place my hand on his extended one and let him lead me

onto the dance floor as the female musician starts playing a new song. Tristan clasps my hand in his and places his other on my waist while I rest mine on his shoulder. We step in time to the music, and I use this opportunity to glance around the room. Everyone seems to be enjoying themselves; I can't help but beam with pride.

"I can feel that," Tristan says, offering me a faint smile.

I lift my eyes to his. "Good."

We dance until the song ends, and he pulls me against him. "Tonight is amazing. The donations are pouring in. Congratulations on a successful event, sweetheart." He smiles at me. "I have to speak to some people, but I'll find you later."

I squeeze his hand before letting go. "Of course. I'll be around here somewhere."

He tweaks my chin, and his signature smirk sends my heart racing as he leaves me standing off to the side of the room, surveying my success.

My chest feels light and happy as I watch guests dance around me. I couldn't picture how this event would turn out—nothing would measure up to how wonderful this is.

As I'm grabbing another drink from the bar, I catch Skylar waving me over from behind the donation table. I'm heading toward her when one of the hotel employees taps my shoulder and leans close to my ear. "Your phone keeps going off."

I forgot I'd left it on one of the tables. "I'm a little busy right now," I say, not wanting to keep Skylar waiting.

"It appears to be your mother."

I huff out a breath and take the phone from her, my drink in the other hand. "Thank you," I say, trying to be polite.

I exit the room and walk into the lobby as my phone buzzes again. "Mom, what's going on? Is everything all right?"

"Aurora." Her tone makes my heart stop. "Aurora, honey, we need you to come home."

I swallow. "What happened?" The room feels too warm, too small as it closes in on me, so I retreat outside. The cool night air touches my skin, but little relief follows.

"Your brother got a lot sicker," my mom says, and her voice breaks at the end. She sniffles as if she's fighting back tears, and my stomach plummets.

"Mom, I need you to keep talking. Tell me what's going on."

She takes a deep breath. "Adam got pneumonia while he was in the hospital. His body is so weak from the chemo . . . he's struggling to fight it off."

The glass slips out of my hand and shatters against the marble step. I squeeze my eyes shut. When I open them, my vision is blurry.

"Your father and I are both here at the hospital with him."

I cover my eyes with my free hand. "I'm coming home," I cry.

"Your father can come get you," she says in a hoarse voice.

"No." I wipe my cheeks, but it's pointless; more tears spring into my eyes and fall. "I'll take the train or something. I'll find a way home." A lump forms in my throat, making it hard to speak. "I'll be there as soon as I can." I end the call and stand frozen in place, staring straight ahead as I sob. Too many things are rushing through my head. Oh god, Adam must be terrified. How are my parents functioning right now? I give up trying to fight back tears and cry until my eyes hurt and there's nothing left. My stomach coils up tight, and I think I'm going to throw up all over the steps of the Westbrook Hotel. Willing the nausea to fade, I press a shaky hand to my mouth.

This isn't fair. Adam was doing so well. He's the last person to deserve this.

I walk back into the hotel where the gala is in full swing. I stop at the coat check to grab my clutch and ask one of the employees to tell Tristan I had to leave.

Hurrying out of the lobby to the front of the hotel, I pull out my phone to call a cab. I'm bringing the phone to my ear, and then I'm spinning around at the hands of Tristan.

"Where are you going?" he asks.

Turning my face away, my hair falls forward. "I have to leave." I try to keep my tone casual, but my voice cracks.

He grasps my chin and turns my face to look at him. "Are you crying?" His forehead creases. "I saw you leave. What happened between then and now?

I shake my head. "Tristan, please," I beg, and dammit, the tears are back. I blink, and they fall, dripping onto his hand.

He lets go of me. "Tell me what's going on, Rory," he says in a gentle voice.

I swallow the lump in my throat. "Adam has pneumonia."

Tristan's brows tug together. "What do you need? What can I do?"

"Nothing. I need to go home." I don't want to ask him, but the words fly out of my mouth before I can stop them. "Will you . . . take me?"

"If that's what you want, of course I will."

I wipe my cheeks dry and nod.

"I'll have my car brought around."

We ride in an expensive-looking SUV, speeding toward the hospital where my little brother lies, battling cancer *and* pneumonia. Fucking pneumonia.

We arrive at the hospital after midnight, and Tristan stays in the lobby while I ride up to the pediatric floor. The hallway is dark, the only light coming from the nurses' stations spread out over the floor. The walls are a dull beige punctuated by boxes of masks and gloves, sanitizer pumps, and shelves of gowns. The smell of antiseptic burns my nose and makes me want to hold my breath. My eyes flick around the silent hallway; I can hear snoring behind one of the doors as I pass.

As I reach Adam's room, tears roll down my cheeks, wetting the cloth mask I put over my nose and mouth at the doorway. I walk closer to where he's asleep on the small bed. He's hooked up to a bunch of different machines. His face is pale even against the soft beige blanket that covers him. His hair is a mess, and even though his eyes are closed, the underneath is dark, making his face look hollow.

I pull a chair over to his bed and sit. I reach for his hand and hold it in both of mine. He doesn't stir, so I sit for a while and listen to the sound of his breathing.

A nurse walks in and stops dead when she realizes I'm here. "Hey there, hon. Your parents went home about twenty minutes ago to change and get something to eat."

I lift my head enough to look at her, my eyes stinging from crying for so long. "Thanks," I whisper. "I'm just going to sit with him for a little while." A few more tears slip free.

The nurse nods. She checks the machines and glances over his chart before she leaves the room.

I sweep the hair out of Adam's face and press my lips to his temple.

"Aurora?" a soft voice calls.

I turn to see Tristan leaning in the doorway. "Hey," I whisper. "You didn't have to wait around for me." I dry my cheeks and stand, pushing the chair back against the wall.

"I wasn't going to leave you here. I can take you home if

you'd like," he offers.

I nod.

"Come on," he says, his hand at the small of my back to guide me out of the room as I pull the mask off and drop it in the bin by the door.

We don't say much on the way to the parking lot. I'm not in the mood for conversation, and I think Tristan knows that.

Back in the car, I give him directions and stare out my window. I jump when Tristan's hand touches mine. I look over at him, but I don't pull away when he slips his fingers through mine.

Chapter Nineteen

WE PULL UP OUT FRONT, AND TRISTAN INSISTS ON walking me to the door. I texted my mom on our way over, so she's already waiting for us. It's a struggle to get out with my gala dress, but Tristan helps. He keeps his hand at the small of my back as we approach the front of the house.

My mom glances between the two of us before settling on me as her eyes well up. "Aurora, I'm so glad you're here." Her complexion is splotchy and pink from crying, which makes the dark circles under her eyes look worse. Her hair is frizzy and tied back in a messy top knot.

I step forward and wrap my arms around her in a tight embrace, my eyes burning from hours of crying and the fresh tears forming now. "I wouldn't be anywhere else, Mom."

She pulls away and looks at Tristan. "Who is this?"

"Tristan Westbrook," he says. "I'm sorry to have to meet you under these circumstances, Mrs. Marshall."

She nods. "Please, come in." She ushers us into our small but cozy living room off of the main entryway.

My dad is throwing more wood into the fireplace when we walk in. I give him a hug, and he shakes Tristan's hand before we sit, Tristan and I on the couch, Mom and Dad in chairs across from us.

"That dress is beautiful, Aurora," Mom says in a hoarse voice.

I try to smile. "Thank you."

"We appreciate you bringing her home, Tristan," Dad says, Mom nodding in agreement.

"Of course." Tristan glances at me. "I'll let you talk to your family," he says in a hushed tone.

"You're leaving?" I bite the inside of my cheek. "Please stay." His presence next to me makes me feel stronger, almost as if I have an anchor to keep me grounded, to keep my mind from racing in too many different directions. I don't have the strength to hide the emotions that are tied to feeling that way. In this instance, I don't mind Tristan knowing what's going on inside me.

There's hesitation in his eyes before he says, "Okay."

"We'll head back to the hospital in the morning. Dr. Collins said he was stable and suggested we get some rest while he's doing okay."

I let out a slow breath and nod. "I think I'm going to change into something more comfortable." I rise from the couch and Tristan follows suit.

My dad stands and holds his hand out to Mom while he shoots Tristan a wary look. "Aurora, see if you can find something of mine for Tristan to change into. I'm sure he'll be comfortable in the guest room."

"That's not necessary, sir," Tristan says. "I don't want to intrude."

"Nonsense," my mom cuts in. "You brought Aurora all the way here. We aren't going to let you turn around and drive back tonight."

"It's not a problem," he assures her.

She nods. "Well, thank you again."

He offers her a polite smile. "It was my pleasure."

Mom and Dad walk toward the kitchen, leaving Tristan and me alone. "Thank you for bringing me home," I say, looking at the carpet under my heels.

He cups my cheek and lifts my face so our eyes are level. "I'm glad I can be here for you." His thumb brushes across my skin.

"Will you stay here tonight? Please?"

His forehead creases. "If that's what you want."

"Unless you need to go back. I know tonight was important."

He smiles. "I'm confident Max and Skylar took care of it. If you want me to stay, I'm not going anywhere."

Stopping in the kitchen where Mom and Dad are drinking tea at the breakfast bar, I let them know Tristan is staying.

Dad arches a brow. "Is there something going on between the two of you?"

"Dad, now's not really the time to talk about that." Not with Adam being sick, or with Tristan in the other room where he can hear us.

"The way he watches you," Mom says. "You seem important."

The heat rises in my cheeks. "I can't speak for him."

"Well, how do you feel?"

Oh, hell, what a loaded question. How desperately I wish I could confide in my mom about the feelings I shouldn't have for Tristan, but the timing . . . I can't right now.

"I feel like I don't want to talk about this anymore."

She frowns. "Okay. We'll see you in the morning, honey."

I hug them both before returning to the living room. Tristan looks over at me but says nothing about what I said to my parents. I reach over and slip my hand into his, and we walk upstairs. We pass Adam's room, and I pause. My hand is opening the door before I can stop myself.

Tristan steps inside with me, my hand still grasped in his, and stays silent.

I look around the room, taking in all his old video game posters. Clothes cover most of the floor, and his bed is unmade. All the poor kid wanted was to sleep until noon on the weekends, hang with his friends, and play video games. Now he's stuck living at the hospital. He's hooked up to machines and fighting to stay alive.

I blow out a breath, my chest heavy and my eyes watering again. "This isn't fair," I whisper.

"I know," Tristan murmurs, squeezing my hand. After another few minutes, he guides me out of the room and down the hall until I stop at my closed bedroom door.

"You can't laugh," I say in a tired voice.

He peers at me. "Why would I laugh?"

"Just promise me you won't."

He brushes the back of his hand across my cheek. "I promise."

I nod and open the door before stepping inside. Everything is a different shade of purple. The bedding, the curtains, my desk—everything. "I haven't lived here for, like, three and a half years," I say as though it's some form of explanation.

He presses his lips together against a smile. "Sure," he says.

"It's . . . nice."

"Oh hush, it's overwhelmingly purple. It's terrible."

Tristan shrugs off his jacket, draping it over the chair at my desk, and slowly unbuttons his white collared dress shirt. "It's fine, Rory."

I sigh, guilt trickling in. I don't care about my room right now. Not when Adam is stuck sleeping on a hospital bed instead of his own. "I'll go grab you something to wear." I slip out of the room and find a pair of sweatpants and one of my dad's old T-shirts.

When I return to my room and close the door, I find Tristan sitting shirtless on the end of my bed.

It takes me a minute to find my voice; my head is in too many places right now. "I found these. I'm pretty sure they'll fit." I toss the shirt and pants at him and turn away, walking to my dresser to find something for me to wear to bed. I sneak into the bathroom across the hall and change into an old hoodie from high school and a pair of worn gray leggings. My reflection in the mirror makes me pause. I cringe at the smudged eyeliner and black tear stains running down both of my cheeks from the excessive amount of mascara I had on for the gala. My hair is still curled and set around my face, which makes it look odd. I grab a makeup wipe and do my best to get rid of it before flicking off the light on my way out.

Tristan is dressed this time when I walk into the room. I turn the lamp on and turn off the main light, giving the room a soft golden glow.

"I should let you get some sleep," he says, stepping toward the door.

I pick at the hem of my hoodie. "You don't have to sleep in the guest room."

"It's not a problem, Rory."

I look away. "What if I want you to stay with me?"

"You've had a long day." His tone is gentle.

I press my lips together. "Stay. Please."

"I don't want to upset your parents."

"They sleep downstairs. So long as you don't snore obnoxiously loud or something, they won't have reason to come up here and check where you're sleeping."

He exhales slowly, nodding. "Okay." He watches me crawl into my bed, then walks around to the other side and sits on top of the bedding.

"This doesn't feel real," I whisper.

He nods. "That's understandable." He reaches over and tucks my hair away from my face.

"My head is spinning so fast right now. I'm trying to figure this whole thing out, but I know there's no explanation."

He frowns. "You're right. There isn't. You're doing what you can, Rory. You're here with your family."

"But I can't help him," I whisper as I lie back and stretch out my legs. "I . . ." I choke on a sob, and turn my face to look at him.

His eyes search mine as he gets under the sheets and lies on his side, and then he wraps his arm around my shoulders and pulls me against him. There's plenty of room for two people in my queen-sized bed, but Tristan is pressed right against me; I'm not about to ask him to move.

I press my face into the crook of his neck and cling to him.

He holds on to me until the sobbing quiets. I knew the silence would come in time, after crying for so long, but the fear of the unknown still weighs on my chest.

He cups my cheek in his hand and draws my face away so that I'm looking at him. An idea hits me so fast I don't have time to register it before I say, "Can you use magic to heal him?"

Tristan's face falls. "Sweetheart, no, I can't. I'm sorry."

"But you healed me—the day we met after Max hurt me—you healed me."

"You had cuts and bruises and a mild concussion. I can heal those injuries, but I can't fix this. Fae magic is powerful, but it can't cure cancer or sickness."

It's not fair. What the hell is so great about having magic if it can't cure a human illness?

My bottom lip trembles. "I thought . . ." My voice breaks off, and more tears spring free, rolling down my cheeks.

Tristan swipes the tears off my face with his thumbs. "You should get some sleep," he says softly.

I shake my head. "I can't sleep." I try to shift away from him so I can get up. "I should go back to the hospital and wait for visiting hours. That way I'm there when he wakes up."

He sighs. "Aurora, I don't think you should sit at the hospital all night."

"What the hell else am I supposed to do?" I snap, sitting up.

He runs his hand up and down my arm. "Let me help you," he murmurs.

"How?" I ask, my voice trembling with a fresh onslaught of tears.

"You trust me?" he checks.

"You know I do."

A faint smile touches his lips. "Lie back and close your eyes."

I follow his instruction and reach for his hand. "You're not going to leave, are you?"

He gives my hand a gentle squeeze. "I'm not going anywhere, Rory." He snakes his arm around my waist and pulls me back against him. "I'm going to help you sleep, all right?"

"Okay." I hug the arm he has wrapped around me.

He leans in and whispers words into my ear, soft and lulling, until exhaustion floods in, and I drift off into a black, dreamless sleep.

Chapter Twenty

THE FOLLOWING MORNING, I WAKE UP IN A TANGLE OF limbs. My pulse increases as I become aware that my legs are wrapped around one of Tristan's. Not only that, but my arms hug his midsection, and my cheek is pressed against his chest. His heart beats against my ear as his chest rises and falls in time with the rhythm.

Glancing around while trying to keep my head still, I try to think of a way to get off the bed without waking him. I pull back, freeing one arm, but he's lying on the other. I flick my eyes to his face to make sure his eyes are still closed, and I shift to the side so I can slip my legs free. Of course, I lean too far back and lose my balance. I'm heading for the hardwood floor, and I'm going to smack my tailbone hard.

At the last minute, Tristan grabs my wrist and pulls me back onto the bed.

I suck in a sharp breath and wince. "How long have you been awake?"

"Oh, long enough," he murmurs, a slight curve shaping his lips.

I laugh sheepishly. "Great." As I look around the room, the events from the past twenty-four hours come back in a painful rush. I rake my fingers through the mess of curls on my head and swing my legs over the side of the bed. "I should get ready and head to the hospital with my parents."

"Okay."

Tristan Westbrook is crawling out of my bed—where he slept beside me last night. I've imagined this moment, and it didn't include having to go to a hospital let alone downstairs to see my parents.

He kisses my cheek on his way out of the room.

I use this opportunity to change into a pair of dark jeans and a loose T-shirt. I'm sitting at the end of my bed to pull on some socks when Tristan knocks on my door. I tell him to come in and force a small smile when he closes the door behind him.

"You should head back to the city," I say, standing and grabbing my phone from the table beside my bed. "I'm sure you want to check in at the office and see how the rest of last night went."

"I don't need to check in. I'm fine right here."

"Tristan," I say, looking at him. "I don't know how long I'm going to stay here. I'm not going to ask you to hang around for me. I haven't forgotten everything you have to deal with right now. You were here for me last night. Now you need to be there for your people."

He sighs. "You'll call me if you need anything?"

I nod. "Go home. Deal with the light fae. No one else needs to die. Work with them and figure out a way to coexist."

"All right," he concedes.

I walk toward him. "Thank you," I whisper, "for everything you've done for me."

He leans in and kisses my forehead. "If anything happens, you call me."

"I will," I promise.

We walk downstairs together, and he says goodbye to my parents. They stay in the kitchen while I walk Tristan to the door.

He smiles and pulls me into his arms. "I'll see you soon," he murmurs, his lips brushing my ear. His fingers splay across my cheek, and he rests his forehead against mine. "Hang in there, sweetheart."

The rush of tears that gathers in my eyes doesn't surprise me at this point. "I'm trying," I force out in a hoarse voice.

His lips press against mine in a whisper of a kiss. It's slow and tender and unlike anything I'd expect from Tristan. He smiles at me once more before he walks outside and heads for his car. My cheeks are warm when I close the door, flushed from the mixture of emotions that accompany kissing Tristan.

Mom and Dad are drinking coffee at the kitchen table when I walk into the room.

"Morning," I say as I pour myself a cup.

"Morning, honey," Mom says. "Tristan didn't want to stay for breakfast?"

I shake my head. "He had to get back to the office."

"He seems like a decent man," Dad says.

I peer at him over my mug. "Yeah, I guess." Where is he planning on taking this conversation?

"He also appears to care about you a great deal."

I shrug. "He's . . . it's complicated."

Mom chuckles, but it sounds nowhere near her normal,

carefree laugh. "All the best things are, Aurora."

I'm not sure that's true, but I keep that to myself. "We should go over to the hospital," I say.

"Visiting hours don't start for almost an hour," Dad says.

"I want to be there when they do. Adam is probably scared to be alone in that place. We need to be there for him." Being stuck at school while he's been fighting through treatments has been difficult. Now that I'm here, I want to be with him as much as I can. If I can bring him any amount of comfort, I'll do whatever it takes.

Mom and Dad exchange glances and both nod.

"All right," Mom says. "Let me get dressed, and we'll head over."

My hands are shaking by the time we pull into the visitor parking lot at the hospital. I don't know how I'm going to face Adam if he's awake. The three of us ride to the pediatric level in silence. Mom's hands are clasped in front of her, while Dad has one arm around her and the other shoved in his pocket. They look as out of place here as I do.

I let the two of them lead the way to Adam's room. I know where it is from stopping by last night, but I can't be the first one to walk in, so I slowly trail behind them.

Dr. Collins is sitting in the chair beside his bed. She looks up when the three of us walk in, and stands, offering a smile. Mom, Dad, and I all stand in the doorway. I think we're all a little hesitant to approach Adam, which makes my chest ache.

"Good morning," she says in a pleasant voice, turning her attention to me. "Would you mind sitting with Adam so I can talk to your parents?"

I glance over at Mom and Dad, catching their subtle nods. "Sure," I say. After a short moment of hesitation, I walk over and sit where the doctor was when we came in.

"Hey, Roar," Adam says, waving at my parents as they leave the room with Dr. Collins.

When I look at him, my throat burns. He doesn't look all that sick right now. His eyes are still the same bright blue they've always been, and his hair still falls in messy brown curls around his face. His cheeks even have some color they didn't last night. "Hey, buddy. How are you doing?"

He sighs. "Every time I try to sleep, some nurse or doctor comes in." His eyes flick around the room before he shrugs. "At least I'm not in any more pain."

"You were in pain?" I ask. "When?"

He stretches his legs out, sighing. "Yesterday and last night when I woke up."

"The doctors gave you medication to take it away?"

He scratches his head. "I don't think he was a doctor."

I frown. "What are you talking about?"

"He was wearing a suit. He didn't look like a doctor, and he didn't give me any medicine."

"I'm not sure what you're saying."

"He sat with me for a couple of hours early in the morning before the nurse came to check on me. At least, I think it was the morning. I was pretty out of it. I remember there was so much pain, and then there wasn't. It was like he absorbed it."

My breath catches, and before he can say more, Mom, Dad, and Dr. Collins walk in. There are fresh tears on Mom's face, but she forces a smile.

Dr. Collins leaves the room after saying goodbye to Adam, promising she'll get someone to send a snack later on if he's feeling up to it.

I glance between where Adam lies, attached to machines, and where my parents stand at the end of his bed. No one has said what the doctor and my parents talked about, but if my Mom's reaction walking back into the room is any indication, things aren't looking good.

"Roar, please don't look so scared," Adam says in a small voice.

I turn to him and force a smile despite the wetness gathering in my eyes. "Sorry, buddy." The last thing I want is for Adam to worry about me; *I'm* the one who needs to worry about *him*.

He smiles. "It's going to be okay. If I can fight cancer, I'll fight this too."

I close my eyes against the tears. His optimism is painful, but I can't bring myself to say anything that might diminish it. He deserves it. Hell, he deserves so much more than this shitty hand he's been dealt. "Okay," I say in a hoarse voice. "Okay."

Chapter Twenty-One

MOM, DAD, AND I HEAD HOME FOR DINNER AFTER promising Adam we'd come back in the morning. I don't think my parents can handle sitting in a room with their sick son when there's nothing they can do for him. I want badly to stay with him, but it turns out, I'm no stronger than they are. If I continue to sit in that hospital room, I'm going to burst into tears in front of Adam, and that won't help.

Mom and Dad both seem pretty out of it after we get to the house—understandably so—which is why I cook dinner. Knowing how much they love it, I make garlic bread and penne in a rosé sauce. We sit around the table, but we're all picking at our plates.

Dad breaks the silence, saying, "Your mom and I understand that you'll need to get back to school soon—"

"I'm not going anywhere until he's better," I cut in, trying to keep my tone gentle. My parents are just as concerned about Adam as I am. I don't want to make it harder on them.

"Aurora, we don't want your education to suffer because of this, and neither does Adam. You've accomplished so much, honey, and you're almost there."

The food in my mouth suddenly tastes sour. I have to force myself to swallow it. "Education isn't *always* the most important thing. Especially when Adam is sick. I've made my decision." The two biggest factors that typically trigger my anxiety are attacking simultaneously, forcing me to choose between my sick brother and my education. My degree has been my life for the past three years, but my family takes priority over it. I'll figure it out.

Mom sighs. "Okay."

After dinner, Dad offers to clean the kitchen, so I retreat upstairs and stand in the shower far longer than necessary. I'm drying myself off when I notice my phone going off on my bed. I rush over and answer it before it goes to voicemail.

"Hey."

"When the hell were you going to tell me he got worse?" Allison asks. "I would've gone with you. You shouldn't be alone right now."

"Yeah, I'm sorry. Everything happened so fast. I found out last night while I was at the gala." I explain how I got home as I pull a comb through my hair.

"Yeah, Tristan told me all of that. Do you want me to come there? I can be at your place in a few hours."

"No, it's okay. I appreciate you wanting to be here for me, but I'm going to stick around for a while."

"Okay. Do you need me to talk to your professors? I can let them know what's going on if you want."

The idea of missing lectures makes my stomach queasy, but I say, "would you mind? That'd save me from emailing them.

I'm sure they'll understand. I have all of my placement hours done plus extra, so that won't be a problem."

"Of course. Consider it done."

"Thank you, and—oh, shit! With everything . . . I forgot to call Tristan. Have there been any more attacks on the dark fae?"

"Not that I know of. I think Tristan got off his high horse and planned a meeting with Jules."

"That's good. Let me know if anything happens, will you?"

"Sure," she murmurs, "and let me know what happens on your end, okay?"

"I will."

"You know I love you, Aurora. I'm here for whatever you need. Always."

"I know, and I love you. Thank you."

I end the call and let out a long breath. I sit on the end of my bed and fidget with my phone. Not knowing how the following days are going to go is killing me. My skin itches, and my nerves are jumpy. My mind is racing with so many what-if scenarios, I can't think straight.

I crawl under my sheets and try to relax. Tristan's absence is almost tangible. As I gaze at the empty spot beside me, my chest aches. *That's new.* I roll around to face the other way so I'm not staring at the blank space and close my eyes.

I drift off, grateful for the darkness pulling me under and away from reality. At least when I'm asleep, I can pretend everything is fine.

A scene materializes around me, and it takes a minute for me to realize I'm dreaming. I blink a few times, focusing on the fireplace in front of me. I'm in Tristan's bedroom.

I stand, turning to glance around the room. "You can't invade my dream and leave me here alone," I call out.

Tristan enters the room out of nowhere. "I wanted to give you a safe space," he says, approaching me at a comfortable pace. "I didn't intend to make you spend time with me. I know you told me not to do this, but I needed to make sure you were okay."

"It's okay." I glance at him. "I wish you were here," I blurt.

"I'm right here, sweetheart," he murmurs, brushing the hair away from my face and tucking it behind my ear.

"You know what I mean," I say. "How are things there?"

He shakes his head. "That's not why I brought you here. We don't need to talk about that."

"Well, I don't want to talk about what I'm dealing with."

"Then we won't," he says. "We can talk about whatever you want, or we don't have to talk at all."

"So, you brought me here to—?"

"To hopefully offer you some comfort. I spoke to Allison after she talked to you. I know what you're dealing with, and I want nothing more than to be there with you, so this is what I'm doing."

I reach out and take his hand in mine. "Thank you. You continue to surprise me."

He gives my hand a gentle squeeze. "Is that a good thing?" he asks.

"Some days it really is," I say.

We sit on the loveseat in front of the fireplace with my back pressed against his front and his arms wrapped around my waist.

"Adam told me," I whisper.

"Hmm?" He leans down, tracing his lips along my jaw.

"I know you went back to the hospital after we left," I say.

"Why do you think that?" he asks, tracing slow circles on

the back of my hand.

"Because I remember what it felt like when you healed me. The pain was there, and then it wasn't. That's what Adam told me, and he said the man who made him feel better was wearing a suit. You didn't want to go back to the hospital in my dad's sweatpants?"

"Ahh," he murmurs, refusing to confirm my suspicion.

"Why didn't you tell me you went back?" I push.

"You didn't need to know, Rory."

"Right. God forbid I think positively of you."

He chuckles. "I didn't do it for you," he says in a soft tone.

I smile. "No, of course not." I tip my head back and whisper, "Thank you."

He kisses the spot right below my ear. "You're welcome, sweetheart."

I press my lips together, debating whether I should go through with what I'm about to say. "I saw your dream," I blurt. "I mean, I was in it, like you're in mine now. Except you didn't know I was there."

He shifts, peering down at me with a shocked expression. "You *what?*"

Swallowing, I say, "I don't know how it happened. It was that first night you did it. You left my dream, and then when I fell asleep later on, I somehow entered yours."

He frowns. "That's unusual."

"Random fae magic?" I offer.

He chuckles, but it holds no amusement this time. "Random fae magic sounds about right."

"It only happened that one time." I don't want him to think I've been snooping through his dreams, especially since he's stayed out of mine.

He shakes his head. "I'm sorry you had to see that," he murmurs, and covers my hand with his.

I shake my head, wanting him to know he has no reason to apologize. I run my finger along the collar of his shirt. "I'm sorry *you* had to see that."

We lie together in silence for a while after that. I didn't know it was possible to fall asleep during a dream, but I find my eyes drifting the longer I stare at the flickering flames in the fireplace, basking in the warmth it's radiating.

"You know," I mumble, sleep tugging at me. "I think I'm falling for you."

Tristan exhales, his breath stirring the hair at my temple. He brushes his lips against the skin beside my eyebrow, and I close my eyes.

Before he can say anything, the scene fades away, and I'm staring at my mom's frantic face as she shakes me awake.

"Get up, honey," she says. "We have to go to the hospital."

The silence is deafening. From the time we leave the house to the moment we step off the elevator on the pediatric floor, none of us says a word. I don't need fae abilities to feel the terror we're all experiencing.

We round the corner, and the moment I see the crowd of hospital staff surrounding Adam's door, I freeze. My heart stops. Everything. Just. Stops.

We all move at once, sprinting toward his room, pushing through the nurses and doctors. Mom's scream tears through the room, and once I manage to squeeze past a nurse, my hand flies to my mouth, and my legs wobble, no longer wanting to fight to hold me upright. I stumble back against the wall and stay there, unable to take my eyes off the mop of curls on Adam's head.

Dad grabs Mom, crying as he tries to pull her away from the bed. *No. Please, no. This can't be happening. He was getting better. This isn't—*

A young doctor steps forward and faces my parents. "We tried to revive him for as long as we could, but his heart wouldn't restart. His body wasn't strong enough to fight off the pneumonia. I'm very sorry for your loss."

My mom chokes on a sob, and Dad catches her before she collapses. "How did this happen? Where is Dr. Collins?" he demands.

"She was called away for an emergency out of town. We've notified her. Take as much time as you need, there's no rush. Please let us know if you need anything."

I shake my head, a faint ringing in my ears. "This isn't happening." My hand raises slowly and covers my mouth, my fingers shaking against my skin. Dr. Collins leaves town the night my brother loses his battle. *Oh my god.* Is Adam's doctor light fae—the *leader?* There was always something I didn't trust about her. What if . . . *No.* The light fae would have no reason to go after my family. *Would they?* I can't think about this right now.

The doctors and nurses file out of the room, and I stand, staring at the wall, forced to listen as my parents sob over the death of their son, knowing there was nothing they could do to make him better. They pull me into a hug, and the three of us hold each other up as we cry for the loss of Adam.

I'm not sure how much time passes before any of us move. We leave the room; Dad is all but carrying Mom through the hospital as she wails into his chest. I walk in front of them, oblivious to, or not caring about, the people who turn to look at us. Have they never seen people leaving the hospital after losing a loved one? It's ridiculous.

We sit in the parking lot and stare at the building where Adam is lying dead, his body not strong enough to fight off pneumonia because it was weak from the medicine meant to make him better.

"Okay?" Dad asks, breaking the silence in a voice so beaten down my chest tightens.

Mom says nothing, just sits there staring at her hands while her shoulders shake with soundless sobs.

"Drive," I mumble from the back seat. I rest my head against the window and close my eyes. More than anything, I wish that I could go back in time and never have left his side.

I didn't get to say goodbye.

Once we get back to the house, Dad helps Mom into the living room, and I retreat to my room, not ready to endure what comes next. We'll have to call the family and tell them that Adam got worse and didn't make it. Nothing makes sense right now, not now that Adam is gone.

Gone. He's never coming back. I'm in a state of confusion and denial. I think about him being gone, and it's as if I don't believe myself. It doesn't matter that I stood at the hospital and listened to the doctor tell me he was dead, or that I saw his still body, covered in ugly hospital bedding. I still don't believe it.

Tears leak out of the sides of my eyes and fall down my cheeks. I turn my face and press it into my pillow to muffle the sob that rips free from my throat. I scream at the top of my lungs, then cry, my entire body wracked with tremors until there's nothing left, and I'm dry heaving. Every muscle in my body aches. I can't force myself to move, to get up and drink some water to ease the terrible burn in my throat. A part of me doesn't want the pain to stop. Once it does, I'll either start crying again or feel nothing at all, and that fact scares me so much I can't move.

Adam didn't deserve to spend the end of his life as an invalid, enduring treatment and being poked with needles. He didn't deserve to have cancer or to die, but I figure most people who have suffered the same fate didn't deserve it either.

chapter
Twenty-Two

IT'S BEEN A WEEK SINCE ADAM DIED AND WAS CREMATED. My parents are holding off on a funeral to give our extended family time to arrange travel plans, so his service isn't until next Sunday. They're both off work on bereavement, but I've already missed a week of classes.

I've learned in the last several days that everyone grieves differently. While Mom and Dad can't think about going back to work yet, I *need* to go back to school. I need *something* I can put my energy into that isn't thinking about my little brother. He wouldn't want me to be sad forever, even if deep down that pang of loss will always be there.

I've spoken to Allison a couple of times since it happened. Tristan calls every night and stays on the phone while I cry myself to sleep. Both of them wanted to come to Mapleville, but I wouldn't let them, fearing it would make everything feel more real. I'm barely hanging on as it is.

My parents drive me back to Rockdale after dinner Sunday

evening, and it's never been so difficult to say goodbye to them, even though I'll be home again in less than a week.

"You don't need anything before we head back? Groceries or anything?" Mom asks.

I manage a small smile. "I'm okay."

They're having as much trouble saying goodbye as I am. If I think about them driving back to an empty house, I'll never let them leave. I'm sure Tristan would give them a suite at the hotel, but I wouldn't ask that of him, and they wouldn't want to live in a hotel for a week—no matter how fancy it is.

I hug them both for a long time, praying Mom won't cry again. I won't be able to hold back my own tears if she does, but I'm thankful she keeps it together.

Once they're gone, I head to my room and dump my duffle bag on the floor beside my desk. Allison isn't here, so I write her a note that I'm back in the city before I leave, walking with my head down through the residence building. I feel eyes on me everywhere; word travels fast around here.

At the campus streetcar stop, I stand in the pouring rain without so much as a hood to cover my head. When the street-car arrives, I stare out the front window the entire ride and get off at the stop I've gotten so used to over the last few months.

I swipe my all-access employee card and ride to the pent-house suite. My reflection in the mirrored panel of the elevator makes me cringe. I look like a drowned homeless person. My hair and clothes are soaked through, and yesterday's mascara that I'd put on to meet with the funeral director streaks down my cheeks.

Once I get off the elevator, I stand in front of the door for a lifetime before I knock. My hand shakes as I rap against the dark wood with a closed fist. Water from my hair drips down my face and onto my shirt. My body shakes, and my toes are all but numb—like the rest of me.

The door swings open, and I lift my head until our eyes meet. His expression is hard, the sharp lines of his face defined by the dim light behind him.

He closes his eyes and lets out a breath. It's such a human thing to do. "Aurora," he says in a hushed tone.

When he opens his eyes, he reaches for me, but I flinch away. If he touches me, I'll come undone.

"I . . . don't know . . . why I'm . . . here," I admit through chattering teeth.

He ushers me inside. My skin sings at the warmth of his living room, but I feel awkward dripping rainwater on his floor.

"You're going to get sick," he says.

I don't respond.

He sighs. "Skylar," he calls.

The door to his home office opens, and Skylar walks out, frowning when she sees me. "What's this?" she asks.

"I need you to help Aurora into the shower. Get her warm so she doesn't get sick." Ha. Wouldn't that be tragically ironic? Me getting pneumonia.

She blinks a couple of times. "Okay. They're waiting for you." She jerks her thumb back toward his office.

He nods, shifting in front of me, and grasps my chin in a gentle hand. "I'll be back. Please let her help."

Once he decides I'm not going to respond, he drops his hand and walks away.

Skylar eyes me as she approaches with hesitation. That's a first.

When she puts her arm around my shoulders and leads me through the suite, I don't protest. Once we make it to Tristan's bedroom, Skylar leads me into the en-suite bathroom and flicks on the light.

"I know we're not friends," she says.

I glance at her.

"But I'm sorry," she continues. "I know what it's like to lose someone important. No one deserves that."

I nod in acknowledgment.

Skylar turns on the shower and turns away while I peel off my wet clothes. Under other circumstances, I would be mortified, but right now I couldn't care less. She gathers my clothes and leaves me alone.

My eyes travel around the room, taking in the elegance. Marble counters line one wall with two massive sinks, a white porcelain clawfoot bathtub, an all-glass shower, and a fireplace with a flat-screen television installed in the wall above it. Over-the-top is an understatement.

I stand in the hot spray of the shower until I stop shaking and can feel my limbs, and then I continue to stand there, letting the water mix with the tears rolling down my cheeks.

"I love you, Adam," I say to the empty room.

The last words I should've said to my little brother keep playing over in my head until my legs give out and I slide down the glass wall onto the floor of the shower. Hell, I don't even remember what the last words I *did* say to Adam were.

I pull my legs to my chest and wrap my arms around them. I'm shaking again, but it's no longer from the cold.

My brother is dead. My brother is dead, and I didn't get to say goodbye.

"Aurora." Skylar's voice makes me glance up. "Oh." She frowns. "Tristan asked me to check on you."

I don't say anything.

"You should get out now," she suggests before reaching over to turn off the water.

"Don't!" I scream.

Her eyes widen as she steps back. "Aurora—"

"Get out! Leave me alone!"

"It's okay—"

"*Get out*," I cry.

She shuts off the water, getting the front of her blouse wet. She wraps her fingers around my wrists and pulls my hands away from my knees. "You can't stay in here," she says in a firm tone, holding my hands in hers.

When I don't say anything, she sighs, reaching behind her to grab a towel, which she wraps around my upper half.

"Stand up," she instructs in a softer tone.

I blink at her. I don't want to move.

She tucks the towel under my arms and lifts me until I'm standing in the shower, holding onto her arms. She guides me out and onto the bathmat.

"Your shirt's all wet," I inform her.

"I don't care."

"Okay," I mumble, staring at the delicate buckle on her belt.

"Aurora," she says in a quiet voice.

I glance up to meet her gaze, and my bottom lip trembles. I blink a few times, but the sting of tears is too strong. "Adam is dead," I say as a sob tears free.

"I know," she says and wraps her arm around my shoulders. "I'm sorry."

She hugs me to her side while I cry in the middle of the bathroom.

Skylar leads me into the bedroom and hands me a shirt.

It's one of Tristan's. She looks away when I drop the towel like she didn't see me naked in the shower a few minutes ago, and I pull it on, buttoning it until it covers my breasts. It falls to just above my knees, and I roll up the long sleeves.

"I'm going to get Tristan," she says, heading for the door.

"Skylar," I call after her. "I'm sorry I snapped at you."

She pauses, turning to face me. "It's okay, human. You're forgiven. This time." The faint quirk of her lips manages to make me smile. For once, the tone of her voice when she calls me human doesn't sound like an insult.

I'm fidgeting with the hem of the oversized shirt I'm wearing when Tristan walks in. His eyes darken as they take me in.

"What?" I ask.

His jaw works. "You, in my clothes . . ." he trails off as his eyes continue to devour me where I stand. "Are you warm enough in that?"

I nod, closing the distance between us and grip his arms. "I'm sorry I showed up without any notice," I whisper.

He dips his face down, and some of his hair falls into his eyes. "Don't apologize, Rory. I'm glad you came," he says. He wraps his arms around me, and I press my face into his chest, inhaling, comforted by his clean, crisp smell. It's familiar—it's Tristan.

"Stay here tonight," he murmurs.

I peer up at him. "In your bed? With you?"

His lips twitch. "In my bed. With me."

I nod. "Okay."

He leans down and brushes his lips across my forehead, alleviating the pounding behind my eyes. I'm not sure when the dynamic between the two of us shifted so significantly, but it's during moments like these that it's clear that it has.

I slide my fingers along the fabric of his collar. "Thanks," I murmur.

He nods. "Can I get you anything?"

"I'm okay."

He grazes my cheek with the back of his hand before he walks away and takes off his dress pants, tossing them into a hamper. He takes his time undoing the buttons on his shirt before adding it to the laundry, and pulls on a pair of dark gray sweatpants.

I sit on the end of his bed, staring at my hands in my lap. "Skylar was nice to me."

He chuckles. "You sound surprised."

I lift my head to look at him. "Aren't you?"

He tilts his head. "Maybe a little, but I think you've grown on her."

I find myself hoping he's right.

Tristan sits beside me and sighs. "'I'm sorry' isn't sufficient for me to say to you, but nothing is right now. Adam was a kind young man who didn't deserve to have his life cut short before he had a chance to live it. I know you're in pain. I know you're devastated—I can feel it. But try to remember, through all of the pain you feel, Adam is watching over you. He's right there with you, always. He's proud of his older sister, and he loves you. That love will last forever," Tristan continues, "long after tonight and long after his memorial when you'll say goodbye to him for the last time."

My lower lip trembles as I nod. "Th-thank you," I manage to say.

"Why don't we get some sleep?"

"Okay," I say, standing to walk around to the side of the bed and crawl under the covers. Tristan does the same on the other side.

We lie facing each other for a while before I slide over and wrap my arms around him. He circles an arm around me and runs his hand up and down my back.

"I don't think I can do this," I cry into his shirt.

He tips my chin up with his other hand. "It feels that way right now, but you're the strongest person I know. This pain, this heartbreak, is the worst thing you've ever experienced in your life, but you will bear it, and it will make you stronger."

I shake my head. "What if I don't want to? What if I can't?"

A hint of a smile touches his lips. "You underestimate your own strength, sweetheart. I thought you knew better than that."

I cast my eyes downward, my damp lashes fanning my cheeks.

"Rory," he murmurs. "You don't need to be brave or strong right now. Just know that when all of this is over, and you have a minute to breathe and start to move on, you will do so with a grace that continues to captivate me every day. That's who you are. You know that."

Somewhere, deep down, a part of me that isn't broken and grieving knows he's right, even if I don't believe it right now.

chapter Twenty-Three

THE DAY OF ADAM'S MEMORIAL, THE SKY IS BRIGHT AND clear—the first day without rain in a while.

Mom and Dad spend the morning locked in their bedroom, which leaves me to get ready in silence. I sit on the end of my bed in the plain, knee-length black dress I picked out last night. I drop my gaze to the notecards in my lap and sigh. I spent hours working out what I wanted to say about Adam, but right now nothing seems good enough. I stare at the words until they blur into black splotches on the cards, and then I tuck them into the pocket of my jacket.

There's a soft knock at my door before Mom peeks her head in.

"Almost ready?" she asks. Her dress is similar to mine aside from the short sleeves on hers where mine is sleeveless. Her hair is up in a soft twist, and she applied a bit of makeup that she has already cried off. Her eyes are puffy and red. How else should she look?

"Yeah," I say. "I'll be right down."

She nods, a solemn expression on her pale, tear-stained face, and closes the door.

I take a shaky breath and let it out before I slip on black heels and shrug on my jacket.

I walk out of the room and pause at the closed door before the staircase. My hand reaches for the handle, but I stop myself, biting my lip. I shake my head and keep walking, meeting my parents downstairs in the front hallway.

"We can do this," Dad says.

I nod. "We have to. For Adam."

"For Adam," he agrees, and Mom covers her mouth to muffle a sob.

We're escorted into the back of a car, and I stare out the window the entire drive to the cemetery.

Adam would be happy. So many people sit in rows, facing where his silver-and-black urn sits on a podium. We sit in the front row with Mom's parents and Dad's mother, and behind us sit family members I don't remember that well or have never met. Among the crowd are teachers from Adam's school, some of his friends and their parents, and more faces I'm unfamiliar with. Allison and Oliver are two of the only ones I recognize, and they offer small, sad smiles when I see them.

The pastor talks about love, life, and loss, and a bit about Adam and his short life. Dad chokes back a sob beside me, and I reach over to grasp his hand. He looks over at me and smiles through the tears, squeezing back.

The time comes for me to speak, and I stand, giving my dad his hand back. I walk the short distance to the podium and pull out my notecards, the crowd silent as I prepare myself.

As the wind blows and the faint smell of the roses surrounds me, I close my eyes and inhale, letting the breath out a few seconds later. I lift the notecards and read the first line in my head before I stop and set them face down beside the urn.

"Adam was this incredible person that my parents brought into this world—into my life—and who I had the privilege of calling my brother. We all knew him differently. Some were friends, some were family, and if you were lucky enough, you were both." I stop to take a breath, and my eyes connect with familiar stark blue ones in the crowd.

Tristan holds my watery gaze, his expression soft and solemn.

For the number of moments he's made my head spin, his presence now is steadying. It's exactly what I need to get through the rest of Adam's eulogy.

I return to my chair and stand with my parents as the urn is placed into the ground. Mom, Dad, and I step forward and drop roses on top of the soil after it has filled the spot where Adam's ashes now lie. I close my eyes as wetness trails down my cheeks, and my parents wrap me in a sob-filled hug while we all say goodbye to Adam one last time.

My house is filled with people after we return from the cemetery. I don't remember whose idea it was to have a reception here, but if it was mine, I'm regretting it now. A grieving person can only handle so many offers of condolence and hugs from people they should know the names of but don't. That's what happens when you have a huge family. I've been offering smiles and accepting hugs from family members I don't know for over an hour now, and all I want to do is sneak to my room and lock myself inside until everyone leaves. Allison and Oliver are around here somewhere, helping my parents by handing out drinks and whatever sympathy food people brought with them. I feel guilty, but they're such social people, they don't mind chatting with my family.

I'm leaning in the doorway to the living room when a hand touches my shoulder, and Tristan shifts closer to kiss my cheek.

"How are you doing?" he whispers.

"Honestly?" I sigh. "I want to get the hell out of here."

He slides his fingers through mine and gives my hand a gentle squeeze. "Why don't we get you something to drink?"

I lean back into his chest and glance up at him with an arched brow.

"Tea or coffee, sweetheart," he says.

I purse my lips. "What about coffee with something a lot stronger?"

"I'm not sure that would be a good idea right now."

"Yeah, you're right," I grumble.

"What's that now?" he checks.

I roll my eyes. "I'm not going to say it again, Tris. Nice try."

Before he can say anything, Mom approaches, offering a small smile. "Hello, Tristan," she says.

"Mrs. Marshall," he greets in a warm tone, reaching out to shake her hand. "Please accept my deepest condolences."

"Thank you for being here today and for being so supportive of Aurora."

"Of course. It's been my pleasure." He steals a glance at me and smiles.

I look over at my mom. "How are you doing?"

Her smile fades. "I'm hanging in there. Your father has barely left my side since we walked in the door. He's talking to your uncle right now, so I thought I'd sneak away and check on you."

"You don't need to worry about me, Mom. Please take care of yourself and make sure Dad is doing the same."

She blinks, trying to clear her watery eyes. "You're my daughter, Aurora. I will always worry about you." She glances past me to where Tristan stands. "Maybe you two should get out of here for a bit," she suggests. "Go grab lunch or something. I'm sure we can hold the fort for an hour or so. You've been so strong during all of this, Aurora. Take a break."

I shake my head. "I don't need to, Mom. It's okay. I'm not going to leave you and Dad to talk to all of these people."

"Please, Aurora. This is your mom taking care of you."

"Okay," I concede. "Please call me if you need anything."

"Deal," she says, stealing a quick hug before walking back into the living room, where a group of people pull her into a conversation.

When Tristan pulls into the parking lot of one of the most expensive restaurants in the city, I shoot him a look.

"We're not eating here," I say, glancing over at the people walking into the building with suits and formal wear. "We could've gone for something more casual."

"Is that what you want?" he asks, tapping his fingers against the steering wheel.

My stomach growls at the thought of kung pao chicken. I glance over at him and offer a small smile. "Maybe."

"Whatever you want, Rory, say the word."

"There's an amazing hole-in-the-wall restaurant a few blocks down."

"You got it." He pulls back out onto the street and holds one hand out to me, keeping the other on the wheel.

I slide my hand into his, resting it on the gear shift. "Thank you," I murmur.

It only takes a few minutes to get to the locally owned Chinese place I told Tristan about. My family has been ordering from this restaurant since I was born, and from what I can tell, it's still as amazing as it was over a decade ago.

One of the waitresses I've chatted with on several occasions, Tess, seats us in the far back booth and leaves us with menus. I scan mine as if I don't already know what I'm going to order. I peek over at Tristan, watching him for a moment before his eyes flick up and catch me staring.

He shoots me a wink and sets his menu on the table. "Do you know what you want?"

I nod, dropping mine on top of his. "I knew before we walked in the door."

He chuckles. "You're always prepared."

I tilt my head. "I spend so much time with you," I say. "I have to be."

Tess returns to the table with our drinks, so Tristan doesn't say anything in response to my remark. I hand her the menus and order my kung pao chicken and vegetable chow mein before Tristan orders. She scribbles down what we want and hurries off to get our order in.

"Crap," I mutter. "I left my phone in the car. I should go grab it in case my mom calls."

"Stay here. I'll get it," he offers.

I shake my head, standing. "Toss me your key, and I'll be right back."

He fishes the key out of his pocket and drops it into my open hand. "Always so stubborn," he murmurs.

I walk backward to the front door and blow him a kiss.

Outside, I head toward the parking lot at the back, clicking the unlock button as I approach the passenger side. Swiping my phone out of the cup holder, I slip it into my jacket pocket and lock the car after I shut the door.

Before I can turn around, a hand clamps over my mouth. Someone slams me against the car. I cry out, pain shooting across my face where it hit the window. I spin around to face my assailant and wince when he grabs me by my throat. His dark brown eyes narrow, his white blond hair flying all over the place with the wind.

"Aurora," he purrs, cocking his head to the side. He looks over my face as his fingers dig into my jaw.

I try to smack his hand away, cringing at the sharp pain. "Who the hell are you?" I growl, as two others step into my line of sight—a guy and a girl who both look my age.

He presses his knee between my legs and leans in until his face is inches from mine. "Keep quiet," he snaps.

"Ease up," the other guy barks.

"Fuck off, Nik," the guy snaps but lets go of me.

"We were told not to harm her," the guy—Nik—says.

"So what?"

Nik rolls his eyes, thrusting a hand through his messy black hair, and shrugs. "Your funeral, asshole."

The girl sighs. "Can we hurry? I'm getting bored."

I shove the guy away from me. "I'm going to take a shot in the dark and guess that you lot are light fae."

Nik slow claps from where he's leaning against one of the parked cars.

"What gave us away?" the guy still blocking my escape asks with a snicker.

"Well, it certainly wasn't your friendly demeanor," I

remark dryly.

The light fae whose name I still don't know growls and rears back to hit me, but his fist never connects. I blink, and he's flying through the air until he smacks against the brick side of the building.

I suck in a sharp breath as Tristan prowls toward the guy crumpled on the ground. "Don't." I grab his arm. No matter how much that fae deserves what he'd have coming to him, I don't think I can watch Tristan kill someone.

"Nice suit, Westbrook," Nik laughs from the same spot against the side of the car.

"You want to live, Sterling?" Tristan snaps.

Nik snorts. "Oh, threatening. Showing off for your girl?"

Tristan steps around me, and faster than my eyes can register, he has Nik by the collar of his jacket. Seeing fae shifting from one place to another so fast makes me queasy. "Since when do you do Jules's dirty work?"

Nik cocks a brow. "Who says Jules sent us?" He shakes his head.

"Nikolai," the female fae snaps.

"Why *are* you here?" Tristan demands, and his knuckles go white as he tightens his grip.

"Now where's the fun in me giving that up?" Nik's eyes glimmer.

"Well, you might get to keep your life. That could be *fun*."

"You're so uptight, Tristan." Nik glances over at me. "Anytime you want to get away from Mr. Broody over here, you let me know."

Tristan growls and slams him into the car, which shatters the passenger-side window.

I offer a tight-lipped smile. "Not in your lifetime."

He chuckles. "I'm immortal."

"Exactly."

Nik rolls his eyes and twists Tristan's arm enough to slip free, stumbling to the side. "Believe it or not, Westbrook, your fight isn't with me."

"My fight is with the light fae," he barks. "Until they—*you*—stop killing my people, my fight *is* with you."

Nik fixes his jacket where Tristan wrinkled it. "I haven't killed anyone."

"You're going to act like you weren't going to kill me?" I cut in.

He licks his lips. "I wasn't." He shrugs. "I was going to watch."

Tristan backhands him so hard, he falls to his knees. Tristan hauls him to his feet and strikes again and again, slamming his fist into Nik's face until blood is spraying from his nose and mouth. The female fae disappears at that point.

My eyes focus on the battle in front of me. Nik isn't getting many hits on Tristan, but it doesn't look as if Tristan is putting much effort in either, and he's practically pummeling Nik.

Nik disappears, and Tristan whips his head around, growling.

A hand snakes around my waist and a hand clamps over my mouth. *This shit is really starting to get old.*

"Let. Her. Go," Tristan says in a voice so hard, so low it hurts my ears.

"Relax, Westbrook. I'm not going to hurt your girl, especially not today." Nik spins me around to face him and tucks my hair back. "I'm sorry for your loss."

My mouth goes dry. I blink at him, and then he's gone.

The fae on the ground comes to, groans, and gets to his

feet. "Your days are numbered, Tristan," he grumbles. "Jules will make sure of it." With that, he disappears, too.

"Are you okay?" Tristan asks, stepping in front of me.

"I'm fine," I say.

He tilts my head back to look over my face, and his features sharpen. "Does it hurt?"

"It doesn't feel particularly good," I answer.

He closes his eyes and exhales through his nose before he traces his fingers along my skin to heal the marks from being thrown against the car.

When he leans down to kiss my cheek, I cup the side of his face and guide his lips to mine, kissing him fiercely.

After we break apart, I say, "What the hell was that about? Jules has people tracking us now?"

He shrugs, tucking my hair behind my ear. "It's possible."

"Tris, you don't think my parents are in danger, do you?"

"We can't be sure of anything, sweetheart, which is why I've had a team of my people watching them for a while."

I let out a breath. The idea of Jules targeting my parents makes my pulse surge with nervous energy, but knowing they're protected eases the weight on my chest. "Thank you."

"Maybe we should take this food to go?"

I'm not about to argue with that.

chapter Twenty-Four

I T WOULD BE A LIE TO SAY THE NEXT MONTH IS ANY easier than before Adam's death because it gets harder after the day of his memorial. Tensions are high with the dark and light fae so close to war. After I was attacked, Tristan explained that his meeting with Jules was unsuccessful in putting an end to the war. He said I was targeted because of my affiliation with the dark fae. Because of that, I now have one of the dark fae with me most of the time—including when I go home for Christmas break. It's quite the sight, Skylar drinking hot chocolate in our kitchen with my parents. Either she's an amazing actress, or she didn't hate spending time with humans as much as she wants me to think.

Christmas is hard. Mom and Dad make an effort for me, I think, but it isn't the same. We do the tree thing, open presents, and Dad cooks a turkey, but we go through the motions of celebrating as if we're being forced to do it.

After the first real snowfall of the season, I drive over to the cemetery and clear off Adam's stone. Kneeling in front of it for a while, I wish him a merry Christmas before I leave. I can never spend much time there. It still hurts too much.

I travel back to campus a few days later, unable to spend any more time in that house with nothing to do.

With the first semester over, I don't have anything to work on for a week and a half. I thoroughly clean my room, leaving Allison's side alone. There isn't much I *don't* do to distract myself. I shift my furniture only to move it back an hour later and wash my bedding and all of my clothes. I clean the bathroom. Hell, I sweep and mop the floor.

Now, almost two weeks into my final semester of college, my life falls into a comfortable routine. I go to class, study in the library or the lounge, and help out at the Westbrook Hotel. My placement is over, but I'll use any excuse to spend time with Tristan, something I never could've predicted would happen.

On the couch in Tristan's office, I'm half sitting, half lying, reading over the preliminary papers for my business proposal final assignment when he storms into the room and slams the door behind him.

"Long day?" I ask, glancing at him over my paper.

He lets out a heavy sigh. "I didn't know you were here."

I frown. "I don't have to be. Do you want me to leave?"

He approaches the couch. "That is the last thing I want, Rory." He rakes his fingers through his hair, messing up the already tousled strands.

"Okay," I murmur, offering him my hand. "Do you want to talk about it?"

He slides his hand into mine and sits on the edge of the coffee table beside the couch. "Four more of ours were found dead this morning. I sent Max out to get some answers."

"What happened at that meeting, Tris?" I ask. He's been keeping quiet about the light fae since Adam died. I think he's worried about putting more on me, but I want to be there for him like he was there for me.

He bows his head, looking at our hands as he brushes his thumb across the top of my knuckles. "Let's just say a ceasefire isn't in the cards. Jules is hell-bent on seeing me fall."

"Jules doesn't want to coexist," I say. "What could the light leader *possibly* want? Power over the light fae isn't enough?" I sit up, dropping my paper onto the couch beside me, and my knees touch his.

Tristan shrugs. "To lead all of the fae, the dark included. Some are open to the idea of coexistence. On both sides. Except in Jules's plan, I'm no longer included."

My jaw clenches. "We have to do something about this. Now."

A hint of a smile touches his lips. "Are you worried about me?"

I raise my eyebrows, pulling my hand free from his. "Are you kidding? Of course I'm worried! Your enemy is planning to kill you!"

"It's been that way since we both became leaders, sweetheart. This isn't new. To be honest, this wouldn't be a priority for me if not for the light fae killing mine. Skylar is still preparing the retaliation group."

I press my lips together, hesitating before I say, "The war is about to start, isn't it?"

He shakes his head. "The war started the moment they killed one of ours."

I nod. "What can I do to help?" I shoot him a look when he chuckles. "I'm serious. I want to help."

He leans forward, brushing the hair away from my face. "I know you do. After everything you've been through over the last four months, you still want to help. You can't imagine how that makes me feel."

"Tristan Westbrook, Leader of the Dark Fae, *feels*?" I gasp mockingly. "Alert the press."

He tweaks my chin. "Smart mouth," he says.

I press my lips against his in a quick peck. "Touché," I murmur.

His eyes flick over to the paper I was working on. "What's that?"

I pick it up and hand it to him. "My business proposal for class. It's not great, but I think I can make it work. I couldn't come up with anything else. Nothing seemed good enough. I'm hoping my professor will accept it."

It's something I've been thinking about for almost a decade. I want to open my own independent bookstore and café. The exact plans have changed several times since I came up with this business proposal. I've known since Adam passed that I wanted to make it a charity where all profits after operating costs go to financially struggling families with sick children.

Tristan scans the pages, and I become more nervous by the second. "I think you should do it," he says.

"You think I could use this for my assignment?" I check.

"Sure, but that's not what I meant. I think you should do it," he repeats.

"Do it? As in—?"

"Open the business, Aurora."

"What? I can't do that." I shake my head. "That requires a commercial building, marketing, employees, and, oh yeah, money. I've spent thousands of dollars getting my degree. I'm dead broke."

"Let me pay for it," he says in a casual tone.

My brows tug together, and I gape at him. "No. No way. Absolutely not."

His lips twitch. "Then partner with me."

"What did you just say?"

"You've made it clear you can't start this business venture as a sole proprietor, so partner with me. I have the necessary funds, and you have the ideas. It's simple."

"I think the word you're looking for is *crazy*, Tristan. This is a college assignment. I haven't graduated. I can't open my own business. I have approximately zero experience, and—"

"You have plenty of experience, sweetheart. You've worked here for months. Do you think I would've given you the responsibility I did if I didn't think you could handle it?" He sighs. "Aurora, I arranged that placement for your protection. There was no way to know what would happen after you found out about the fae, and with your lineage being a dead end, I couldn't count on that to protect you—from my own people as well as the light fae. That aside, the choices I made in regard to your working at my company were smart business decisions. You impressed everyone, though most would never say it. You can do this. *We* can do this."

I thrust my fingers through my hair, and try my best to wrap my head around the idea of Tristan protecting me from his world—even back then. "I don't know," I mumble, biting my bottom lip.

He smiles. "I'm not expecting an answer right away, Rory. Think about it. Talk to your professor about using it for your assignment, but think about how amazing it would be to create it."

"You're serious," I breathe.

"I'm serious."

I wrap my arms around his neck and pull him forward until our lips meet. I close my eyes and kiss him hard, my fingers gripping the ends of his hair as a lump forms in my throat. He grips my waist and lifts me onto his lap, taking control of the the kiss as his tongue teases its way into my mouth. I gasp against his lips when he presses against me, my heart racing when his fingers trail up my shirt until they reach the edge of my bra.

I pull away enough to look at him, my chest rising and falling fast. "Maybe we should slow down," I suggest, every nerve in my body tingling with need. Everything escalated so fast, I need a minute to catch up.

He shifts me back onto the couch. "Are you okay?"

"Of course," I say. "That was . . . I have a lot to think about."

He nods, his eyes flicking back and forth across my face. "You do."

I glance at the floor, pressing my lips together. "I haven't made this thing between us easy for you, and I'm sorry. I thought the first day I met you would be the last day." I lift my gaze until our eyes meet. "It's no secret that when I did see you after that day, it wasn't a good thing. I dreaded those moments when you popped up out of nowhere with your hidden agendas and ridiculous fae charm."

He chuckles, and I shoot him a look.

"We challenge each other every single day; it's our thing," I say.

He tilts his head to the side, a hint of a grin playing at the corner of his mouth as if he agrees.

"It was easier to hate you than to admit I had feelings for someone who kidnapped me, someone *fae*, who I didn't know

241

existed until said kidnapping." Glancing away, I sigh. "I'm rambling. I promise there's a point to this whole thing."

"I'm listening," he says.

"I'm still struggling with . . . this. You're so sure of yourself when it comes to us, and I'm over here with no idea what I'm doing. Every other aspect of my life is under my control, for the most part. Everything has a plan. That's how I've chosen to live—it's what keeps me sane. So, when you came along and I fell for you, I panicked. You being in my life forced me to consider a different future for myself than the one I've had planned forever. You didn't just nudge me out of my comfort zone, Tris, you freaking launched me so far away from it, I'm not sure what it feels like anymore."

"Aurora—"

"No, listen for a minute." I need to get this out. "I'm not saying this is going to be easy, but . . ." I flick my eyes up until they reach his. "I want to try."

Tristan leans in and cups my cheeks, his thumbs skimming across my face. "You're too good for me," he whispers, and rests his forehead against mine.

"That's not true," I say. "Please, tell me you'll try, too."

He kisses my brow and offers a soft smirk. "Oh, I'm all in, sweetheart."

chapter Twenty-Five

ORCING MYSELF TO TAKE A BREAK FROM EVERYTHING fae-related and get back to focusing on school, I text Grant to meet up to get our presentation done. I was lucky to get another elective class with him this semester after working together during our last class turned out to be mutually beneficial.

He sends me the address for his apartment a few blocks away from campus, and I head over there mid-afternoon.

"It's open," he hollers from inside after I knock, so I turn the knob and let myself in.

"Hey," I say as I walk into the kitchen where I find him chopping vegetables at the island counter. "You're cooking." I glance around at the clean, white cabinets and cupboards that line two of the walls, forming an L shape with gorgeous gray marble countertops. He has all stainless steel appliances, including a fridge with an ice dispenser like the one I've always wanted. I never pegged Grant as someone who had a fancy-ass kitchen, but this thing looks like it should be featured in a home and style magazine.

He tosses me a lopsided grin when I look at him. "I *am* cooking. I thought we could eat and then work. Food is always better than homework."

I lean against the counter and watch him chop a few more pieces off a carrot. "You don't have to convince me. I'll do anything to avoid this presentation at this point. Can I help with anything?" I ask, glancing at the garlic bread on the counter.

He wipes his hands on his pants. "Uh, sure. Want to slice some tomatoes?"

"I've been waiting my whole life for this moment." My tone is light with sarcasm.

He laughs. "Perfect." He walks around the counter and hands me a knife, setting me up with a couple of tomatoes and a cutting board.

I slice into one of them, Grant watching beside me, his shoulder brushing mine, as if he's worried I'll screw it up. The idea brings a smile to my lips . . . until my head starts spinning. Squeezing my eyes shut at the familiar sensation, I drop the knife and grab the counter.

"Easy there," he murmurs, his hand flat against the small of my back.

"W-what . . . ?"

"You're okay," he insists as his eyes meet mine. "I want you to sit down." His hand drops away from my back, and he returns to his place on the other side of the counter.

I stare at him without moving.

He peers over at me and frowns. "Interesting."

Wait a minute.

My eyes go wide. "You just tried to . . ." My mouth goes dry, and my ears ring. "Oh my god." My fingers grip the countertop until my knuckles go white.

"Would you look at that. You finally figured it out." He pops a piece of carrot into his mouth. "All those months of slowly feeding off of you so you wouldn't notice." He claps his hands together, and I flinch at the loud sound echoing around the room. "Phew, I'm glad I don't have to hide it anymore."

He's been feeding off of me? *In class*? My stomach churns, and my throat burns with bile.

"You son of a bitch," I growl.

"Uh-uh," he purrs. "Be nice now, or I'll be forced to respond unpleasantly."

My eyes flick around the room. "Let me go," I demand in a tight voice.

He smiles without looking at me. "Why would I do that? You're what I need to win this war."

My jaw clenches so tight my teeth ache.

"*Jules*." His real name comes out as a growl. I spent so much time thinking Dr. Collins was somehow involved, I didn't even consider that Jules wasn't a female, or that *he* was Grant. I was so focused on it being Richelle Collins because of her involvement with Adam. How she always made me feel like something was off about her, and her disappearing when he died. I blinded myself to the real light leader who was using me the whole time.

His eyes flick up and meet mine. "Well done. That's one point for you."

No points for me. I was *so* wrong.

I scowl. "What the hell do you need me for?"

He frowns. "Isn't it obvious?" He walks back around to stand at my side.

I try to lean away, but he grabs my arm and forces me to

stand before him. I swing my fist toward his disgustingly attractive face. "Why are you doing this?" I demand after he catches my fist before it connects. I pull my hand back, growling at the tingling sensation left behind, and try to shove him away.

Quick as a snake, he wraps his arm around my shoulders and holds me against him, his grip too tight to break no matter how hard I struggle. He smoothes a hand over my hair, and a sickening drowsiness trickles in. I should be fighting him off, but standing seems like too difficult a task. My eyelids flutter, and I lean into him to stay upright. "That's it," he croons. "Close your eyes."

Once awake, I blink several times before my vision clears and I can focus on the ceiling I'm staring at. I turn my head so I can look around the room. It's simple, fair in size, set up with a dresser, closet, desk, and bed. The bed that I'm lying on. I bolt upright. *Where am I?*

Before I can panic, the door opens and Grant—*Jules*—walks in, carrying a tray of breakfast food.

"You're awake," he says in a pleasant voice and sets the tray down on the table beside me.

I try to scramble off the bed but my legs get tangled in the sheets, and I almost fall off the edge. I catch myself on the mattress at the last second, managing to get the sheets away from me, and slide off, trying to put as much distance between us as possible.

"How are you feeling?" he asks.

My lip curls. "You don't give a shit about me."

He frowns and walks around the bed toward me.

I jump onto the bed to get across to the other side, away

from him, but he catches my leg and pulls me back, maneuvering himself on top of me, and pins my arms to the mattress above my head.

"Get off of me," I scream, tears pricking my eyes as I buck my hips to get him off the bed. I grunt, digging my nails into his hands, and he bares his teeth at me.

"Scream away. No one can hear you." He grins, and I think I'm going to be sick.

I lift my knee and catch him in the stomach as hard as I can. He grunts but doesn't move, so I do it again and again. He lets go of one of my hands to try to cage my leg, so I use that opportunity to lash out, dragging my nails across his cheek.

He hisses and rolls off of me, standing beside the bed. "You should eat something," he says in a tight voice.

There's no way I can stomach a glass of water, let alone a plate of eggs and pancakes. With a snarl, I kick the tray off the table, sending it to the floor in a pile of food and shattered glass. My temples throb with an impending headache. "Why are you doing this?" He didn't answer me the last time I asked.

He exhales through his nose. "Because, sweet Aurora, you're the way to Tristan's heart. And to destroy him, I'm going to destroy you."

My eyes widen. "I thought you were my friend," I snap. "What's your plan? You think you can just keep me here?" I clench my hands into fists so I'm not tempted to scratch my nails down his face again—though I'd like nothing better. Right now I need information.

"Help me destroy Tristan Westbrook so I can become the *only* leader of the fae, and you can go back to your mundane life and do whatever you want. You can live the life you've planned. All you have to do is say yes."

I stare at his shoulder because I can't force myself to look at his face. That's his angle. Tristan was right. He wants to rule the fae—all of them. Maybe if I play along, I can figure a way out of this. Jules is crazy if he thinks I'll help him. He couldn't offer me anything significant enough to have me agree.

"Take some time and think about it. Consider what this could mean for *you*, Aurora. You could have your old life back, just like that."

"Fine," I say, and that one word feels like I've already lost.

Jules narrows his eyes as if he might not believe me, but then he says, "You're making the right choice, Aurora."

I wait until he's far enough away before I press my face into the pillow and sob.

It's dark outside the window when I open my eyes. I use the bathroom, and while I'm washing my hands, I catch my reflection in the mirror. *What am I doing?* I need to find a way out of here before Jules has the chance to force me into doing something that will hurt Tristan.

When I leave the bathroom, I find Evan standing in the other room. The bedroom door is open.

My eyes narrow on him. "Are you involved with this?"

He hesitates. "In a way, yes."

"What the hell are you doing here?" I demand.

"Jules asked me to see if you'd like dinner now."

I stare at him. "You knew," I say, tasting the venom in my words. "You knew he was going to do this to me."

"Listen, Aurora—"

"Shut up," I growl. "You don't get to speak." I squeeze my hands into fists at my sides, inching toward him. "Does Allison know what's going on right now?"

Evan shakes his head. "I do care about her. While things may not have started that way, I came to care for her. You have to believe—"

"You knew that I knew Jules, but that I didn't know *what* he was," I accuse.

He nods.

That's when I snap. I launch forward and slam my fist into his face. He stumbles back, and I follow, swinging at his face again and again, almost surprised that I'm getting some decent hits in. Either he's letting me, or he isn't as coordinated and fast as most fae. Blood sprays from his nose and drips from a cut on his lip, but watching them heal as fae magic works through him makes my rage burn hotter. I hit him harder, faster, over and over until someone grabs me around the waist and pulls me away.

"Aurora." Jules's voice doesn't help the part of me that wants to murder Evan with my bare hands.

"I'll kill you," I hiss at Evan, trying to break free of Jules's hold. "I swear to god, I will end you."

Jules pulls me back and turns me to face him, grasping my chin with his free hand.

I try to break his grip. "Get the fuck away from me."

"Stop fighting me," he orders.

I swallow hard and stop struggling. It's not doing any good, anyway. "You sick son of a bitch," I growl. "He deserved that." My heart pounds from the adrenaline rush, making my hands shake as they grip the front of Jules's shirt. My knuckles are bloody and already bruising—I didn't notice until now.

Jules holds his hand over them until the cuts seal and the bruises fade. He sighs heavily. "Come on. Let's have some dinner. I did cook after all."

Evan grumbles, getting up from the floor, and walks out of the room without a word.

Jules and I sit across from each other in a small, modern dining room. He brings out two plates with chicken breast, broccoli, and roasted potatoes. He pours me a glass of white wine and one for himself before he looks at me. "Eat," he instructs.

I narrow my eyes at him but pick up my fork and knife. I slice into the chicken, watching the serrated metal cut into the meat. I wonder how fast I could—

"I wouldn't," Jules says in a casual tone, lifting a piece of chicken to his mouth. My eyes snap to his, and he smirks. "Your rigid posture and permanent scowl are fairly telling, Aurora."

Glaring at him, I drop the utensils and cross my arms. "You can't blame me for thinking about it."

He tilts his head, chewing and swallowing before he says, "I don't. However, I know how it would end if you attempted it, and I'd rather not see that come to fruition."

"How kind of you."

"There's no reason for you to get hurt, Aurora. It wasn't your fault you became a part of this world. The way I see it, once we deal with Tristan, you can go back to your life, and you'll be happy. I'm giving you an out that benefits me as well."

"You're forcing me to take it," I correct in a sharp tone.

He sets his fork down and takes a sip of his wine. "It's for your own good. You'll see that eventually."

"You know, I'm not sure that I will," I say. "You don't need me for what you're planning. You overestimate Tristan's feelings for me." I know how Tristan feels about me, enough to know

Jules's plan to use me against him could work. The thought makes my chest ache. For all those weeks I dreaded seeing Tristan, he's the only person I want to see right now.

Get it together, blondie. Why Max's snippy voice is what booms in my head, I'm not sure, but I latch onto it. Regardless of what the voice sounds like, it's right. I need to get through this myself.

He laughs. "I don't think so. I've seen the way he is with you. That's never happened before in all the years I've known him. Humans don't do it for him, but you do."

I push away from the table and stand. "I'm done talking about this. You started this war when you let your people kill the dark fae. You want to destroy Tristan and rule the entire fae race? You're on your own. Good fucking luck." I storm toward the door with no idea where I plan on going, but I have to get out of this room, away from him.

I'm about a foot away from the door when he grabs my wrist and spins me around. "Stop," he says.

"Go to hell," I snap.

His lips curl into a twisted grin. "Your fear and anger are intoxicating," he murmurs. "Such strong, genuine emotions."

My heart races at the intention behind his words. "It's called being *human*. You've tried it, remember?"

"That's right." He blinks, and I stagger back, free of his hold. "It's a shame that didn't work out, but college can be *so dull.*"

My forehead creases. "So then you know what it's like to spend time with you." Ah, there's the inappropriately timed witty comment. Well done, Aurora.

He sucks in a breath that almost sounds like a laugh. "Maybe you need more time to think about my offer." His eyes flash with an unprecedented anger, and I barely catch sight of his fist before the sickening sight of him goes black.

I blink a few times, my head already pounding, and my ears ringing. I spit out a mouthful of blood before I gag on it and groan.

"You hit her?" Evan says, but his voice sounds far away.

Jules grumbles. "Put her back in the other room. I've got shit to deal with."

I watch his shoes as he walks out, and I barely see Evan approach before my eyes shut on their own.

When I pry open my eyes this time, I recognize the room around me. I'm in Tristan's bedroom. I struggle to keep my eyes open long enough to see him sitting on the end of the bed and watching me with an angry, dark expression. His hair is a mess. It looks like he hasn't brushed it in days.

"What . . . ?" I stop. My head is spinning so fast I have to squeeze my eyes shut, or I'm going to throw up.

Tristan shifts closer and lays his hand across my forehead. The dizziness recedes enough for me to open my eyes again and look at him. He brushes the hair away from my face and assesses my appearance.

"Am I dreaming? How did I get here?" I ask, trying to figure it out in my head. There's a chunk of time missing, but I can't fill in the blanks.

His jaw clenches, and I wish I hadn't asked. "You don't remember?" he murmurs, his eyes on me. "This isn't a dream, Rory. Evan brought you back to us a few hours ago."

I shake my head, confused and unsure whether I'm able to speak anymore.

"You know Grant Taylor, yes?" he checks, his voice clipped.

My throat goes dry, and I force another nod. "Is he okay?" I ask in a small voice. Grant and I aren't all that close, but since I met him in class last semester, he's been a good friend.

His eyes darken. "I imagine you didn't know that he's fae. Or that Grant isn't his real name. It's Jules."

My eyes widen, and no words come out when I open my mouth.

"I didn't think so," he says. "It would seem that he has been—" Tristan stops, clenching his fists in his lap. It's like the night I was poisoned all over again. I can *feel* the anger rumbling through him like dark, violent waves, and I immediately want to make it stop.

My hand is shaking, but I reach over and place it over his fist. "Tristan," I whisper.

He sighs heavily and looks at me. "The bastard has been feeding off of you."

I play that sentence over in my head, and then I lean over the side of the bed and hurl.

When my stomach calms down, housekeeping comes to clean up the mess, and Tristan and I sit in his living room. The fireplace casts dim light on the room, reflecting off the prints of the hotel on his walls.

"This whole time . . ." I trail off. "I've been friends with him since before I met you. I've spent time with him all semester, and I didn't know he was the leader of the light fae, that he was your enemy."

"I'm sorry," he murmurs, putting his arm around my shoulders.

I lean against him and try to take a few deep breaths. "I think it's coming back, Tris," I whisper, squeezing my eyes shut as images of me attacking Evan and memories of Jules feeding of off me play over in my head like a twisted movie.

"Shh," he soothes. "Listen to me, sweetheart. Listen to my voice. You're okay. Keep breathing." He runs his hand up and down my arm, trying to help me through the montage from hell.

The pictures stop, and all I want to do is kill Jules for what he did to me. Some things are still blurry, like how I got here. I remember being in the back of a car and someone carrying me into the back entrance of the hotel. I don't understand why Evan brought me back.

"It's all right, Rory," Tristan says, grazing my cheek with the back of his hand. "You're safe now. We'll figure this out, and then I'll deal with that bastard. You need to rest and recharge." He lifts my chin until our eyes meet. "I gave you my blood so that you'd be up to par faster, but you should eat something."

My stomach churns, and bile rises in my throat at the idea of trying to put food in my body. "I'm not sure I can."

"You can," he insists. "You'll get through it, I promise you."

I don't say anything else, but after a moment, I nod.

I find it difficult to remember what my life was like before the fae. When I think about Jules's offer to give me that life back, I know I could never take it. I can't give this life up. I can't give Tristan up. I won't.

All I can do is hope he feels the same about me.

Chapter Twenty-Six

I SPEND THE FOLLOWING DAYS STAYING AT THE WESTBROOK Hotel, sleeping in Tristan's bed at night, and working in the office when I'm not in class or studying. He's calling it an internship now that I've finished my placement. I'm glad most of the employees don't seem to have any issues with me hanging around.

I've come to enjoy working with Skylar, even if she does still boss me around. I think we've both decided to pretend that night she helped me in the shower after Adam died didn't happen, and I'm grateful for it.

Max is still a total asshole, but I accept that as his nature now. I've tagged along with him and Oliver at lunch a couple of times since the two of them became an item. It's taken a while, but I can look at Max and see someone separate from the fae who kidnapped and almost killed me all those months ago. Oliver doesn't know any of this, or anything about the fae, and I'm glad Max plans to keep it that way.

It's been three days since I was returned from Jules's clutches, and we have yet to hear from him. No epic battle has broken out; no more dark fae have been killed. Nothing has happened. I think we're all going a bit crazy waiting for *something*. I've tried to think about the time I spent with him, as hard as that is, to remember exactly what happened, but I haven't come up with anything.

In the office boardroom, I glance up from the stack of papers on the table in front of me when the door flies open, and Allison charges in with determination in her eyes.

"We have a problem," she says, setting her hands on her hips. Allison has been spending time at the hotel since she ended things with Evan over his involvement when Jules kept me captive. I think him helping me escape was his way of trying to make things right, but Allison didn't care. I don't blame her, but I'm also sorry she got hurt. She didn't deserve that.

"Is it a dire emergency? I'm swamped with paperwork right now, but we can get drinks later and chat."

She shrugs. "That's the thing. I don't know."

I frown, flipping through some of the papers, and pull out the one I'm looking for. "This problem. Is it human or fae?"

She curls her fingers around the belt loops on her washed-out jeans. "Fae."

Before Allison can answer, Tristan walks through the other door from his office and flicks a glance between us. He smiles. "Ladies."

"Perfect," I say, jerking my thumb toward where he stands. "Allison, I'm sure he'd love to help with this problem, as he is the beloved leader of your kind." I drop my eyes back to the marketing report I was reading and uncap my pen to make some notes. "We can talk about this later, I promise, but until then,"

I point at Tristan again without looking up, "fae leader," I say, then point back at Allison, "fae problem."

She sighs. "Okay, but I'm holding you to that drink. I think we could both use it."

Tristan chuckles. "Why don't we step into my office?" he suggests, and the two of them walk through the door, closing it behind them.

I'm still buried in paperwork when they come out almost an hour later. Allison says a quick goodbye before she leaves, and I offer her a wave.

Tristan approaches and perches on the table next to me. He watches while I work, and I can only ignore his presence for so long.

"What's with the lurking?"

"Am I distracting?" he inquires in an amused tone.

The crispness of his cologne tickles my nose. I want to envelop myself in that fresh scent like a soft, comforting blanket of Tristan. I knock the thought out of my head and say, "You're blocking my light."

"My apologies," he purrs, leaning down so his lips are in line with my ear. "You've been sitting here for hours." He shifts so he can place his hands on my shoulders, and massages them slowly. "You look like you could use a break." His breath is warm against my lips as his eyes search mine.

I swallow, my chest rising and falling fast. "Tris," I mumble.

His mouth curls into a wicked smirk, my only warning before he drops his hands, gripping my hips to pull me up, and lifts me onto the table. I suck in a sharp breath, and my eyes land on his. He dips his face close to mine and presses his lips against my jaw, trailing his mouth along the length. He sucks my earlobe into his mouth, and I gasp, pressing my lips together to muffle a moan as my eyes drift shut.

I grab his waist to steady myself and lean into him as he ravishes me with his mouth against my skin. Goosebumps rise on my arms as he takes his time exploring each inch of bare skin, bringing heat to my cheeks knowing someone could walk in at any moment.

We should stop.

Oh god, I don't want to stop.

He pauses briefly before his lips collide with mine, and my belly gives a happy flip as I move with him. He groans, and we fight for control, always pressing closer.

I wrap my legs around him, and he responds with a growl and teases my lips with his tongue. They part, and his tongue grazes against mine, sending a pleasant warmth deep into my belly. I grip the material of his suit jacket as our tongues dance, and he gives my hips a gentle squeeze before dragging his hands up my sides. One hand dives into my hair, holding the back of my neck while he kisses me slow and soft, and my body jerks forward when his other hand skims my breast over my shirt. His lips curl against mine as his thumb deliberately brushes over it again. I gasp, but the sound is muffled by his insistent mouth.

Breaking away before I'm even close to wanting it to end, I succumb to the need for air. I rest my forehead against his chest, and he slides his hand out of my hair to cup my cheek, his thumb brushing across my skin. I lean back and meet his deep blue gaze, unable to help the grin that touches my slightly swollen lips as I push my fingers through the mess of soft blond hair hanging across his forehead.

"I'm never going to get this paperwork done," I mutter as I catch my breath.

"Keep talking about work, and I'm going to take you to my room and give you something else to do with that mouth," he warns, making the warmth in my belly spread lower.

I arch a brow, pressing my thighs together as if that'll relieve the pulsing between them. "I might believe you if I didn't know you have a meeting tonight," I say with a sweet smile.

His eyes narrow. "You think I won't cancel that to be inside you?"

My heart wants the world to know how that makes my blood warm. "Do it," I say in a defiant tone.

He smirks. "You're adorable when you're feisty."

I scowl, but it's halfhearted. "You think I'm not serious?"

"Oh, I know you are." The hand holding my hip slides down and grazes my thigh. I watch his fingers move lower before he tips my head back up. "You're never one to miss out on a challenge."

I sigh. "For someone who was complaining about me talking, you're sure slow to shut up."

He raises a brow. "Clever."

I nudge him back far enough so I can slide off the table and straighten my shirt. "If you're not going to follow through with your threats, you shouldn't make them," I mumble as I reach for my notes to get back to work.

Tristan grabs my wrist and pulls me back against him. His lips are quick to find my neck, and his teeth graze my skin, sending shivers down my spine. "Upstairs," he breathes.

I manage to nod before he shifts, transporting us from the boardroom to the master bedroom of his penthouse. I lean up on my tiptoes and brush my lips over his bottom one. His arms come around me, sweeping me off my feet as his mouth closes over mine. He presses me back against the closed door and nips my lower lip, making me suck in a breath. He chuckles as I wrap my legs around his waist. I bury my fingers in his hair, tugging at the ends as my lips move against his. Our mouths are frantic, losing coordination in our desperation for more.

His lips leave mine for a second, and I drag air into my lungs while he trails his mouth along my jaw, kissing and nipping gently. His hands grip my hips, his thumbs moving in slow, sensual circles.

"Aurora," he breathes.

"Kiss me," I demand.

"This isn't the slow pace you mentioned before."

I lean back enough to look at him. "I don't want slow," I say. "I want *you.*"

The hue of his eyes darkens into a look so filled with desire, heat floods through me. My entire body is tingling with a wicked sensation, a need to be touched.

"You're saying—?"

"I'm saying *kiss me*, Tristan."

I don't have to ask again. His lips are on mine in an instant, pulling soft whimpers and moans from me with ease. He spins us around and walks across the room, setting me on my feet when we reach the side of his bed. My heart surges forward, and my eyes snap to his.

"Are you sure?"

I nod, reaching for him.

He catches my hand and presses it flat against his chest, over his heart. I can feel it pounding against my palm. "I need to hear you say it, sweetheart."

A smile touches my lips. I lift my free hand to his face and cup his cheek. "I want you, Tristan Westbrook, so much it terrifies me. I want you so badly it hurts."

His eyes go wide. "You can't possibly understand how long I've waited for this moment."

My breath catches. "Then stop talking and kiss me."

He slides his hand up my neck, cradling my head as his lips seal over mine. He lays me on his bed and leans over me, planting short, soft kisses along my jaw, down the side of my neck, across my collarbone. My skin heats at his touch, pulsing between my legs each time his lips brush across a new part of me.

He lifts his shirt over his head, dropping it on the floor before reaching for the buttons on my blouse. "I need to know you'll tell me to stop if this gets to be too much," he says.

"I will," I assure him.

He undoes each button with care until he can push it off my shoulders, then tosses it on the floor with his shirt. He dips his head and licks along the top swell of my breasts, making me gasp. I grip the waistband of his pants, tugging on his belt until I can get it to unbuckle. He steals my hands and pins them above my head with one hand, using the other to unclasp my strapless bra. It falls away, leaving my upper half bare and bringing a new heat to my cheeks.

His eyes catch mine as he releases my wrists, and he smiles. "You're so beautiful," he murmurs and brings his lips back to mine in a sweet, slow kiss. He drops his mouth to my chest and kisses around my breast, flicking his tongue across it, hardening the nipple before he sucks it into his mouth. I groan as he circles his tongue around it while tweaking the other with his fingers. I arch my back, and he answers by switching sides and delivering the ministrations all over again. The heat between my thighs pulses with need, and almost as though he senses it, he presses his knee higher, and my hips jerk in response.

He trails his lips the length of my stomach until they reach the edge of my pants. His eyes flick to mine, and I nod. He smirks and pulls them past my knees. I kick them the rest of the way off, and Tristan helps me slide back further so my head rests against the pillows. He hovers over me, kissing each of my cheeks, my forehead, my nose, before his lips return to mine. His hand presses against my stomach and slides lower. My hips buck when his fingers brush over my panties, making me gasp against his lips.

"You like that?" he murmurs.

"Yes," I breathe.

My head spins when he slips his hand into my panties, and I grip the black silk sheets on either side of me as he slides a finger inside. His thumb circles my bundle of nerves while his finger thrusts in and out, making me writhe against the sheets.

He takes his time stroking me, stealing my moans as his lips move against mine in a feverish kiss.

Shifting his body, he trails his lips down my neck and across my collarbone. My pulse kicks up when I realize where his mouth is heading. His free hand slides down my side as he moves his lips lower to my stomach while his fingers still move slowly inside of me, eliciting small, soft moans from me. He kisses just below my navel, then lifts his eyes to mine. The sight of him before me almost does me in, and when a smirk touches his lips, my heart races.

He pulls my panties off and tosses them behind him, then lifts my leg over his shoulder, and raises a brow at me. An invitation.

I take the cue, and lift my other leg. He lowers his gaze to my core, his dark lashes fanning his cheeks. His fingers slow and slide out, making me sigh, but before I can protest, his tongue replaces them. I press my lips together so I don't make a sound, and my eyes shut on their own accord as he flicks it against my bundle of nerves.

I let out a breath that sounds more like a moan and bite back a string of expletives when he pushes his tongue inside. *Holy shit.* Doing this has never felt *this* amazing before. *You've also never had Tristan Westbrook between your thighs.* If I'd known it would feel like this, I don't think I'd have been able to hold off this long before admitting what I felt for him.

"Tristan," I murmur his name, my hips jerking off the bed. He chuckles, shooting vibrations straight to my core, and holds me against the mattress with his hands. My fingers grip his hair, holding him there while he pulls more moans from me, making my head spin and setting my body on fire.

My breath comes in short, quick gasps, my heart pounding in my chest as my hips grind against him even as he holds them down. He flicks his tongue over me once more, thrusting in deep, and I explode, crying out my release.

He presses a kiss to my stomach and gets off the bed, giving me a minute to catch my breath while he steps out of his pants and boxers. My mouth drops open, in awe of him.

Sliding his hands up my thighs, he crawls over me and reaches into the nightstand, pulling out a condom. He tears it open and rolls it on with ease, kissing the corner of my mouth. He tilts my chin up until our eyes meet. "You're still sure?"

"Yes," I say, running my fingers through his hair.

His leg nudges mine apart as he settles between my thighs. His lips find mine as he leans forward, and I feel him against me. He dips inside of me, and I wince at the discomfort, squeezing my eyes shut. I may not be a virgin, but it's been a while.

"You need to relax, Rory," he murmurs, his lips brushing my cheek.

I take a deep breath, and let it out, forcing my muscles to relax. He slides in a bit more, groaning as he rests his forehead against mine.

"You're so tight, sweetheart." He pushes in a bit further before sliding almost all the way out. He thrusts back in, stealing my breath, and doesn't move for several beats. "Are you okay?" he checks.

It takes me a minute, but I manage a nod. "Don't stop," I breathe.

He slides out once more and then fills me again, making me clench around him. "Christ, Rory," he groans.

A few more thrusts and the discomfort dissolves into a pleasant fullness. He quickens his pace, making me moan, and kisses the pulse at my throat.

"That's it," he encourages, reaching between us to tease me with his thumb. He thrusts a few more times, and I can feel another orgasm building. My head spins with pleasure as he thrusts into me again and again until my orgasm hits, and I cry out his name.

"You still with me, sweetheart?"

"Always," I murmur, still basking in the aftershocks.

He grips my hips and dives into me hard and fast, changing his pace every few thrusts. Some are deep and slow, others quicker. His eyes shut as he groans, the sound rumbling in his chest, and seals his mouth over mine, kissing me sweetly.

I meet his thrusts, lifting my hips off the mattress each time. We pull each other closer, our lips battling for control with each stroke, each thrust, until Tristan reaches his own climax, growling deep in his throat.

Our heavy breathing mingles as we break away slightly. He takes his time sliding out of me and gets off the bed. "I'll be right back," he says, still a little breathless, and less than a minute later, he's lying next to me again, his head propped on his hand. His grin is wicked. "We should've done that the night we met. I could've won you over a long time ago."

I roll my eyes and push him clear off the side of the bed, smiling at the thud he makes hitting the floor.

He gets up, unfazed, and kisses my shoulder. "I'm sorry. I didn't mean to ruin the moment."

I flick a glance in his direction, unable to stop the smile from touching my lips. "Nothing in the world could ruin what we just did."

We lie together in silence. The only sound is our quiet, steady breathing. Tristan traces slow circles on my shoulder with his finger, lulling me into a sleepy, content state. He pulls the sheet across my naked body and wraps his arm around my waist. Despite the number of times I've slept beside Tristan in this bed, anticipating this day, it is so much more satisfying than I imagined.

In this moment, there are no dark fae or light fae, there's only us, and that's all I want.

chapter Twenty-Seven

I WAKE UP WITH THE MOST DELICIOUS ACHE BETWEEN MY legs, and a smile curls my lips before I even open my eyes. Last night was incredible. It felt like something I've been waiting my entire life to experience, and it surpassed my expectations of what being with Tristan would be like.

I blink a few times, squinting at the sunlight shining in through the window. With a quick glance beside me, I see Tristan is still asleep. I lie on my side, watching the rise and fall of his chest. I could watch this forever, basking in the normalcy of it, but the longer I lie there thinking about how great last night was, the more panic trickles in. Each passing moment makes it harder to breathe as a clear picture forms in my head. The light and pleasant feeling I had when I woke up is gone, replaced with a pit of unease in my stomach. Even while looking at Tristan's calm and relaxed face, all I can think about is Jules plotting his next attack in his grand plan to destroy Tristan and rule the entire fae race. My chest tightens, and I fight the urge to reach over and touch his face. I don't want to wake him.

Sliding off the bed, I head into the bathroom, pulling my clothes back on and tying my hair up. I peek over to the bed, relieved to find him still asleep, then slip out of the room. I grab my jacket and bag, putting on my shoes at the entryway before I step onto the elevator and ride down to the lobby of the hotel.

There's a good chance I'm the only girl who has left Tristan Westbrook alone, naked in his bed, after a night of mind-blowing sex, but I have to do this.

It's not even ten o'clock, so the lobby is empty aside from a few employees. I wave to the concierge on my way out the door and get on the streetcar heading toward campus.

After I take the fastest shower I've ever had, I change into black leggings, a sweater, and boots. I pull a comb through my hair and tie it back so it's out of the way. Standing in front of my desk, I hesitate before I open the bottom drawer and grab the iron stakes. The night Tristan and I met, he confirmed the myth about fae and how iron is poisonous to them.

I slide one into each of my boots and another one at the back of my leggings. I hold the last one in my hand for a moment and slide it up my shirt, securing it between my breasts. I hope my bra will keep it in place until I need to use it. I pull on my jacket, check the time on my phone before tossing it onto my bed, and walk out of my room.

When I woke up this morning, I knew where Jules was. Maybe he wanted me to know where he is. Maybe he screwed with my head more than I can remember. The smart thing to do would be to call Tristan and tell him where Jules is, but I need to do this for myself. This whole thing—the fae war—isn't about me, but the moment Jules messed with my life, my feelings, it became about me on some level. He made it personal when he decided to manipulate me and feed on my emotions, and now he's going to answer for what he did.

Campus is quiet as I walk across it to where Jules is—in the basement of his pub. I'm not surprised to find the door unlocked even though it isn't open yet. My heart hammers in my chest as I step inside. The place is empty, televisions off, and chairs on tables. My shoes feel like they weigh a thousand pounds each as I walk across the old wood floor toward the basement stairs. I hesitate before reaching for the door handle, my mind racing through the ways this scenario could end. I push them away, knowing it's too late to think about that now.

My eyes do a quick scan of the space. It appears to be a simple basement storage area that's been partially converted into a hangout space. Boxes cover half of the room, while the other half has been decorated with an antique-looking rug to cover the concrete, some old couches, and a coffee table, along with a couple of rolling chairs.

Maybe I was wrong. Maybe he isn't here.

"I have to say, I didn't think you'd come alone," Jules says, walking out of another room at a relaxed pace. He looks at ease, no creases in his forehead, no sharp, calculating expression.

My jaw clenches at his cliché line. "No one else could be bothered to deal with your pathetic ass," I say, my tone laced with sarcasm.

He tilts his head to the side, his eyes wandering over my face. "I'm surprised you came at all, especially after Evan took you back to Tristan. It's a shame I had to kill him for helping you. He didn't know what loyalty was."

My eyes widen, and the sting of tears surprises me. I was never crazy about Evan, but he helped me get away from Jules, and I'm grateful for that. He didn't deserve to die. "What do *you* know about loyalty?"

He smirks, ignoring my remark. "Why are you here?"

I bark out a laugh. "I need to spell it out for you?"

He prowls closer, stopping a foot away, making my back stiffen. "I want to hear you say it," he says.

I swallow. "You used me."

"It was never about you, Aurora, not really."

I shake my head. "The light and dark fae can coexist. You and Tristan can lead *together*."

"You don't get it." He swipes his hand through his hair. "I won't lead *with* someone. I want the fae race to grow, become more powerful, and to do so, they need a leader that'll do anything to make that happen. They need *me*."

"You're insane if you think Tristan's people would follow you if you kill him. They'll destroy you for it and make all of your people watch."

It's silent for several moments, and then he sighs. The soft sound makes my blood run cold. He slams me into the wall. I cry out, seeing stars.

He shoves his hand up my sweater and rips the iron stake out, growling as it burns his skin, and tosses it across the room. It clatters against the cement floor. I wince, trying to break free of his grasp. "It's a shame," he says, tightening his grip on me. "This could've gone a different way, Aurora."

"I doubt that," I say through my teeth, shoving him hard.

He backs up a couple of steps, a dark smirk plastered on his lips. "So, you came here to kill me?" he lifts his arms out, palms up. "Have at it," he taunts, letting his arms fall back to his sides.

I bend and pull the iron stake out of my left boot, holding it in a tight grip.

Jules laughs, flicking his gaze from my face to the weapon

in my hand. "Did you stop at the hardware store on your way here?"

I step forward, swiping the air in front of him so he'll move back a few more strides. I circle around him and kick out with my right leg, but he catches it, pulling the other iron stake out of my boot. *Fuck.*

He pushes me back, and I almost lose my balance, managing to catch my footing at the last second.

"I'm curious, Aurora. Do you believe you can win this fight?"

"I have to," I growl. "I will."

Jules charges forward, throwing me to the ground and holding me there. "I'm almost sorry," he murmurs, trailing his fingers along my jaw. "You might be my one regret."

I choke on the lump in my throat and try to push him off. I knee him in the stomach over and over, but it doesn't faze him.

The pity in his eyes makes me want to hurl, and then he slams me against the cement floor again, making me suck in a sharp breath.

I lift my leg and kick him in the groin as hard as I can, screaming at the top of my lungs when he rolls off of me and onto his back with a loud groan. I throw myself on top of him and wrap my fingers around his throat with one hand, using the other to grab my last iron stake out of the back of my leggings.

"You've got quite the collection," he grumbles. "I guess that's smart, considering the crowd you choose to spend time with."

"Shut up," I shout, tightening my grip around his neck, digging my nails into his skin. Claws would be more convenient; I could slash his throat, his chest, the soft, charming face that made me befriend him, that made me *trust* him.

In a second, he has us flipped over, and now he's on top again, holding my arms at my sides. "You're making this too easy." He leans down until his lips brush my ear, which makes my stomach clench. "Do you think Tristan feels bad for what he's put you through?"

I buck my hips, trying to get him off, but all it does is exhaust me.

"He should, you know. If it weren't for him, I'd have had no reason to enter your life."

I stop. "*What?*"

He cocks his head to the side. "You were always part of the plan, Aurora. From the day we met." He grasps my chin in his hand and guides my face up until our eyes meet. "I'm the reason you were taken from that party instead of Allison."

My mouth goes dry. My ears ring, and my vision falters. A panic attack has never hit me so hard, so fast.

"I set you in Max's path."

"Stop," I say, my voice cracking.

"I've been watching you for a long time. I got to know everything about you. You were the perfect pawn. I knew the dark's beloved leader would be taken with you. It was only a matter of time before he fell for you. It was you falling for him in return that worried me in the beginning. Especially with the whole kidnapping thing. But look how that turned out." The sly twist of his lips makes my blood run hot with rage.

I glare at his passive, relaxed expression. "So, what the hell does Allison have to do with it?"

"I sent Evan to corrupt her allegiance. I needed her to break a rule in order for Tristan to send someone after her."

"How did you know I would be close enough to her for

that to work?" I don't know why I ask, but the words tumble out of my mouth. "What would've happened if she didn't fall for Evan?"

He grins. "Allison was easy to manipulate, and you met her because I made it happen that way."

My brows inch closer. "You're saying this was in the works before I knew her?"

He nods. "Immortality has its perks. I've been planning this for some time."

Oh my god. The day Allison caught him checking me out in first year. *She knew who he was.* It makes sense now. That's why she warned me off him, and why she never tagged along when our friends wanted to eat at Taylor's Brew.

Everything I've experienced over the past three years has been for some scheme for power? *Was anything real?* My feelings for Tristan? Oh god. My friendship with Allison? How much is my own and not a byproduct of Jules's plot to rule the fae?

Tears blur my vision. "He will destroy you," I say through my teeth.

He laughs, and then the snap of bone echoes in my ear. My left arm explodes with such intense pain, black spots dot my vision, and a scream rips from my throat. He frowns, but his eyes hold a sick glimmer of amusement.

The room blurs, and I fight to keep my eyes open. I refuse to pass out, and by the frustrated, borderline angry expression on the face above me, I'd say that's exactly what Jules wants me to do.

"You shouldn't have come alone," he says with a snarl.

I bark out a laugh. "You really wanted to see Tristan, didn't you?" I wince as the throbbing in my arm intensifies. "Do you have a thing for him or something?" Sarcasm laces my tone. Good. At least I'm holding on to my wit. "I don't blame you. He's hot."

Jules growls and wraps his fingers around my injured arm, squeezing hard, and I scream.

"Where's your fire now?" he taunts.

I close my eyes, hot tears rolling out of the corners. I bite my lower lip hard so I'll stop screaming. If I'm going to die, I refuse to give him the satisfaction of seeing the devastation course through me. I've experienced too much over the last six months from learning about the fae to losing my brother in one of the most human ways possible. I can't do it anymore.

"Are you giving up?" he whispers in a cold voice. There's a moment where his grip on my wrists loosens. I've been waiting for it with bated breath. When it happens, I rip my right arm free and raise it, ready to slam it into his chest.

"Wait!" he shouts, a smile creeping onto his lips. "I can bring your brother back."

My whole world stops. My arm freezes halfway to where the stake was heading for his chest, and I snarl. "You bastard! You don't know anything!" There's no way to bring Adam back. His body was burned to ashes the day after he died.

He nods. "Touché, Aurora."

I growl and drive the iron stake into his ribcage.

He cries out in pain, a sound so excruciating, I want to cover my ears. He falls, rolling off of me, but still holds my broken wrist in a weak grip. "There she is," he mumbles.

His mouth forms a perfect *o*, his eyes widening in shock before they close for the last time.

My eyes snap to where his fingers remain wrapped around my wrist when the contact starts burning. It becomes unbearable, but I can't get free. Tingles shoot up my arm, traveling to the rest of my body, and my heart pounds in a panicked frenzy. Fire races through my veins, burning everything in its path. I throw my head back, screaming in agony that seems to last forever.

The pain is slow to recede. I've cried my eyes dry and my throat raw. I manage to pull my wrist free from Jules's lifeless grasp, and everything goes dark.

Chapter Twenty-Eight

"AURORA. AURORA, YOU HAVE TO WAKE UP." THE VOICE tickles my senses. He shakes my shoulders, and I open my eyes. "You can't stay here. Please go back. You're not ready. It's not time for you to be here yet, Roar."

Roar.

I suck in a sharp breath and scramble back across the stark white floor. My eyes whip around, and I find that I'm surrounded by nothing but whiteness. My eyes land on him as a sob catches in my throat. "Adam?" I whisper.

He smiles, his blue eyes bright like before he got sick. His brown hair is still a mop of messy curls on his head, and he's wearing his favorite band T-shirt. He waves. "Hey."

I blink several times. "Am . . . am I dead?"

"I don't think so," he says, walking closer and sitting next to me.

I frown at him. "Why am I here?"

"Something bad happened, Roar." Adam's brows tug closer

together. "I'm so sorry."

I wipe the wetness from my cheeks. "I don't understand," I whisper.

He touches my shoulder. "I know, but we don't have a lot of time. You need to get back before it's too late."

"Too late? Adam, what are you talking about?"

"I don't want you to get stuck here. I miss you, Roar, but I can't let you stay."

I nod. I'd rather return to the world of the living, no matter how much I miss Adam. There's still so much I want to do with my life. I'm not ready to be here yet.

"You're going to wake up, and things are going to be harder than they've ever been, but I need you to remember who you are. Promise me you'll remember, no matter what happens."

More tears leak free as I nod again. "I promise." I wrap my arms around him in a tight embrace. "I miss you." I cry against his shoulder.

"I know, Roar. I miss you, too."

We sit like that, holding onto each other, and I realize I'm getting the goodbye that was stolen from me when he died.

"Adam?" I murmur.

"Yeah?"

"I love you so damn much."

"I love you, too."

The beautiful white walls crumble as the blank scene around me fades. I'm about to leave Adam for real this time.

"You'll see me again, Roar," he promises with a light kiss against my cheek, and then I wake up.

The cement floor is hard against my back, and it takes me a minute to sit up. I glance sideways where Jules's body still lies with the iron stake sticking out of his chest, and I wonder how long I spent in that in-between state. I peek at my arm and frown when I find it's uninjured. I move it with care, confusion flooding through me. Did Jules heal me before he died?

I hear shuffling upstairs, but I can't move fast enough to hide from the two people that come barreling down the stairs. I'm not sure why, but I know they're light fae. There's one guy, appearing to be in his late twenties, with sandy brown hair, and another, younger-looking guy, with dark red hair. They both look as if they could take me out in a matter of seconds. Against muscles like that, I wouldn't stand a chance.

Glancing back and forth between me and Jules's body, the redhead growls deep in his throat. He takes a step toward me, and I kick my feet, pushing myself away so I can scramble upright.

"Back off, man. You know we can't touch her now," the older one says.

"The hell we can," he snaps. "She killed our leader."

"You know what that means," he replies.

I lift my head. *I* don't know what that means. "What are you saying?" I speak for the first time, and the men look at each other.

"You took his life, which means you took his position in our world."

Any response dies on my lips.

"You're the new leader of the light fae, Aurora Marshall."

My eyes widen. "I'm no leader and certainly not of the light fae."

"Jules was our leader," the brown-haired one says. "You took his place when you took his life."

I shake my head. "I'm human. I can't be your leader." When the men exchange looks, my stomach twists. "What?" I demand.

"You're not anymore."

My mouth goes dry. "I . . ."

"You're fae," he says.

"Get out," I say. "Now." They look at each other and leave without another word.

You're fae.

Those words play over in my head until it's spinning. My legs give out, and I drop to my knees on the floor beside Jules.

"You son of a bitch," I say through my teeth as tears fill my eyes. I rip the iron stake from his chest and cry out when it burns my skin.

The back emergency exit flies open and breaks off its hinges, slamming onto the floor, and Tristan storms into the room with Allison and Max flanking him. His eyes find mine right away, and my breath halts.

The three of them stop dead in their tracks, staring at me with wide eyes. Max glances at Jules's lifeless body, and the recognition that flashes in his eyes is mirrored by Allison's and Tristan's expressions.

I cast my gaze down as Max and Allison move around me to grab Jules and haul him out the back door.

The room is silent, and then it isn't. I can hear Tristan breathing, his heart pounding. I can hear the faint sound of his shoes against the floor as he closes the distance between us. I can hear everything I couldn't before.

I can't bring myself to look at him. If I do, I'll shatter.

"Aurora," he murmurs, and his voice cracks.

My chest tightens, and my hands shake at my sides.

"Aurora, look at me," he says in a deep, tight voice, as if he's struggling to hang on.

I shake my head, clenching my jaw.

I feel his presence before I see the tops of his shoes reach mine. He reaches out and cups my face, allowing me to keep my head down. His thumbs brush across my cheeks. My heart drops, and tears well in my eyes.

"Look at me, please," he begs.

I lift my face enough to meet his gaze, and the tears slip down my cheeks, wetting his fingers. His eyes are wide and panic-filled. His face is pale, and his expression is strained; he's terrified.

"What have I done?" I breathe. And then I shatter.

Tristan catches me before I hit the floor and cradles me in his arms, brushing my hair back out of my face as his eyes search mine. He guides us the rest of the way to the floor and pulls me against him. I bury myself there as he holds me to him, and it takes me a while to realize the unfamiliar movement in the rise and fall of his chest. He's crying.

Tightness snakes around my chest, making it hard to breathe as I grip the front of his shirt and rest my forehead against his. Seeing Tristan like this—I can't bear it. "I couldn't let anyone else get hurt," I cry. "Please, Tris, you have to understand." I don't know if his tears are because I went after Jules without him, or for what happened because I did.

"This wasn't supposed to happen," he grinds out. "You weren't supposed to . . ." He stops and clears his throat. He leans back and wipes his face with the back of his hand.

"I'm sorry," I mumble, the burning in my eyes threatening more tears. "If I had known this would happen—"

"It doesn't matter," he cuts me off. "It did happen." Tristan stands, pulling me with him, and I wrap my arms around myself. "Come on, let's get you out of here."

We meet Allison and Max in the parking lot and drive back

to the Westbrook Hotel. Tristan and I ride up to the penthouse, and he guides me into the bathroom. "I'll be right outside," he murmurs before leaving me alone.

After getting undressed, I stand under the hot spray of water, staring at the marble tile for a while before I wash myself off. Maybe if I stay in here long enough, everything will sort itself out, and I won't be the leader of the light fae anymore. I almost laugh at the thought. I'm not naive enough to believe that could happen. I'm stuck with this because of the choices I made.

How much did Jules manipulate my life to work in favor of his goal to destroy Tristan? What was real? What *is* real? There's no way to know for sure. For all I know, Jules screwed with my head to make me fall for Tristan. My stomach twists, and I wince. The thought makes me feel sick.

I step out of the shower after I've rinsed the soap off and wrap myself in a towel. I change into the set of dry clothes Tristan left me and dry my hair the best I can.

Standing in front of the large vanity mirror, I study my reflection. I look the same. Same hair and eyes and skin. Nothing about my appearance has changed. If it weren't for the drastic difference I *feel*, I could almost pretend that none of this happened, that I wasn't the new leader of the light fae. Almost. However, the changes are too significant to ignore. I can see and hear better, but shifting scares me too much to think about. In fact, nothing about this new situation *doesn't* scare me. Every breath I take is an effort, and I don't know how long I can keep it up.

Running my fingers through my damp hair, I let loose a heavy sigh, not wanting to leave the room. I don't want to go out there and face Tristan—face what I did by killing Jules. I'm still so confused. Did Tristan know a human killing a fae leader would make that person fae? If he did, why didn't he tell me? *He didn't think you'd be so reckless as to go after Jules alone*, a sharp voice in my head says.

I open the door and step into the bedroom to find Tristan sitting at the end of his bed. He looks up when I enter the room and stands, waiting for me to approach.

"Hey you," he murmurs.

My lips form a smile, but it isn't real. "Where are Allison and Max?"

"Max said he was going to see Oliver. Allison is downstairs with Skylar trying to keep everyone calm. Word travels fast around here."

"As if I needed to give the dark fae more reason to hate me." I tug at the hem of my shirt.

"It'll be an adjustment," he says. "For everyone."

I chew my bottom lip, my eyes burning. "Maybe it shouldn't be." My voice is small.

Tristan's gaze intensifies. "I'm not sure what you mean."

Swallowing the lump in my throat, I sigh. "I think I need some time." The words leave an unpleasant taste in my mouth.

His jaw tightens. "Of course. It's not going to be easy, but we *will* figure this out, Rory. You're not alone."

"I did this, and I need time to process it. Alone." Time to go through these last months and decide what was real.

Tristan drags his hand through his already messy hair and down his unshaven face. He looks as wrecked as I feel. "You want to leave?" The confusion on his face makes the ache in my chest blossom.

"No," I shake my head, "but I have to."

"You're overwhelmed. That's understandable. Let me help you through this." He reaches for my hand, but I step away before he can touch me. I'll lose the strength I need to leave if I let him touch me.

"*Don't*," I breathe, my lower lip trembling. "Please let me go." My chest is so tight it feels as if it's about to explode.

"Why?" he challenges, desperation creeping into his usually confident tone.

"Because," I snap, "Jules did whatever *this* is." I gesture between us. "I would never have been at that party if it weren't for him. You and I would never have met."

"You're saying because of the way we met—?"

"How can we be sure what's between us is real? What if it's nothing more than some fucked up byproduct of Jules's plan to rule the fae?" My eyes sting, threatening more tears.

He frowns, his brows inching closer. "Do you honestly believe that?"

"I don't know what to believe right now! I just killed a man who has been screwing with my life and hurting the people I care about. Now I'm not only fae, but the light fae fucking leader *because* I killed him!"

His hands clench into fists, as if he's fighting the urge to reach for me. "Jules might be the reason we met, but he's *not* the reason we care about each other. What's it going to take for you to realize that?"

I bite the inside of my cheek, then sigh. "Time," I whisper. "I need some time."

"Remember what you told me? About not putting down a book before you finish the story? Our story isn't over yet." His words knock the air out of my lungs in a swift, painful whoosh. "Aurora." My name is a prayer on his lips. He's begging me not to leave. I can see it in his eyes. In fact, it's the last thing I see before I back out of the room and walk out of his suite.

I almost don't make it into the elevator before my chest explodes in a shower of fiery pain. I made a mistake by going after Jules. It was stupid and reckless. I screwed up, and now I'm facing the consequences—I'm going to face the consequences. Forever.

I walk back to campus. My hands and face are frozen by the time I make it to my dorm. When I get to my room, I'm thankful for the first time that Allison didn't lock the door when she left, because I'm pretty sure my key is somewhere at Tristan's. I can't go back there, not now—maybe not ever.

I close the door and lean against it, scanning the room. Everything looks the same, except different. Nothing has been touched or moved, but it's as if I'm seeing it all through new eyes. Panic rises to the surface again as I think about everything. I fall back against the door and slide until my butt hits the floor. Pressing my knees against my chest, I wrap my arms around them and hide my face. My shoulders shake as I'm overcome with sobs, and I hug my knees tighter.

I should've stayed with Adam. I dig my fingers into the side of my leg as tears fall down my cheeks. This isn't what I came back for. If I knew what was going to happen, if I'd had the choice, I never would've woken up.

For the first time since Adam died, I experience a pain stronger than what I felt that day. There's a physical emptiness in my chest. I don't know how to describe it, but I feel it there.

Sitting with my head in my hands, I cry until there's nothing left. It's like losing Adam all over again, except this time I feel as if I've lost Tristan. I don't know how I'm going to get through the night, let alone the rest of my life as not only one of the fae, but as the light fae leader. The thought of everything I felt with Tristan being fabricated by Jules's meddling makes the bile in my stomach rise; I have to swallow it.

Sometime after midnight, I pull myself off the floor and crawl into bed. I lie awake, staring at the door as if I'm expecting Tristan to walk through it and refuse to leave. For all the times he showed up and I wanted him to leave, I'd give anything to have him here now. To know that what I feel for him is real. Until I know the truth, whatever we were is over. It has to be. After everything we've endured together since we met, we end in the most tragic way I can imagine—in a cruel twist of fate.

STAY TUNED FOR *TWISTED GIFT*,
THE STEAMY, FAE-FILLED SEQUEL TO
TWISTED FATE, COMING FALL 2018.

Author Note

Reviews are everything to an author. If you enjoyed *Twisted Fate*, please consider leaving a review on Goodreads and your favorite bookseller's website.

Acknowledgements

First and foremost, I need to thank my family. Without them, this book wouldn't exist. Their love and support is the most important thing to me. They are my inspiration to work hard for the goals I want to achieve.

To the friends who have supported me since the day I announced I was writing a book. Special thanks to the ones who said they would buy it before they knew what it was about or if it was any good.

To my incredible critique partner, Allison Alexander: I don't have sufficient words to express my gratitude for your friendship. I can't imagine going through this journey without you, and I'm so excited to continue working with you in the future.

To my epic critique partners, Beck Wilkinson and Destiny Murtaugh: thank you for your unwavering support and suggestions.

To my amazing team of beta readers: thank you for loving Aurora and Tristan (and the rest of the gang) as much as I do. Your honesty and compassion makes my heart happy. Special thanks to Jenna Streety for being an awesome friend who let me bounce ideas off her too many times to count.

To Jacquie Pugh who wrote the lyrics Aurora sings in the ballroom scene: thank you for helping add a beautiful level of authenticity to the story.

To my cover designer, Sarah Hansen at Okay Creations: I'm in awe of your work. Thank you for bringing my vision of the perfect cover for this book to life.

To my editor, Maggie Morris of The Indie Editor: You are a-freaking-mazing. I can't imagine working with anyone else on my debut novel, and I can't wait to work with you again in the near future. Your suggestions were pure gold and took *Twisted Fate* to the next level.

To Kim Chance: for not only proofreading *Twisted Fate* but for being such a bright, encouraging light in the writing community. *You* are the bee's knees, Kim.

To Stacey Blake at Champagne Book Design: thank you for working with a debut indie author and for making *Twisted Fate* look amazing.

To the wonderful ladies at Love Between the Sheets Promotions: thank you for making the release of *Twisted Fate* so smooth and epic.

To the bloggers who reviewed and pimped *Twisted Fate*: I did the book blogging thing for a long time, I know the work that goes into each post, so thank you for taking the time for my book.

To all my amazing online writer friends: I'm not going to list names because I *know* I'm going to forget someone and then I'll feel terrible. You guys know who you are, and thank you.

Last, but in no way least, thank *you*, the reader, for giving *Twisted Fate* a chance. I want to hug each and every one of you.

About the Author

Jessi Elliott is a newly graduated law clerk and debut author of both young adult and new adult romantic fiction. Her love of writing was born after many years of reading and reviewing books on her blog.

She lives in Southwestern Ontario with her family and two adorable cats.

When she's not plotting her next writing project, she likes to spend her time hanging with friends and family, getting lost in a steamy romance novel, watching *Friends*, and drinking coffee.

You can find Jessi at www.jessielliott.com, on Facebook, Twitter, and Instagram, and you can sign up for her newsletter to stay up to date on book news and upcoming releases.

Join her Facebook reader group, Jessi Elliott's Twisted Sweethearts, for exclusive news, promos, review opportunities, and giveaways!

Facebook: www.facebook.com/authorjessielliott
Twitter: twitter.com/AuthorJElliott
Instagram: www.instagram.com/authorjessielliott
Newsletter: www.jessielliott.com/newsletter